GW00645098

The White Night

Kathleen Clare Waller

Palette et Papier Publishing

ISBN 978-0-9906283-1-6
Palette et Papier Publishing

Cover photograph by the author.
Saint Malo, France, June 2013.

www.kathleenwaller.com

For Evey and Peg

The White Night

Nuit Blanche

A nightlong festival. People forget about time, about schedules. Normal sleeping hours become the time of living. Art, music, dancing, and conversation as dissonant experiences in the twisted warp of hours and moonlight without a worry for tomorrow.

I

La Rentrée

Saint-Germain-des-Prés, Paris
June 1999

She wakes without the alarm. Early, but past June's daybreak. For the first time in four months, her initial thought is not about her own imminent death. She is not overwhelmed by obligation, does not consider what *it* may feel like, questions not why this has happened to her, nor does she plead with God or Allah or any other deity to allow her to live. She does not wish these unpleasantries away; they are simply absent from her mind. This beautiful absence takes over completely.

A chill has whistled through the closed shutters during the dark night. After a few minutes in bed, not sure where reality lies in the haze of forgotten dreams, she stretches toward the day. Blindly putting on soft clothes, running shoes, she nimbly spirals down the stairs, soft as a cat.

The hollow void of the courtyard holds spiraling thoughts from yesterday and tomorrow. She willfully merges into the open space. Her sneakers make no noise as they amble from her building's door to the massive entranceway, large enough for horse and buggy or modern delivery trucks. Stretching her arms toward the sky, the keys around her thumb jangle off her open hand, a small echo bounces off the windowpanes that protect their inhabitants from simple morning sounds as they sleep. She pushes the release button for this porthole to the city outside and slowly heaves it ajar, just enough to slip through.

Clicking the ancient emerald-green wooden door to the courtyard shut, she springs forward into the morning fog before the pedestrian commute that will break through the grayness and kill the night's dreams.

Rue de Seine is dead. Shutters are closed. Cars are parked quietly in their usual positions: the yellow vintage Renault coupe, the red supermini Peugeot 205, the black Ferrari. Scooters and motorcycles are scattered in crevices that they seem to have wiggled into like belly dancers, reshaping themselves to fit available negative space. The sidewalk before her is empty and shadowed from opaque clouds, although just three weeks from the summer solstice. This shrouded morning hour buys extra time to a life's hourglass filling up with sand.

Moving toward the junction with *Boulevard St. Germain,*

she sees the other early risers. Lean ghosts emerging in the fog. Living Giacometti statues. Café owners clean their espresso machines letting the hot steam hiss through relieved pipes, while waiters wipe down wicker chairs on the terraces. Bus drivers move freely down the open street with only occasional passengers. They hum morning tunes, savor the speed. Running past the man unleashing newspapers into the hands of *Tabac* owners and sidewalk vendors – black and white pages that continue to inhabit café tables, inspiring debate in leisure time that Parisians, of all classes, guard – running past the homeless man, now asleep, who always politely greets her with '*excusez-moi, madame*' before asking for change – running past the closed shops' metal gates that open in invigorating swoops at the same time each day except Sunday – she arrives at the edge of the *Jardin du Luxembourg*, just as the guard opens the gate with a fatigued, flirtatious smile. This time, she ignores him, lost in the matrix of her thoughts. They vibrate incessantly alongside the cherry-sized brain tumor. One physical, the others mere energies, jiggling juxtaposed, involuntarily creating unbidden images as a mélange in her mind.

She opens her mouth to the oxygen surrounding her, breathing much more than necessary, but slowly and consciously, as if directed by a yoga instructor. The breath from her engaged nostrils visibly merges with the fog – giving her misery over to this garden where Marie Medici once built a palace. Like the horse that delivers the mail to Dover in Dickens' imagination, a mysterious cloak of moist carbon dioxide forms around her. Soft respiration and perspiration envelope her. Toxins are released through her skin and evaporate into the morning where they will later be condensed along with the rest of Parisians' breath and sweat, binding to the exhales from their cigarettes and uncaught spray from perfume bottles, in an evening rain that will catch commuters on their walks and rides home or toward *apero* on a *terrasse*. Purged confessions and fears falling heavily to the stone pavement. The sky's release will allow for an evening of refreshed, innocent reverie.

The protective envelopment travels with her, though she threatens to outrun its effect, constantly juggling desires for knowledge and ignorance. She feels a calmness now unlike anything she has experienced since the diagnosis. Yesterday morning, she did not even have those thoughts of tragedy as the plane took off from Logan Airport; the ones that would have come to her in the past. She did not need to squeeze a lucky keychain, a gift from her daughter, when the turbulence would have normally created thoughts of a long tragic drop from sky. She instead drifted seamlessly between sketching and sleeping, so that the drawings became a part of her dreams.

At the airport she had always had an encounter with mortality. *How would it feel to die today? What would people say about me, my life?* Would she panic if the plane were to go down? She knew she was statistically safe in the sky, but like many people, she felt disconnected with the reality of this safety. Imminent danger was synonymous with takeoff.

But when she went to the airport after her diagnosis, she was no longer afraid . It was the first hint that she could accept death and even defy it. The plane was instead an adventure, an activity less dangerous than everyday life. A chance to take oneself out of the world, literally out of worldly time. Who is to say what time it is when you travel through time zones and arrive before you left? She always finds it depressing traveling East. Although she knows she would gain back the day as she traveled West, this loss of hours or even a date on the calendar seemed to erase time that was owed to her. But this seven hour flight could have been twenty minutes, or three days; time was absent. She begins to wonder if all time could be this way and the day before her could flash without awareness or spread into a lifetime.

She floats through the rich space of the park. Continuing in even pace over the gravel without asking her body to move. Closing her eyes a few seconds while moving freely on the vacant path. Drifting to the soundless grass. She lets the cold dew on the grass nip her ankles slightly before returning to the gravel. Her shoes make a beautiful textured sound that lasts longer than staccato steps on the pavement outside the park.

Upon reaching the Medici fountain, she pauses to look, allowing its hidden beauty to take over the chaos that once was in her mind. It reminds her of her time in Florence. It had been an escape, an awakening after tragedy. This fountain had been modeled after Florence's Boboli Gardens well after Marie's husband's mortal stabbing. Marie placed her heart in these stones -- an eternal beauty, a mourning, a celebration. Melancholy or romantic Parisians sit at its edge each afternoon. They converse, kiss, read, or simply reflect. Now empty metal chairs painted green and with permanently reclined seat backs sit scattered around the rectangular water basin, waiting patiently for earthly visitors to enjoy their picnics or contemplation. The statues wait, too, forever in frozen emotions, longing to be human.

As if to get farther from the people who are not yet in the park, she drifts back behind the fountain's façade. There, she can intimately view the eccentricities of the stones that were laid there. Although they have almost become one large mass of polished rock, fused closer over the centuries, a rough surface lives on to hold the scars of Marie's personal traumas and the pains of visitors over time. She reads the neatly chiseled inscriptions every time, never aging in their fresh impression on her mind. There is something important in the dates and names of things. Data that should be chiseled all over the city, not only guarded for the parks and cemeteries.

Moving again, she impulsively grates her knuckles along the wall to feel the hardness of the rock. These stones of Paris that have witnessed the rebellious transition of power that Dickens wrote about so beautifully in the novel that first introduced her to this city. A numb morning suddenly has sensation as the deeply exposed epidural layer reveals virginal white before the blood begins to seep through. She continues with a sharp movement downward on the rock, catching flecks of dirt and dust that lie in the crevices of the rock's jagged undulations. *It is like I am floating away from my body, witnessing this act.* If she cannot carve her name in them, like the prisoner of the Bastille, she will allow them to carve a scar into her skin. There, forever joined, she feels the gritty reminders of her impulsive act mixed with her blood. It is not pain she feels but awareness, part of her strategy to wake herself up. She is not sure this dream is real, that she could feel so light in face of death. This run, this blood, this crisp wet air of June that will burn off and open up to the day.

As she circles the fountain once before moving forward on the path, she notes again the beautiful stonework of an unnamed artist, most impressive at the Roman arch. One summer when she was sick of her painting and wanted to work with her hands in a new way, she joined a group of historians, hippy-tourists, and stone masons who refurbished medieval castles near Saint-Vincent-la-Coste. She had gone alone, leaving them at the base in Naples. In the pulsing Provence summer sun, they headed to the hilltop château with pick-axes, wheelbarrows, and water bottles.

There, she would jog in the vineyards, becoming part of the landscape as the cicadas began their daily song. She was both alone and a member of an intimate, ephemeral group. They ate onions, tomatoes, and watermelon from the earth; they drank wine from the vineyard down the road. They built for the future generations to enjoy the fruits of their labors. They captured the people from medieval times in the form of essence, like an eau de vie.

But at the same time, they built for the present. Although it was physically demanding, so much so that most of the volunteer workers would nap all afternoon after lunch, their toil gave a sense of peace and purpose, creative energy that molded with the ages and the elements alike.

Their task on the first day had been to cut away rock, to build a smooth slant where *pavage* of carefully chosen stones would be laid down. At first she was disappointed, thinking she had come to lay rock in beautiful patterns, not take the place of modern machinery. However, it slowly became apparent that the removal of earth and stone could be just as a creative a force in the world. Without much direction, she attacked relentlessly with the pick ax, finding strength from the breakfast of simple yet plentiful bread and butter with large bowls of coffee poured from Italian carafes. The mere motion of the stone mason's flat hand like a mime over the production he expected gave her a simple guidance. Her working space slowly changed shape, creating a slope she had already formulated in her mind. Its appearance was a moment of *déja vu*. Later, she noted that this was like the work of great sculptors. Michelangelo knew how to chip away at a beautiful piece of expensive marble. He had already imagined what it would turn into. Sculptors who could not see beyond the rock turned to other materials, because they could not afford to waste marble if it did not come out the right way. Here, those limited to the present carried away dirt and brought water to those experiencing the collapse of time.

And here on this burning hilltop in Provence, they were working on a slope that could not be recreated for any cost related to Modernity's progress. Her leveling of the surface had to be perfect. The old man with the large, warted nose shook his head and gave many directions to the group. 'Not so deep! It is not even and cannot be undone.' *Can't you see how it is wrong?* He needed their help but was constantly dissatisfied with their work. Stone masons are hard to come by these days. But as the first day wore on, he moved closer to her, remarking with his big eyes what was taking shape under her angled body. He was silent and continued with his own digging. She watched, then tried to let the practice come to her.

Passively, yet with strength, she played the role of a stone mason from long ago.

The work continued by selecting long, stable rocks with flat faces, like molar teeth long pointed roots. The stone mason would systematically pull rocks neatly placed by the volunteers. As the sun rose toward its noon placement and breakfast was longer in the past, patience wore thin. Even Catherine thought many of these extractions were unnecessary. A furled brow told her otherwise. The apprentice occasionally swore as he took out a series of fittings, avoiding eye contact with the volunteers as he concentrated on swiftly remaking the area. With his shirt tied around his dread locks, the others could see ripples of back muscles engaged in this process. *'Merde! Touristes!'*

More difficult than extracting, these bones of the earth had to be fit together in the hopes they would rest side by side for centuries. We assume our descendants will want to continue to hold onto the history we are so desperately trying to restore. So far in the past, so deep into the future, as the sweat, dirt, and rock mix with the energies of the present.

Later on the way to the car, the old man with the big nose very simply declared to his young apprentice: 'Catherine understands the work.' The frustrated Olivier glanced at her from beneath his dreadlocks and let his eyes linger a moment in careful study of her character.

This experiencing of the present was ironically so engrained in the lifestyles of these people upholding an ancient tradition. Each volunteer also had a day in the kitchen to understand how the simple, delicious meals were constructed. The list of recipes that made its way into Catherine's journal was deep: watermelon with yogurt and local cheese, Tunisian roasted eggplants, tomato and onion salad, ham and mushroom quiche, apricot tart. In the kitchen, she, like the others, began by cutting up a full basket of white onions. The task was like an entry into Margeaux's kitchen. After positioning the still sleepy adventurer in front of a large wooden cutting board and proper kitchen knife, she would hand the full basket over to the morning's volunteer with an ironic smile. 'Cut the onions like this, please.' It was one of the few phrases she knew in English. And with that, she would grab a baseball-sized, pungent bulb from the basket, layer off the dry skin, and slice it into translucent pieces that appeared to have been cut by an industrial chopper all within seventeen seconds.

As she left to gather the other ingredients for the day's cooking, Catherine glanced at the full basket and wished she could instead transport herself to the van filled with buckets, shovels, and quiet workers that was winding its way through several tiny villages toward the renovation site. She recalls now actually wishing the onions into rocks, but of course it was futile and she knew she had to 'earn her way' by cooking one day in the kitchen. She fumbled through the first two onions in no less than four and a half minutes. But on the third, Margeaux came by halfway through to silently reposition her grip on the knife, which cut down the time for each one significantly. She began to glide her way through onions, feeling more and more proud of the growing pile of translucent morsels she would push into another bowl after each one's thorough dissection. The onions' pungent smell also brought clichéd tears, but this time Catherine welcomed them. She felt more aware of this moment and now fully awake. It was like the episode in *Como Agua Para Chocolate* when the onions and the tears created allow deep sorrows to emerge, purging the soul in detoxification. *I am so far from him, from the base. He wouldn't last a day here.* When Margeaux came around again, she simply smiled approvingly and led her over to an area where the girl from Morocco who worked in the kitchen and taught the volunteers how to dance with their hips in the local bar at night was placing wedges of Mirabelle plums in patterns on pastry dough. *I am lost in this moment, in this timeless village.*

The local bar was another part of the experience. There was a nightly mix of volunteers, wine makers, migrant workers, and locals who seemed to have no other occupation than sitting at terrace tables with espresso, Pastis mixed with water, or the local rosé. The wine – one euro a glass – was crisp and easy to drink. The atmosphere was jovial, but sometimes Catherine wanted to avoid the crowds and their displays of drunken behavior. Instead, she would often linger at dinner long enough for the non-francophones to leave the table. The locals would refill the wine pitchers and they would embark in philosophical discussions, varying from whether or not France should legalize marijuana, the French method of not mixing food on the plate, and the perils of Modernity. Olivier often looked angry, not understanding why people didn't see the world his way. The French hosts seemed rarely to talk about themselves or their families, perhaps hiding a traumatic past. Or perhaps free of any bounds to memories. Despite massive absence of information one would have about childhood friends, she felt she had known these people for years. She felt she could give herself fully to them without talking of her dark places.

After the first day at the chateau, he found her in the bar and loosened his tight face. "Would you like to escape?" He guided her toward the book entrance and they scrambled up the mountainside, pausing collect cans of *1664* and a joint from Olivier's cavernous room. Then they continued until they could no longer here the voices from the tiny village.

Up on the rocks, Olivier's demeanor would oscillate between an unpretentious prune-faced silent laugh and a high-nosed open-eyed defense of French traditions. She asked him why he liked the rocks. He said it was spiritual, his religion. Olivier asked her why she was alone. Here, they *would* talk of their memories, their families. Sometimes, though, they would simply sit in the refreshing timeless night and watch for shooting stars in the pure sky, so far from city lights. There, she had found a part of herself she had left behind. It was one that existed before her husband, one that was pure and dependent on nature.

Now with the open pebbled path before her, she tries to recall what she had wished for on those shooting stars. And if they had come true. It was the stuff of childhood, but why must those romantic truths disappear as we age?

She has made it to the opposite end of the park and glances briefly sideways at the open view of the fountain and the *Palais du Luxembourg*. She then scans the possible paths before her that this single road branches into. She chooses one that brings her deeper in the interior, even quieter than before, as she is removed from vision of those who may pass by the sidewalks outside the gate.

Her pace quickens. *Where is this mysterious evader of society now? The one who embraced childhood's realness?* Would he have given her a different life? Would she have this tumor now if she had run away with him? And if she had met him before she had given birth to her daughter? But looking around again at the *Jardin du Luxembourg*, Catherine realizes she also enjoys too much of what the Modern world has given her to give it up and live as isolated as the stone mason. And she would never wish away her daughter. He is a part of her dreams only. He drifts back to her at moments like this. Maybe this is more real, more a part of her, than the real husband she once had.

After passing by the beehives and tennis courts, she tries to remember why she had volunteered in the middle of nowhere as she eases back to a trot, weaving through different paths in the hidden edges of the park. She took this trip the one time that Esmé stayed alone with her father. Even though she knew she had to leave them there, she had felt guilty for going away to do something only for herself. It was an impulsive act. She had never told her sister about it, fearing she would judge her a careless mother whom was likely already being judged by the other army wives. It was one of those moments she kept locked inside her next to many feelings of shame and guilt, but this was one of those moments she had lived the most, defying and outweighing the associated avoidance of social responsibilities. This morning, this lock has opened and the moisture expelled from her body is bound to the memories, carrying them outward, upward toward tree limbs and into the clouds before falling again later to nourish their roots.

Having always admired the New England stone walls of

her youth, she was intrigued by this project after a recommendation. An acquaintance from the *Napoli* military base was constantly looking for diversions. She was childless and an army spouse. She would have become a friend had her husband not been moved to northern Japan several weeks after Catherine and Thomas' arrival in Naples. After enjoying the cheap shopping and manicures on base and then the well paved, empty roads perfect for many leisure sports, she found there was not much to do if one did not have kids to tend to. So she would save up her money and whenever her husband would allow it, she would drift off on an adventure in the region.

Catherine did have a baby already at the time. She had been content at first with looking after Esmé, riding her bike with the yellow baby-seat on the empty base roads, teaching an art class to displaced teenagers at the Department of Defense high school, and cooking new Italian recipes for her small family — *ravioli con la zucca, melanzane parmigiana, polenta con gorgonzola*. But then he began to expect things of her *like other army wives*. It starts simply with a shifting of political loyalties. With the indoctrination of the base television channels, it's easy to see how this could happen. Her liberal mindset was in conflict with most of what she saw on it: support for the NRA, new ways to drill oil in Alaska, how to know if your neighbor is a Russian spy, personal messages from President Reagan about Communism, fundraising for base CCD classes, and fights to keep the 'Don't Ask Don't Tell' policy in place. She felt like screaming at the television set that would not allow a dialogue.

Thomas warned her to hold her tongue at dinners with

other officers and their wives, the only people they were allowed to socialize with on base where rank was strictly adhered to. She had received a lecture after debating with a wife who was planning to lobby for the death penalty. She was mid sentence in bringing up the point about *even if you look at it economically, it costs the government more money in legal appeals for the death penalty than it does to keep a prisoner behind bars for life* when she had received a kick under the table. Thomas wanted to impress their new friends; Catherine didn't understand the value of a friendship that was based on lying and acting only to please others. Besides, isn't argument the only path toward truth? She almost outed him at the dinner table. It was so tempting to expose him, make him look stupid with his friends. But she couldn't be bothered. Their response would not have been related to the political debate she was trying to have, and the pain in her leg was not the one she cared the most about.

It was as if she were a stranger on this base. She even felt more at home outside the security check, on Italian soil, than what was supposedly an extended part of her home country. When one feels a stranger, there is no backbone left. There is no ability to verbiate the identity; rather, one may still be what one is, but may not extend that being to action, and without that, what use is identity at all? She thought about this in the base library where she would visit old and new philosophers, escaping and making the most of the non-place like a prisoner seeking education. She seeks answers: *What is the value of art? The purpose of our senses? Of family? Of solitude?* And not: *What is the meaning of life?* but *How to live?* Questions that come to her when she is alone.

These were the types of things she would think about as a stranger on that base, but she found no one to share them with. She read deeply and widely, noting her thoughts in a journal always nearby. She enjoyed reading Derrida's books the most, even with the extreme difficulty to interpret them. She found his language a welcome puzzle, but Thomas never wanted to contemplate it with her, or anything of the sort. Her supposed friends would just laugh at her when she tried to ask philosophical questions. The more she asked, the more she felt like an outsider.

She remembers asking Thomas at dinner one night, 'What do you think about energy healing?' after reading an article on the subject. He stopped chewing the rosemary pork chops and stuck his fork into his polenta with a blank expression. 'Are you serious?' he asked slowly. He then continued to eat methodically and complained about the nurses at the hospital, 'They are always talking about other things, like gossip or cooking, and wasting time at work.' She tried to change the subject by asking how he liked the new recipes she had tried out (because he had yet to comment on her three hour toils, which she enjoyed, but would have liked appreciated) and he replied rather pleasantly, 'I like the meat.' He did not even seem to notice the flavors of rosemary and gorgonzola adorning the dishes. Catherine closed her eyes to taste the food. To block him out.

Later she was asked to join the wives for church when he was away, to go get her nails done with the girls, to stop wearing those artist outfits. *Wear something a future Ambassador's wife might wear.*

The couple of art classes she taught at the base school

were her one solace besides the time spent with her daughter. Although the teenagers in her class often lacked artistic talent or much direction in their lives, they were fresh and unjaded. Their talk was unfiltered. But when the principal asked her to change the senior art project to focus on the theme of nationalism, she knew that even the school had a short life span for her creative freedoms.

She was a mismatch from the start. The years on base changed her so that she felt self-indulgent whenever she actually felt in her element. These rocks she molded with her hands, the smooth yet irregular *pavage* she created were memorable moments and long-lasting imprints of her being. She could paint the apprentice's wild dreadlocks from memory but had long forgotten the results of a two-hour perm many of the officer's wives were so proud of.

Her hair now lightly taps the back of her neck where it becomes damp and will become cold as she finishes later with the walk back to her apartment, propelling her into the hot shower. As she continues to run on the gritty path, she refocuses on her gentle movements. After losing ten pounds in chemotherapy, she seems to move within her clothes without disturbing the fabric, and it is as if she glides over the sand and pebbles barely making a sound. An opening at the right is a path she doesn't remember taking before; she pivots on the next swift step. Like a private corridor, the evergreen trees hide her presence from the guards and a few other early risers with dogs or babies. She counts four more relaxing breaths before rejoining a route toward the central fountain. She exposes herself to the morning sun, diffused but strong. It is at these moments in the morning when Catherine opens her arms toward the sky, facing the sun, closes her eyes and opens her mouth. It is an Ode to Joy. Her mother had taught her to take her very own, every day, and she now feels like she is greeting her mother beyond the earthly world.

She listens to the gravel, two beats per step - the forefoot strike followed by the toe lifting off behind her. She tries to match certain words and names with it: *Esmé, matin, happy.* But they do not work. As she continues she finds the rhythm is longer, swallowing on the first beat, more like: *gooey, Louis...*she loses herself in listening to these soothing rhythms, taking in the different shades of white and gray of the pebbles lining her path. *Louis, Louis, Louis...Louis, Louis, Louis...Fouy, fouy, fouy....*

And then something strange happens for the first time. Defined edges of pebbles blur as does the sound. She passes into a millisecond or maybe several minutes of whiteness. Her senses are gone. She simply *is.* She continues forward in space softly.

As she comes out of the trance, she is startled back to the experience her senses compile for her. *Had it been a single flash or a prolonged state of unawareness? Or was it the opposite - deep awareness?* She is not sure. It intrigues her and she hopes for it to happen again.

Her feet take her back out the gate, moving now with steps on autopilot toward her apartment that she missed so much in America. The guard wishes her *bonne journée* as she says the same. A few scooters with suited passengers buzz by and she crosses the road, continuing forward, passing shops still closed but the beginning of commuters and morning writers or newspaper readers. Still a hundred meters away from her destination, she stops at the tiny corner open-air market and takes some Francs out of her pocket. She carefully chooses the five apricots in the sharpest contrast to the grays of the air enveloping them. But the shopkeeper waves his finger, takes two more from the back of the pile closest to him, closes his eyes and opens his nostrils in a deep inhale before exchanging them for two already in her bag. She smiles at him, then also takes freshly farmed yogurt and raw almonds with a bottle of *Badoit*. The aproned man with a thick white mustache who takes her money and tells her to have a good day reminds her vaguely of the old stone mason. They are both much more knowledgeable of their craft than it seems anyone in her or her daughter's generations could ever be.

She continues down the mainly empty street, walking in exaggerated motion to stretch her legs still in knots from the red eye flight from Boston the night before last. She slows further each time she arrives at a gallery window-front until finally arriving at the gigantic door, which shall remain closed until the inner courtyard gallery's opening hour at eleven o'clock. She types the code. The discreet click echoes through the vacant stone courtyard, its tiny noise in huge contrast to the size of this porthole. It takes her full body weight leaning into the door to slowly release it until she is able to gingerly hop over the threshold and let its own mass move it back into place.

She enters the fifty-year-old elevator and manually closes the gate behind her. This brings a smile. She remembers the way Esmé preferred to climb the six flights of wooden spiral stairs, not for fitness or pleasure, but out of fear of the ancient mechanism's safety. Esmé would throw her luggage or groceries or books in the 'death trap' with her mom and pray for her as she ran up the stairs. *The dangers of our daily lives are vast, she used to tell her daughter, but you cannot live in fear.*

The contrast between this European versus American mentality astounded her at times. Her American friends would not take a taxi with their newborn, missing half the sites they visited on a trip to Bangkok. They cringed at dirty hands, insisting on Purel while their baby lost any hope to fight off life-long disease. Meanwhile in Sweden, women were leaving their babies outside of restaurants in little social circles. A Swedish visitor in New York City made the news when she tried the same thing in the East Village. Rather than thinking of the kidnappers and crazy people in the streets, she thought of the beautiful sunny day that her child could enjoy while she ate fresh Maine lobster for the first time. Each could have her independent experience.

She must think of it like this Swedish woman. She left her daughter in America; rather, her daughter let her return to Paris. Esmé still has a year to go at Tufts University, where she is majoring in French and Environmental Studies. Of course she wouldn't come back to Paris to live right now, but she will visit for the summer months. She recalls Esmé's reluctant and slightly cold face just three days ago. 'So you'll come this summer like last year?' she felt compelled to ask, since the subject had not been brought up by her daughter. After a slight pause, Esmé replied, 'Yeah, that should be OK.' 'Don't worry, I can buy you your ticket, you can even come with me now...' She was cut off slightly, 'But you know I want to work on this environmental project first with Professor

Ramnath. She really has such a cool idea...it's a really great opportunity...'

Yes, Catherine had agreed it was important that she stay for it. That she could meet her later when it was convenient, but they did not pick a date before her departure. She had meant it sincerely, feeling that ideas and discoveries are important, especially for the young. But Esmé seemed to interpret it more coldly, perhaps hoping deep down that her mother would beg her to board the plane or that she would stay and smother her with mother-daughter outings. Her reply was matter-of-fact, 'Fine, well, OK. We have our first meeting tomorrow so I can't go to the airport to say good-bye.' 'It's alright, just stay for dinner then...' 'I can't, Mom, I'm just...I just can't stay tonight, I'm really busy.' Catherine was confused, disappointed. She tried to understand and couldn't, but she let her go all the same.

There were no tears as Esmé turned to retreat to her dormitory. *Does she think of me when I am here? Does she need me?* She missed the days when they were together in Paris and all her free time was taken by Esmé' activities or teenage conflicts. Was she pushing her away or was it all in her head? Was she busy, more independent, exactly what Catherine had wanted he to be? Or was she trying to imagine her mother's death in advance so the blow wouldn't be too strong?

She had gone to the airport by herself. Afraid it would be too emotional for her father, and maybe herself; she insisted the flight was too early and that she would take a taxi. They stayed up together watching old Italian movies her mother had collected and eating takeout broccoli and olive pizza until he fell asleep on the couch and she retreated to her childhood bedroom one last time.

She realizes she has slumped down on a yoga mat where she has been stretching for some time and peels her body up to wash herself off and get ready for the immense day before her. After a French-style shower with the head in hand massaging her body and finishing with a cold rush of water, she prepares some toast for breakfast. She peers in the oven, rising several times to her tip-toes and bending her knees as inner-thighs face forward. A morning plié. She stands lightly in her cotton underwear and long-sleeve t-shirt, a heavy white towel covering her hair, pressing the top of her ears outward like Dumbo.

Although she loves this breakfast and morning ritual, which only feels just right in her apartment on *Rue de Seine*, she cannot help but feel unsettled. She knows this when she cannot open the fig jam. Her hands are unsure. She had the same problem with the key in the door. It was as if her anxiety blocked the door from a willingness to open; it did not want her tormented energy to unsettle the calmness within.

Now that she is inside, it starts to dissipate, but there is something that lingers. With Esmé, it will be ok. She understands place, the topography of feelings. But her newly retired father is scared. Scared about his daughter's mortality and loneliness. But if he is really honest with himself, Catherine knows he would find it is his own mortality and loneliness that he really fears. Her decision to return to Paris, away from all the tests and doctors and special care and attention from her doting family members, marked an understanding that she will die and she is happy. It seemed too contradictory to explain. The connection to place and the topography of feelings. She tried to talk with her sister about it. Undine started crying and exploded in the misery that this sibling of hers was not facing the fact that she must try to live and be with her loved ones as much as possible until her final day. She called her 'selfish' between tears. 'What about *my* children, Catie? What am I supposed to tell them? It's not fair of you to leave. You're always running away from reality…' She couldn't even finish talking and ran to fetch her husband for support.

Undine placed her frosted hair in a messy bun in order to let her facial expressions project raw emotion. It reminded Catherine of when they were young and their mother would help them to sort out an argument. Once Undine had finished her explanation, she collapsed on Lawrence, sobbing. She clung to the fat that had been his buff arms when they were married. Lawrence raised an eyebrow at Catherine who sat still, breathing deeply, in the arm chair. After a brief pause, he responded, 'Honey, Catherine is an adult and can do what she wants. We've done all we could to help her, but if she won't listen…' He had always dismissed her as a bit crazy anyway. *The artist.* The decision went right along with her character.

The painting of her sister's face from high school sits in view of the tiny breakfast table. Innocent and pensive, filled with ideas about becoming a doctor, traveling to Asia. Her eyes move from this painting on a wooden slab toward the books on the shelf she has read, lent out. Her eyes rest on *Invisible Man* then *Madame Bovary*. The apartment itself seems to reflect her feelings. It knows she is sick but does not mourn her absence, both when she was gone for tests in the States and when she will be gone forever. It seems to close the curtains on her, the wind whips them shut each time she attempts to keep them open, playing a game. Her bed is dressed in crisp white sheets and comforters . She looks at it now, crumpled and leaps onto it with a photo of herself as a child, letting the towel unravel from her head and freeing her hair in wild wet Medusa curls. She notes the smoothness in her face, the crooked teeth, the carefree gaze at her father's camera. He still uses that complicated lens. The more she stares into it, the more it seems like a mirror as she floats back to that time of innocence. It was just before a stressful adolescence. Hers was no different than most— expectations for university, for friends, and for ambitions she thought she owed to her parents.

It seems to be the time when we figure things out or rather ourselves. Some people never seem to leave this stage. That's what Psychology 101 had taught her, and she had seen it in her sister, anticipating its duration. This pre-destiny had been fulfilled. Although Undine was married with two children, she could never be satisfied with anything. She would always say life is grand, but could not sit and talk for more than thirteen minutes. There was always something to do, to mind the children, cook some food, or take care of some business. Just as in high school and college, there had always been a party. She was afraid to be alone with her thoughts more than she feared all the dangers of society. Catherine used to stay at her sister's house once or twice a year. She always had her own guest room and could even use one of the family cars. But the problem was that as soon as she would arrive, it would feel like a tropical cyclone. There was clutter all over the house ('…because of the kids, you know…'). Dinner was a constant struggle between what had been made and what the kids wanted to eat and her sister often ended up making two meals, sitting only tentatively on the edge of her chair as she checked on one of many pots on the stove or served upon request. There was normally at least one fight in the middle of dinner after Daddy allowed something he shouldn't have. In any case, Catherine was happy to leave the table since all of the attention was centered on the children: 'Look at what he likes to eat.' 'Tell Auntie about your school.' 'Robert, don't let him do that on his plate.' But after dinner was even worse because bedtime meant an hour or more of reading books followed by screaming so as not to go to bed followed by another book, more screaming, one last book, more screaming, a door closed, more screaming. Her sister always said, 'Oh you remember what it's like with little ones!' But the thing is that it hadn't been like that with Esmé. Sure, she had her share of tantrums and bedtime blues, but Catherine would gracefully abandon the child to her own thoughts, to learn to be by herself and learn who she is. Catherine would retreat to read her own books or go back to the company she had left with dessert or a game of Trivial Pursuit. Perhaps her daughter had listened to the adult conversation on these nights. With her door ajar, conversations about travel or relationships, of political scandal or upcoming art shows would cross the threshold into that tiny mind for processing.

But now she thinks that maybe she had got it wrong, that constant attention to one's child is selfless and worthy. Meaningful and right.

As this thought swirls in Catherine's mind, she superimposes her daughter's face on her own on the

25

photograph she still holds. The morph of images is completed by her teary regard through eyes wet with nostalgia, as if the memories had condensed, purging the salty tinges of guilt for leaving. *Is it selfish to go and live the way I want? Even, or especially, with only a few months left to live.*

She tightens for a moment, gripping the skin on her arms. She then releases slowly, as her fingers rubs a soft circle on her forehead. Light returns to the room as she opens her eyes. She is present.

A few seconds or minutes pass. She hears her dear old neighbor, Cecilia, fumble toward her door and knock, 'Are you there? *Ça va?*...Catherine?' She doesn't have the courage to reply, fearing pity and questions about her treatment back home. Fearing sadness and mourning of a disease that deserves no more of her time. She remains silent until Cecilia's footsteps retreat slowly down the stairs. One day she will have to face her just like the rest of them, but she hopes that this one will not look for solutions or discuss how terrible it is.

She had accepted her fate one day in the middle of her trip to New England. One day during all the visits with relatives and friends, the trips to the doctors, the chemotherapy, the attempts to seek what one should seek for comfort in the place of her roots. In boarding the plane for Paris, so many of them thought she was running away from reality. She had gone crazy or was hardened and angry by disease. They did not realize that Catherine had learned to live with the growth that is not foreign, but something that her own cells had created. It is a new way to live. A new framework of experience. And so she moves back to the place where she has always uncannily experienced comfort with displacement and acceptance with foreignness.   In Paris, life is eternal.   She moves between portholes, tricking Time and spreading her energy through the city where visitors from the future will feel the infra-red and ultra-violet rays of her presence.

II

Devenir

She wakes up suddenly from a nap. Repetition of just hours ago. A morning nap. *It's ridiculous to sleep again in the morning.* She faces herself in the mirror and passes a hand in a vertical motion like a mime.   The face revealed is smooth.   She forces herself up and this time makes the bed.   It only takes thirty seconds and immediately the space opens up and refreshes her.   She pulls on a silky purple robe and opens all three courtyard windows as wide as they will go, securing them with the metal rod that holds them at a fixed sixty degree angle. A neighbor nods from the apartment across then quickly disappears.

There are twenty identically laid out apartments, two

on each floor for five floors and two buildings facing each other. The third building is empty besides the gallery on the ground floor. She assumes the gallery has used the rest of it for storage or someone is waiting to earn enough money to renovate it. It has been that way for the fifteen years she has lived there. Most of the neighbors remain strangers, although her curiosity dares her to sip coffee or wine out her fourth floor window in hopes of catching their interiors whose smells leak through the gaps between curtains and travel in swirls toward her welcome home. She has crossed everyone's path at some point, exchanged small conversations, in or across the courtyard, at a nearby café or market. She had the feeling, though, that no matter how often they crossed paths she would merely be constructing an exterior understanding of these individuals. They costumed and painted themselves ready for the public, playing with societal expectations. This is a side of each of us, but there is something hidden in that private interior that even the baby holds separate in his crib. The placement of objects, movement of one's body, sounds created or listened to. All these apartments are in such close proximity but separated, different worlds. More than privacy, the walls give creative freedom of expressions. Inhabitants allow a glimpse, publicizing a piece of themselves, sharing a story. She has seen the green Victorian wallpaper on the second floor across the way. Below her, she has heard the Romanian folk music as it pushes the sheer orange curtains in concave. In the apartment of the woman with whom she just exchanged a hello, she has seen Normandy copper pots, an empty yellow vase, and a large black and white photograph of a handsome man next to the television. The television was often illuminated, even while the woman was cooking or in another hidden room. At this moment through the ivory curtain she could hear a popular game show's buzzers. She imagines the woman cooking lunch and answering the questions out loud.

Retreating to her own private space, Catherine glances around the apartment, pausing on certain objects: the jar of blue and green sea-glass collected with her sister on Cape Cod, her own painting of Florence's *duomo* from the hillside, a worn out box of Scrabble on a bookshelf. She used to play with her parents and sister at the dinner table. The tradition had not continued, but she carries the game with her *au cas ou*. Next to it, a copy of Gilles Deleuze's book about Francis Bacon. A way to look at his paintings with a combination of psychoanalysis, deconstruction, and Deleuze's own theories about the meeting of flesh, thought, and painting. From the spaces between emerge his philosophy on Becoming. *Devenir* - to live in action rather than simply to be, *être*. To find meaning in affecting other people and in doing what brings joy and purpose. Holding this book up against the game is a jade figure of the Buddha from Boston's Chinatown Esmé gave her for Christmas. Her mother's embroidery on the pillowcases. Reflections of her past, no, self. For many relics of her lifetime had already been thrown away and forgotten.

She is hungry. Rather than taking a quick snack, she welcomes the frustration of an empty stomach with the enjoyable discipline of anticipation.

She turns on the espresso machine to warm it while beginning to clean the salad vegetables. Her actions are methodically slow, coinciding with the faint coo of a lazy morning pigeon. She takes a small coffee in between spinning the salad and opening a can of chickpeas. Then she takes another *ristretto* as she finds the correct utensils. Once the salad is finished, she sits by one of the open windows with her full colorful plate and some water, staring off into space between mouthfuls. The neighbor has now left, and all she sees are curtains blowing, sometimes spilling out across the rectangular wooden frames.

Her mind drifts to another quiet morning. She had woken up sick to her stomach a few times, not unlike when she had been pregnant. Her period had also become irregular as of late. She also had this terrible headache. To try to calm it, she remembers opening the window to the chilly January air. It had the effect of waking her up harshly to the fact that she should probably seek confirmation from her doctor that this was the first stage of menopause. She didn't need an appointment with much advance and got in later in the afternoon of the morning that she called. As she ate breakfast, the symptoms seemed to disappear while she read a missive from her daughter. When Esmé had decided to go away to college in America, they made a pact to write to each other at least once a week. Her daughter's letters detailed the strangeness of dormitory life, the genius of her professors, and random explanations or questions about movie stars, fashion, or politics. She remembers the letter that morning, still in the box of letters under her bed, about a stubborn psychology professor, a shop that imports French chocolates, and, at the very end, details of a new crush she had met at the pool. He was on the swim team, he offered to help her make some workouts over a coffee…it was amazing the way Esmé was opening up to her like a peer now that she was an ocean away. Their relationship had changed, offering a new friend. They began to share fatuous information that filled in the lines meaning 'mother' and 'daughter'. She had held her morning bowl of *café au lait* with two hands that morning, looking out toward a photograph of Esmé at Crane's Beach in the summer when she was only twelve years old. The photograph went out of focus as she wandered happily back to the moment on that beach with sand so hot they had to run from towel to ocean water. The hour drive from her father's in Brookline was filled with the new songs of summer: Nirvana's *Smells Like Teen Spirit*, Whitney's *I will Always Love You*, and the Red Hot Chili Peppers' *Under the Bridge*. They had stopped for a lobster dinner on the way home. Those plastic bibs seemed like a funny juxtaposition with such a delicious meal, but they tied them on voluntarily. After happily losing herself in some nostalgia over breakfast, she spent the day working on some sketches for her next art show and took some pain killer to fight the lingering headache.

She remembers feeling so calm on her way to the doctor that she even stopped on the way at a shop to buy a pair of orange leather flats and did not realize she was running late until she left the shop and heard St. Paul's bells striking three times.

Doctor Jacques Caillot had a warm smile to complement his perfectly trimmed sandy gray crew cut and rectangular-framed silver glasses. He was not annoyed by her tardiness and listened to her concerns gracefully and silently. He did a few minor physical examinations, perhaps simply for show or expectation, and then said what he would do. He would order blood tests to check her hormone levels, an ultrasound of her ovaries to check if she were ovulating, and an x-ray of her head. She understood the first two tests but asked what the x-ray was for. In America, her doctor had always explained every minute detail, but in Europe she found that most believed their patients were just content to trust them. Monsieur Caillot was used to her American ways and responded with a light tone, saying he just wanted to make sure it was not a tumor in her head. 'But this would be very rare, it is just to make sure.' The shock of the taboo word passed through her like a spirit that embodied and poisoned her for only a fleeting moment before finding a new host. She felt reassured by the doctor's statistical allusion and went to the radiology clinic the next day with the same air of indifference as she had entered the doctor's office fifteen minutes late the day before.

The image was blurry as it was whisked away by the radiologist, and she did not bother to try to see what might be hidden there. Instead, she was thinking about what this new phase of life after menopause might mean. She knew women who felt that after a year or so of strange hormonal reactions, they had a new calmness about life like no other. Perhaps it was the effects of the hormones telling them that they had entered yet another stage, a completely new life in a way. There is no possibility to decide to have another child, to nurture another baby, and in a way it gives you distance from the parenting role you already have. Your children have become adult, potential parents, and you have moved beyond the parenting stage. Catherine knew Esmé would always be her child, would always seek advice or welcome a mothering embrace that they had at one time even made a bedtime game of. Esmé was allowed three steps to accelerate toward her mother sitting on the bed and attempt to knock her down with a monstrous embrace. The 'big hug' was designed to tire Esmé out, but always resulted in the two of them giggling in bed after a struggle of strength. Now they would move straight to the laughter or the tears, depending on the rhythm of the day. Rhythm and tone change like a concerto. The movements of life may carry different beats per measure or instructions, like *Adesso* or *Allegro*. But the audience knows not to clap at each pause, waiting until the final climax that incorporates the many themes and variations into a crescendo of vitality. With this kind of music, there is no need for an encore.

While visions of independence and visits to grandchildren danced in her head, Catherine caught a burrowed forehead on the ruddy face of the radiologist that took a quick glance in her direction and then disappeared into his office as he closed the door. She heard a muffled voice. She was certain he uttered her doctor's name. Why would he call Doctor Caillot rather than giving her the information?

'I have set up an appointment this afternoon with Doctor Caillot. *D'accord?*' He didn't ask if she already had plans, if that was an acceptable time for her. He didn't let her set up the appointment. She thought this a bit strange, but then assumed it was part of the superior French healthcare system, number one in the world according to the WHO, and extremely accommodating, even offering house-calls, which had been extremely helpful when Esmé was a young child. She should likely start vitamins or hormone treatment, or even be prescribed a cream, as is the case in many visits to the French pharmacies. For headaches, a concoction of natural herbs she could not translate. For arthritis, omega-3 oils and flaxseed. For cellulite, a green tea extract immersed in soft cacao butter. For infertility, prescriptions took another voice by indicating fifteen minutes of sunshine daily and organic eggs and cheese. She had even heard of women ordered to the spa by their doctors when under stress.

But of course this is not what happened. It's clear when she looks back on the afternoon that she should have known this appointment was for bad news. The lack of information from the radiologist, the closed door, the immediate appointment (the French may have excellent healthcare, but efficiency and timeliness are not their strengths).

'...a brain tumor... glioblastoma...usually fourteen months, maybe less, maybe more...'

Her doctor was harsh and direct, but perhaps this was the most kind way to deliver the news. Rather than spa treatments, soft creams, and flower-derived drinks, she heard next, 'chemotherapy' followed soon by, 'Temozolomide.' At least there were treatments available, even if they sounded painful and more like laboratory experiments. She doesn't remember her response to the doctor, only remembering she agreed to his advice to be with family to receive the treatment. He would call a colleague in Boston to re-diagnose her there so she could get around the problems of receiving treatments for pre-existing conditions in America. She was happy he had a way to feel like he was doing something useful for her, because he seemed so lost as to how to help her immediately. It was evident he was hiding a sadness in addition to this helplessness. There was no natural, quick way to attack this disease.

She walked aimlessly that cold evening in mid-March and did not return to her apartment until nine-thirty, when she collapsed without an evening meal and without talking to another soul.

The void of her apartment filled up with light that day after at about eight o'clock. It caught flecks of her breath and dust she occasionally brought in on her shoes that would take flight once sufficiently dried out and then unsettled by the sweep of a broom or the brush of her bare feet on the tile. One speck of clay originally from *Parc Monceau* that had traveled across the city rose in a brilliant ray of light released from behind a morning cloud. It spiraled dramatically before drifting down in slow motion to settle on the tip of Catherine's nose. She awoke.

It had been as if the supernatural pressures of a black hole's spiral were closing in on her. It pushed on her forehead and gave her pain at the point she remembered seeing the tumor on the x-ray. She crawled up and wrapped herself in a blanket, reaching out toward that light flowing in on her from the window. She remembers opening the window and how cold it was, how she would have thrown off the blanket and jumped to her death had it not been for the chill that had snapped her out of a virtual haunt.

So this was disease. An abstract malady that destroyed you from within. The tumor seemed to spread all through her body, invading her cells and blocking her senses. Even after putting in her contact lenses, she could not see clearly. Overwhelmed. It was the worst feeling in the world. It reminded her of frightening nights in high school. The eve before tests and projects, with the looming college applications at bay. Her own mother would recognize the turmoil, sit down to hear what was before her that evening, listen to a plan of attack and then proceed to make her famous zucchini cookies, made rich from the frozen squash picked in the summer months in her father's garden. She would measure and mix while the oven warmed up, humming a Simon and Garfunkel melody as if it were organ church music. Catherine would ease into her work, completing one task before the first batch was baked. She would pause to eat two fresh muffin-like cookies with her mother. As she would move onto the next task, her mother would retreat to the living room to read a book. It did not matter that it was already eleven and there was work the next day. When Catherine would finish her work, usually much earlier than anticipated, she would find her mother asleep on the couch. Waking to Catherine's footsteps, she pretended to still be in the middle of her mystery, happy to be allowed a late night treat.

Her mother was no longer alive to help her through this feeling of being overwhelmed. But she realized maybe with a more structured and familial approach, she could reach this sentiment. She had tried to pass on the same methods to Esmé who didn't seem to need them as much anyway. She was more carefree and easygoing like her father whose pensive nature might overwhelm her further at a time like this. Maybe this time Esmé could help her mother.

When she had called her daughter, she had been calm.

In order not to scare her, she erased the feeling of the gaping dark hole. She also ate a *tartine* after realizing she had not eaten since lunch the day before. They only held a quick conversation, but there was the promise that Catherine would arrive by the weekend. Esmé had a long weekend for Martin Luther King, Jr. Day and would talk to her professors about taking off a little more time. Perhaps shock is what allowed simple parlance on the telephone. Then she had called her father, her sister, and kept it at that. She held herself together for these simple, informative conversations. But she had then broken down that one day, for the entire day, incessantly tearing up just when she thought she would stay dry.

The next day, she had gone for an early swim in the municipal pool, as if to bring the water of her crying back into her body. Like Juliette Binoche in Kieslowski's *Bleu*, she held her breath underwater until she felt the yearning for survival overtake her and push her up to break the surface, head tilting back, gasping for breath. She even heard the overture from the film playing dramatically in her head. The impressive music that had been a joint venture between Binoche's character, similarly named Julie, and her deceased husband. Although the world celebrated it as his piece of music to mark the creation of European Union, Julie's connection to it is filled with personal mourning, anguish, and then vibrant celebration of a life continued, although through the dark cloak of death and adultery. The dissonant music seemed at once triumphant and adequate for the funeral procession of her husband. As the background to much of the film, the repeated, haunting chords with silent rests between seemed to lack any conclusion. The climax of the film became the beginning of Juliette's new life: forgiveness, new love, and independence. She comes back as a lingering, ghostly presence in *Blanc* and *Rouge*, the two following films in the *Three Colors Trilogy*, which was to be Kieslowski's final artistic achievement.

This was the only day she had cried and the only day she had thought about suicide. The frigid January air kept the temptation of her window shut. But worse than suicide was the thought of living out her final days being looked after like a child, taking numerous tests again and again, all with the same result, trying new methods of treatment that felt more like purgatory than a new lease on life. Then there was the idea of watching her sister observe her with those eyes of pity. On the telephone, she could already hear it and she knew every day with her would now be traced with tragedy.

And so after all of that, she has come back to Paris now to live. All our lives are marked with end, so why change the days just when you know they are shortened? She hopes to live past the New Year with her approximate life expectancy set for March in the year 2000 at the time of her diagnosis. Unlike all the morbid people running around worrying about the second coming at this new millennium, she was anxious to live in it. She remembers a day in an environmental studies class at university. There were professors from different disciplines teaching the class in a way that brought exciting debate at the forefront of this discipline that could save the world. One of the professors was a philosopher. He asked one day, 'If you could live at any time in history, when would it be? Replies varied from, 'before Modernity' to 'the Roaring Twenties' to 'the Renaissance.' Students nostalgic for a time they had only read about were seeking simplicity and closer connections to people and nature. But the philosopher's answer was, 'I would live as far into the future as I could.' Responding to perplexed faces, he added why: new medicine, new technology, many people that have yet to be born with exciting innovations. This idea had stuck with her. Since then, she took care of her memories, but anticipated the joys that the future could hold. With a shortened future, she has chosen carefully where and how to live it.

She will now live in this tiny space she has missed so much. She will paint in her friend's studio. She will *rendez-vous* with her dear friends Pascal and Edmond. She will help her blind neighbor again with her English. She will read, write, walk, run, eat, drink, look, listen, feel, dream, reflect, live. Her energy from her being will move outward into those that survive beyond her. Structural survival is what Derrida would call it when he was about to die a few years later.

Like Holden Caulfield, she pulled herself out of the dark hole, seeing life again through the eyes of someone fresh, her daughter. Like Holden's sister Phoebe, she had an intuitive naïveté, something Catherine nearly lost and many others before her have. Without it, life *is* Modernity: work, schedules, clocks, obligations. One need not live on a communist farm to avoid this misplaced focus. Holden perceived this when he reacted to Old Spence in *Catcher in the Rye*. His teacher was right that *life is a game*, but wrong in that the rules can be your own.

Every day in Paris, Catherine feels like she is playing a game, like life is not real. The city is a make-believe fairyland where people speak a beautiful buoyant language.   Two adolescent ladies, each in tight jeans, enormous scarves, and bright ballet flats, behind her on the bus this morning fence with carefully chosen idioms and *verlin* to debate first which restaurant to head to for lunch then which boy is worthy of their attention. *I wish I had known them when I was younger.* The words dance and sing simultaneously in their rich joy of expression in itself.

Everyone is an artist creating this virtual world of French existence.   Waiters conduct rehearsed malleable skits on tourists.   Street musicians do not merely cover classic fare but create their own melodies, raps, or accompanying dance. *Patisserie* chefs glaze already-perfect strawberries placed in careful rows on sweet crust; layer creams, chocolates,   and flaky dough in precariously stacked *milles-feuilles*; and make kaleidoscopic window displays lined with blue floral tiles. Just down the street at the *boucherie*, a young man sells the roasted chickens all day long at a meter's distance from the rest of the actual shop. His autonomous space is filled with his motions and singing voice that give careful attention to each sweet smelling bird; he flirts with her when she buys one. After asking unsuccessfully for an individual-sized meal, she takes a big hen.   He teases, 'I will come *chez vous* to help you with the leftovers tomorrow evening!' A wink.   '*Merci Madame Poulain! A très bientôt!*'

Paris and the French culture and language have become her Lacanian *objet petit a.*   Her desire spirals toward an abstract destination.   It releases another part of herself, close to the one she found up on the rocks of Saint-Vincent-la-Coste, but still evolving. She constantly seeks a *connaissance* of these things that will never come.   How can one fully understand a language spoken in different slangs and dialects? Does she even always know when she has not fully understood? How can one comprehend the full nature of even one's own culture? The difference is that one rarely seeks knowledge of one's own. Instead, the fascination with Frenchness and love of its eccentricities keep Catherine constantly searching, reflecting, debating, and observing before using the minutest newly apprehended aspects in her own daily life that go far beyond sartorial and culinary choices. It makes her more aware of her nascent culture as well. In between their interaction she may find herself. This is why she had come back, to live freely in dissonance.

Although she is not afraid, she has some parts of her life that are unsettled still. There is something inside of her that is not always at peace, but she is not sure what it is. It appears sometimes right before bed, but disappears as she drifts off to sleep.

She opens the window to the cold blue morning and listens to the clank of plates and espresso cups echoing through the courtyard. She closes her eyes and wraps herself tighter in her nightgown. Leaning back on the counter, she plans her day. A terrace lunch of *salade de l'océan* - green and puple lettuce topped with heaps of salmon, shrimp, and calamari - before a trip to the empty studio. She will begin one more painting for the show. This one will be of her father at his writing desk. She chooses the photograph to accompany her. He has one hand midway through his gray, but still full, head of hair. His gaze is toward the moleskin notebook before him, pen in hand, back straight but leaning forward. A pile of books is at his side as usual, a stalagmite beginning at the floor with Ellison's *Invisible Man* and ending near his elbow at Joyce's *Ulysses*. In between are Victorian novels, studies of ontology, and Modernist plays that all fit together somehow. He might never reach for them during his writing, but they gave him comfort in their wisdom that could be accessed at any minute. This scene was structural surivival in its essence. Writers, readers, thinkers each influencing each other, living freely beyond their physical mortality. Translating the words from different languages or different experiences as observers, we connect ideas and people in writing. But she has no book to leave to the world. Perhaps her paintings, her daughter. But she still has more to deliver, more to experience before leaving merely an imprint for those in the physical world to soak up. There is no feeling of desperation. It is the same choice she made in high school. And in Naples. And after her mother's death. These tests have made her stronger, ready to do battle like a dandelion stem breaking through the soil, reaching for the sun, spreading white fluffy seeds.

She has the feeling that there is a good day planned before her and she exits the apartment with a surprising, scintillating energy that takes her down a zig-zag path toward a terrace near the *Centre Pompidou*. The area near the fountain with all the strange sculptures popping out of it. The enormous painting of Dali on the building façade. The tinker-toy like Pompidou building at her right, with hundreds of visitors entering, climbing, looking out through its transparent walls. She orders a *citron pressé* — loves the way it arrives in two glasses…one half-filled with unsweetened lemon juice, the other a carafe of water. She mixes them with a long spoon and does not add sugar. The taste is strong and makes her face pucker. It reaches her organs to nourish and cleanse them. The glow moves through her body, making her eyes glow green. There, she finds the café has an appealing *plat du jour*, *tartare du saumon*, which she eats like a bird until the white rectangular plate is clean, lingers later over an espresso and sits in the full sense of the world before retreating to the studio cave, turning on the Russian piano concerto called *The Lark* by Glinka, and losing herself in painting until she would realize her hunger for dinner of fresh pea soup followed by a thick slice of Roquefort in her apartment, watching whatever film Arte happened to be showing this evening.

III
Le Cauchemar

She is still on her bed, as if posing for a painting.

It is not so late but time to go to sleep. Just like the hunger pangs that told her about dinner, this is known without the consultation of a clock. She does not mind that this day shall end and feels complete relaxation as her breath softens and consciousness escapes like a ghost through the cracked window. There is still a lingering quality of light left from the late setting sun that forms a diffused spotlight across the angles of Catherine's neck and chin.

. . . . .

* * *

Several hours of deep sleep pass.

She reappears from the darkness of slumber, roused by an unknown force. At first she thinks her internal clock, still thousands of miles away, six hours in the past, has woken her up, but then she hears the unmistakable creak of the bed in pulsating rhythm next door. She is not surprised; the young man through the wall has had frequent visitors since he moved in three years ago. She hears different women's voices sighing, 'Oh - my - God!' or '*Mon Dieu!*' or primal screams followed by whispers and laughing. Occasionally they are so loud, the noise prompts several curious neighbors to stick their heads out of their windows, looking, listening. Although they may carry a disapproving look, they are curious, jealous, or filled with joy. Most pretend not to notice, pulling out a cigarette and calmly resting their forearms on the railing of their thirty centimeter by one meter balconies that are made just for this purpose: to relax, observe, perhaps interact.

On this evening and the others when she has heard these noises through her wall, she thinks of many things but she does not think of her own sexual desires. Long ago, she decided those were in her past. Sometimes she giggles to herself; other times she tries to match the voice with one she has heard before, possibly just the previous evening, and imagine who she may be, why she may be here just through her wall. Her imagination goes further sometimes and focuses on the aesthetic intensity of sex. A painting, she has decided, could never do it justice.

Tonight she sees a fleeting flash of all the men she had ever loved, though she had not necessarily been intimately physically connected with them. There was her best friend from high school, her lover in Florence, her husband preserved in his college days, and a handful of others from different parts of her life whom she may have known briefly but whose souls still reach out to her at unexpected moments. Some people just touch you in a way that stays with you forever. In another moment the thought is gone in her tired mind. Then she thinks of nothing, feeling the rhythm and breath as abstractions, like an artistic installation. As the noise dies down after a final orgasmic finish, she, like the young lovers, falls asleep.

.....

Several undisturbed hours pass again. There is no longer a reminder of daylight in the room, but the cold air of the pre-dawn hours sneaks into the room. It carries with it those nightmares that seem to embed themselves just before morning, so that we cannot forget their messages, so real, so vivid it blurs the frontier between fiction and reality.

She wakes up with more energy than she has had in ages. The clickety-clack of high heels above her makes a forward rhythm for the day. Jumping into the shower, she finds herself singing as if she is filming a shampoo commercial. She deeply massages her head with coconut-scented shampoo that penetrate through to the spot that has caused her so much worry and unsettledness, caused her family and friends pain.

As she continues to slowly make circles of fine suds on her temples in the slowly fogging bathroom, the telephone rings. She quickly rinses, then takes an agile step to grab a towel and pivot to catch the receiver with the other hand.

"Oui?" 'Bonjour Catherine! C'est Doctor Caillot à l'appareil.

47

I'm so happy to have caught you this morning. Wonderful news from the new x-ray yesterday - you have been cured! There is no more tumor.' She thanks him profusely. She cannot stop smiling, holding her face in her hands, looking in the mirror to see if it is real. She drops the towel and combs out her hair. Naked and healthy, some beautiful additions of fat and wrinkles since her teenage years give her unique body more life. Less muscular than her competitive swimming years perhaps, but with well-proportioned parts that seemed to arrive within months of moving to France and last without conscientious maintenance. She takes her favorite creamy Vichy lotion and meticulously alternates between squeezing out an almond size lump in her palm and massaging herself in a spiraling motion. She begins on the top of her feet, moves to the ankles, the calves, knees – front and back…

Then the phone rings again. Impossible, she did not even replace the receiver in her haste. And again…she cannot seem to move toward the unhooked receiver this time…frozen…an inner struggle takes over the joy that had just moved through her body…

Catherine snaps awake upon realizing the metallic buzz is coming from outside of her current experience. And the crisp reality of her senses tells her the previous phone call was not real. She is still in her orange silk pajamas. Breathing hard, she unbuttons the top as if it fits tightly on her neck. She can't breathe. She sits up, places her arms akimbo atop her head to open the breathing passages… *respire…respire…*breath arrives finally in a dramatic swoop. Once she can breathe, she allows the tears to explode in a messy splatter on her hands, the pajamas.

The phone has stopped ringing by now and it calms her. She gets up to look in the mirror and instead of the serene aged visage that greeted her in the dream, a ruddy complexion with disappointed eyes and wrinkled brow face her. She tries to recreate the dream. Taking off her clothes she steps into the shower, but she slides down the tile to the cold bath basin. She can feel her protruding spine against the ceramic. The hardness reminds her this is real. She will die from this thing, this organic growth. She made it; is she not responsible for its delivery of mortality, though it was always destined to come at some point? But why now? Why before her grandchildren would be born or her father would be buried? She has more to give the world, more to paint, more conversations with her daughter, more to see for herself. Had this destiny been written in ink long ago? She used to think it would be nice to know when one would die, to profit the most from one's life and be at peace on the judgment day. But now, she can think of nothing worse. The countdown to her death was constantly reflected in the countdown to Armageddon that so many cultish groups were touting in the media. She hadn't seen much of it in France, but she first saw 'special reports' on this frightening subject from the hospital waiting room in Boston. Her nephew had asked her about it one day during her treatment; at the age of only ten he, too, had this fear of an ending.

Just yesterday, she was feeling alright. She has to get herself back to that calm, change the swirls of fear that have stepped forward in her mind. She begins to take out the same shampoo she had used in the nightmare, swirl it through her hair, and breathe deeply. By the time she is massaging herself with the Vichy lotion, her mindset has changed back to a lighthearted spirit that overtakes the protective cloud she has held onto in France.

Suddenly, *tout un coup*, as if to give herself something else to think about, she returns to find out who had called at such an early time. What time is it anyway? The sky is gray this morning, so the summer light had not woken her up. Ten o'clock. Not early after all but still a strange time for a phone call. On the message, she hears the voice of Edmond, her agent, her gorgeous flamboyant friend, whom she had not yet told about the tumor. He knew she had come home and was dying to see her. 'When are you free so I can hear all about the family gossip and go over those new gorgeous paintings you have done? We're all set for next week, so we don't need to talk business. *On déjeune?* Marais, ok? Meet me at *Philosophes* around twelve for aperitif and we'll find a spot for lunch from there.'

She has not even been thinking about the show since she got back to Paris, but now that it is mentioned again, it brings more calm to her in a hope to regain some of the life she loves. This is why she had come back to Paris. She moves to get dressed.

In Paris, she wears dark jeans or black pants, always tightly fitted, a simple dark top, or white shirt when the heat comes, and one of three coverings: a cashmere sweater, trench coat, or blazer. She finishes it with a wool or silk scarf, depending on the season, her Yves Saint Laurent brown leather handbag (a gift from her father after her last gallery show opening), and then the choice of shoes. A rainbow of ballet flats and loafers and two pairs of heels: black and violet – reserved for aperitif *rendez-vous's* or *vernissage* events. Today, she adds a crimson silk scarf and navy patent *Repetto* flats to her otherwise nondescript – but well fitted – jeans, black t-shirt, and black blazer.

As she leaves the stillness of her courtyard and enters

the entrancing energy of St. Germain, her body shifts into relaxed confidence. One could see this in her purposeful walk, high chin, and nonchalant grasp of her handbag. Her wandering eyes hide behind a pair of large tortoise shell sunglasses, despite the grayness of the sky. But she will not forego a smile to a passerby. This is her greeting to old people walking with canes, to young mothers, to admirers. Really to anyone who happens to glance in her direction rather than keeping up the cold façade of coolness that Parisians tend to unintentionally frighten tourists with. It's usually only the symptom of waiting for a first coffee or thinking the foreigner might stop to ask them something in English, which they might not feel comfortable responding in. Or if they do, yesterday they met a rude American or Englishman who wanted to know why 'no one spoke English around here anyway' or 'why the coffees are so small' and it solidified a stereotype in their mind they had been fighting to get rid of.

She welcomes the way men say a little word to her as she passes in the streets. It's only when they are in big groups that it makes her nervous. Then, their intimidating jeers are more like a dare between them and an assertion of power rather than admiration.

Here, she keeps power over herself. French men like to admire. They admire more than a confident well-coiffed woman or impressive bust. She sees them stop to soak in a pair of shoes, watches, jackets, furniture in shop windows, as women who gaze in at Jimmy Choo shoes and diamond rings do. Gay and straight alike, they have a cultivation for the design of things and the small pleasures they receive from them. She saw it often in this upper class and artist neighborhood, but she also saw it in the far reaching districts, no matter what the price of the objects on display, they could be desired, and sometimes had.

They also like to show off their bodies like women do – tight pants, or at least closely-lined, open shirt buttons, fine tailoring and manicuring – even an actual nail manicure at the salon. And they cross their legs like women do, not needing to create visible space to make themselves appear more powerful and important. They are in touch with their cultural, and philosophical sides: subtleties which replace ambition and machismo. She doesn't know why this happened to this culture in particular and how they continue to take pride in it. Perhaps they could alter others to this sentiment, like her brother-in-law. Although probably not in his case, she decides. This is unlikely after his comments during their last trip to Paris with the children. Lawrence, or Larry, was especially embarrassing after a few drinks. He seemed to forget that many people around him could understand English.

She has been disgusted by the extremes of the stereotypical American male habits to enjoy one's drink too much, like her husband. When he would drink, he was a different man. Joking with his friends about her figure or about the way she wanted more children or her dreams to be a famous artist or her desires for a beautiful gown she was saving up for for no apparent reason. It was if he found her femininity a joke, but he still wanted her to be the trophy wife. Each end of the hypocrisy drove her mad. And she realized that she must forgive him before she could forgive herself. Guilt is a complicated burden.

And one person who lacked any guilty and any unfair judgment upon those around him was Edmond, but he did place it upon himself. For this reason, she had decided to keep her 'tragic news,' as Undine had called it, from him, at least until she returned to Paris. His partner Pascal had agreed it might be too much for him. Pascal started as her masseuse but quickly became a reflective and effervescent confidante. He was the first person she had told about the tumor. She had to tell someone, she said, she apologized for burdening him, but she had to tell someone. Pascal handled the news with sadness, compassion, and understanding. It was as if he knew this fate were coming, that it were part of her being already, that it was ok to be disappointed, but that only acceptance could help her to find her balance. She felt she could talk about anything with him rationally. When she went for her weekly massage, they had the deepest conversations perhaps spurred on by parts of her body that held truths and were stirred up by his touch.

She walks now with meditative tranquility. Feeling the soft movements of her feet in her well worn leather ballet flats, Letting the weight of consciousness fall through her swinging arms and out her fingertips toward the pavement where it will swirl up again to be trapped in the trees or rise up to the clouds.

She continues without looking, just moving, almost as if she is blind, until reaching the red doors of Saint Paul Cathedral.

She has arrived in the Marais from the long route down *Boulevard St. Germain* and the *Pont de Sully* and now continues behind *rue de Petit-Musc*. She has walked these streets near *Place des Vosges* at least a thousand times before and knows all the shops and street names she sees. But she refuses to remember how they all fit together, making each visit a willing new discovery. Each time it is put together a different way, like taking the familiar pieces of her wardrobe and mixing them with flashes of colors in the accessories and *maquillage*. And each corner has people passing by from all over that change the experience each time. The waiters, the type of coffee (*allongé, petit, grand crème*), the displays in store fronts, the flowers in bloom each make it different. Today she walks into *Place des Vosges* through the southern arches. Walking by Victor Hugo's home, she glances at a few pictures and explanations on the windows and notices a quote: 'The guilty one is not he who commits the sin, but the one who causes the darkness.' She looks toward the vaulted ceiling above her to seek the answer to this riddle. Rather than figure it out, she finds his inspiration there. She follows the exquisite marble with her gaze and feels the presence of free ancient spirits.

There is something about porticos, the *arcades*, that has always made her feel weak, as if given over to another time or presence. She is drawn to them and goes out of her way to walk through them. Three-sided tunnels, extended archways. A way to be outside in any weather. A way to make a pilgrimage wherever they would take you, knowing that others had walked this way before, for centuries. The first time she walked through them in Bologna, she felt something shift inside her. They are open yet protective, museum pieces of kingly quality for all to enjoy. They trap sound. Their columns make good hiding places. Many have whispered secrets into their walls and ceilings. The porticos at *Place des Vosges* are not exceptions. They were built for royals, but anyone can experience them today. They can simply walk the circle, sit at a café, or find the small inconspicuous opening that leads to the hidden garden at *Hotel du Sully* and escape to small pebble pathway, vines, and blackbirds.

She walks toward the park and feels the calm at the center. There are two mothers with their babies and a few scattered individuals reading the newspaper or sitting with smooth faces. She continues through the park at the same continued pace and opens the dog gate with a slow creaking sound that echoes through the square. Now on the opposite side of the sleepy square, she exits into the lively streets nearby. She passes under monumental archways, feeling a new energy as she emerges. The light changes color; the air holds different smells.

After she exits on *rue des Francs-Bourgeois*, she walks by the MAC counter where a woman helps two teenagers choose their color palettes. She witnesses one reaching for purple with her finger, the other passively allowing the application of coral over her lid. At the corner after, the server is balancing a tray with a complete *petit déjeuner*: a basket with one croissant and half a baguette, a bowl of *café crème*, and tall glass of *orange pressé*. As she turns to the left, she sees the *Tabac* owner fidgeting with his outdoor displays.

Just before she reaches her destination, she sees a door she has never noticed before. It is a wooden, blue arched entryway, too small for a car. What catches her eye is the dog's nose pushing it slightly ajar, revealing a hidden rose garden in a private courtyard. Although only ajar for a few seconds, the entranceway gives her an image to take with her and contemplate as she walks on. The roses are wild and multi-colored unlike the typical Parisian parks, professionally and immaculately manicured. Even the trees along boulevards in the French countryside are planted in parallel rows, often trimmed in right angles. Is it man's taming of nature or his heightened appreciation for her beauty? She is not sure of the answer, perhaps both are possible. There is a calmness to the homogenous flower beds and parallel trunks, but at this moment the hidden wild roses satisfy a desire to lose control. Wild youth is merely untamed, not evil or destructive. Strange premonitions do not come from thinking inside the box of society. There was the time in Lucca when Esmé had pointed to the sky. *Look!* Nothing was there. Half a minute later, a hundred storks flew overhead and landed in the cathedral square. The locals had seen nothing like it and were sure it was a sign of fertility. Of course, babies were born as usual that year and each one of them was attributed to the storks. She yearns for that childhood instinct. Sometimes she thinks enlightenment is merely a state of return to innocence. Known naïveté. Could it exist?

Her eyes flash between recognition of this inner world rich with sensory detail and the exterior of the Marais's full streets. Walking sometimes on the sidewalk, sometimes with the other pedestrians in the road, she gazes at shop windows and inhales the smells from restaurants and drifting perfumes. She hears voices but not the substance of words. Instead, passing tones and rhythms create the music of her promenade.

IV
À Chacun son Tour

Catherine's topographical instincts in the Marais are enhanced through repetition, but she loosens and unlearns her own cognitive mapping freely.   Still, she arrives effortlessly at *rue Vieille-du-Temple* and makes her way past shop windows toward *Les Philosophes,* where she will meet Edmond. She adores the whicker chairs, quiet, not-quite-pedestrian street, and the soft corner of clients who each interact with the waiter like ping pong balls bouncing in and out of a game, sometimes ricocheting toward a bystander.

She chooses a seat *en plein soleil* that she knows will soon be taken over by the cool shadows. A few moments of powerful rays.   Her seat keeps her back to the café window, a chair adjacent to her looks out as well. She prefers to talk this way, side to side. Observing together and allowing more space for their conversation to grow. She is especially aware of this choice today since she plans to finally tell Edmond about the tumor. Here? At lunch? While walking? There is no right moment.

She orders a *Perrier tranche*, sparkling water with lemon, a fitting complement to the June sun. After it arrives, she takes the plastic swirling stick to push the lemon slices through the water and ice cubes, surfacing the bubbles. She does this more for the sound and the pleasure of movement than for the infusion of the citrus flavor. She drinks the water. The bubbles try to activate the conscious part of her brain, but it is mush in the heat. She cannot decide if it is welcomed meditation or an eerie absence of conscious thought. She considers moving to avoid the heat.

But just in time, as anticipated, the shadow's edge reaches her. She feels the breeze that was always there carry away invisible molecules of perspiration. She pours the rest of her Perrier into the glass and signals the waiter, *"Un café s'il vous plaît."*

Catherine scans the scene. Her hidden eyes pick out a woman walking in skin-tight jeans and high-healed sandals, wearing a large black, straw hat. Her fingers are accentuated by dark red nail polish. They move freely, lengthening her body. A man in a suit walks by with two children, golden curls atop their heads. He speaks with them like adults, reasoning out why they will go to the market before returning home for their lunch break and discussing a problem that came up in one of the children's math classes. The child complains, "It's not fair. We were not prepared and no one did well, *Papa.*" The response is swift: *"Ça suffit. Arrête maintenant.* You don't deserve a higher mark." Another woman at the end of the terrace wears a gray T-shirt, jeans, and ballet flats. She is angular in her poise on the circular table. Her forearms rest on the tile surface with her   elbows spread wide. Her dark hair softly falling to her shoulders in order to be pushed back again in a soft waterfall. The woman next to her is heavy, wears a white blouse, pink scarf. She talks intensely with her friend, frequently gesturing and elegantly crossing her legs. Parisian elegance is not about thinness or haute couture. It is about the positioning of one's body, a confidence and directness. A pride in one's body and self that move toward others as finger tips of expression or commanding gates. This is why the 'trick' of Parisian fashion is so hard to master, for it is not about the clothes, other than simply cleanliness showing self-respect. It is about the movement of oneself within them and the animated facial expressions, *bien coiffée,* that sits atop. Sometimes Catherine feels she is only imitating, even after so many years.   Although her American friends acknowledge it, do they see it as narcissism? She feels *les françaises* know she is an imposter, a wannabe. It shouldn't matter what they might think, but it does. She still has yet to be close to a French woman but considers it her own fault, her frequent voluntary isolation.

The terrace clientele hear rough singing from around the corner. An unkempt woman with curly black hair and a curvy silhouette in tattered dress pushing a stroller appears. Inside the stroller is a dog - a wide-eyed pug who turns her head to watch them as she rolls by, mouth agape. As the woman pauses in front of them, the worn out soles of her shoes are apparent. Where in her long path had it gone wrong? The woman continues and begins singing again. Her dog stays put after a quick yelp - either a cry for help or some kind of harmony to the unrecognizable song.

Catherine lets her eyes linger where the woman had stood and sees another archway before her, doors painted red. She wonders what is on the other side, hoping each passerby will stop, enter the code, and grant her a peak. Most don't seem to even notice it is there. She glances South toward the Seine as a glimpse of peripheral vision reveals an opening. Two people have emerged, they are stepping over the threshold like the one leading to her own courtyard. But she can only see a small slice of empty space. The door closes. Now in front, Japanese tourists with heaps of shopping bags stop. They look like three downward facing flowers - the assortment of angular bags encircling them are the petals. She imagines blue bicycles, long window panes, and yellow curtains that blow into the courtyard. The smell of lunch being prepared, the clatter of dishes. Her mother's contagious smile shining as she opens windows and calls out to her - *'Buon giornio principessa!'*

Her warm beaming smile, accented with fresh coral lipstick, as she opened the bedroom door to wake up Undine and Catherine for school alongside this greeting made it difficult to warrant laying in bed. If the morning was particularly cold or dark, the rising smell of toast in from the kitchen below that would sneak through the door's opening, or would be carried along on her mother's clothes, completed the waking signal. She would want to run to breakfast immediately, but knew she had to get ready for school before arriving at the table. A trick that kept the Poulain girls on time for school.

What mothers and daughters inhabit this building facing her?

Perhaps it is best not to know what is on the inside, to never open that door. She shall forever wonder about the contents in her latest *objet petit a,* her object of desire.

As her *café allongé* and glass of water arrive, her attention turns to that first sip that shocks her system just slightly. The coffee itself is never good in this city and she is especially aware of this fact when she orders a beverage without milk. She had first been under the impression that the coffee was the best here, better than in Italy, not only because she was enamored of the terraces on which you could drink it but also because the heated milk had a taste that brought her right back to the farm where it would have been taken from. When she orders an espresso or *allongé* instead (the drawn out *allongé* is even worse, but she takes these on the occasions when she wishes to sip it for a while), they become a bitter harsh reminder of life without Romanticized sugar or milky coatings. She welcomes these moments, to feel life's intensity with the highs and lows.

She can often read a person by the coffee selection sitting on the table in front of him. Typically, Parisians will take their first coffee of the morning with milk, to start the day softer and with some added nutrition and fat. Later, the coffee turns into simply espresso or perhaps a *noisette,* the French version of the Italian *machiatto.* American tourists tend to get the *Americano,* which is more like the drip coffee they are used to. Or they continue to get *café crèmes* and *cappuccinos* all day long. When they ask for skim milk, the waiters pretend not to speak English, then ask the barista inside, '*Pourquoi les Americains aiment le lait écrémé? Peut-être qu'ils se sentent moins coupables de se gaver les glaces!*' she silently counters. Sometimes an ice cream in place of cream is not such a bad exchange. The *Allongé* is long but not as much as the *Americano* and lets her linger over it longer but still taste the coffee in its pure form. Sometimes, it is an espresso served with a little metal pitcher of hot water. It gives the patron a sense of ownership and craftsmanship. Italians, who help others to understand how to indulge, a symptom of their Roman roots, or those not used to coffee, such as tea-drinking British, will add sugars. Children or pregnant ladies in the afternoon might have a *chocolat chaud*. And in fact, anyone feeling a bit indulgent will have this thick chowder of a beverage that does not remotely resemble the Swiss Miss hot cocoa with freeze-dried marshmallows that Catherine grew up with.

She had seen the extreme of these latter indulgences at the famous teahouse on *rue de Rivoli*, Angelina's. A man sitting with his wife or girlfriend, an Italian couple, had ordered *chocolat à l'Africain*, the thick, dark hot chocolate drink they are known for. He had an espresso sized cup in front of him to pour the pitcher of chocolate into. Before pouring, he emptied one sugar packet into the little cup. After pouring the liquid chocolate bar, he opened another packet, then another, and finally the fourth. The spoon perched between his thick dark-haired fingers spun quickly in tiny circles. He drank it in two or three sips, washed it down with water, and made a similar concoction for his second round. He followed this all with a quick unsugared *ristretto* while his female partner still lingered over her first cup of chocolate, albeit with two sugar packets added to her own. As soon as he put down the cup, he spoke with animated hand language representing swearwords that were parts of the female anatomy, but in an endearing way, to talk about the amazing sights they had seen that day. He then proceeded to take her hand and tell her how beautiful she was in this city, then kiss her hand and bow his head. She laughed at him, 'Oh, Armando! *Sempre romantico!*' Catherine imagined they would soon be ready for their afternoon siesta at their room in the Ritz, a time for both romance and sugar crashing. Coffee can tell a story.

Today she hopes coffee will somehow help her to share *her* story. Before she left for her treatments in New England, she had had a long talk with Pascal about the tumor during her weekly massage on a cold January morning. It was always instantly warmer when she took off her clothes an climbed under the soft cotton sheet on the massage table. She felt she could talk about anything, and so he became the first one she told. She blurted it out as soon as he asked how she was, because the answer to '*Ça va?*' was obviously not '*Oui, ça va*' as is the normal response.

'*Ça va pas,*' she paused, searching for the right words that didn't come, 'I have a tumor.' She then recounted what she knew, systematically, until her voice began to crack and she broke off in silence.

'Is there pain?'

'It's not bad, just some headaches.'

'Ok, I can help you with that. Let's discuss how you can beat it.'

He did not ask a million questions. He did not ask how long she would live.

The massage continued as normal, as if he knew some normalcy could help her at this moment. He talked about how he could use massage to make her feel better if she decided to use certain treatments or therapies. She discussed the possibility of using the drug Temozolomide, which at the time she could barely remember how to say, and also some chemotherapy, but she wasn't sure yet, she would decide after talking with a few more doctors in Boston. It was all so overwhelming.

As she said this, she had clenched every muscle in her body, just as she had done half the night before, and the night before that. He talked about how it was unfair, but he hoped she would not stay angry. 'You are so tense when you are angry!' And over the several weeks before she went to America, he smiled a lot, he teased her, he laughed when she cried, but followed it with a hug or some tea. She could go to see him without worrying that he would constantly pity her or want to talk about how she was feeling. He made it clear he was there for her, should she need to talk or need someone to go with her to the doctor, but that he would treat her like a normal person. 'We are all dying people,' he said, 'So you are no different from the rest.' His wide impressive grin and comforting embrace had warmed her up much more than she had imagined was possible. She had been lucky with the first two she had told about the tumor. In the weeks that followed she felt anger, pity, or absence from the others she chose to share this news with. Some had come around to acceptance; some never would.

For a few weeks, they continued to talk about the subject of telling Edmond of the cancer. His center of truth was based on his emotions rather than rationality or logic. The subject of death was one that he could never handle, whether as an abstraction or the actual earthly parting of a friend or famous person alike. He was then and still is dealing with the recent death of his father, Jean-François. A traditional man *de la terre* from Bretagne. In his younger years he had been vibrant and strong-willed, with thick frame and strong appendages from many years working as a ferry man between Saint Malo and Dinard. And from many bowls of cider, *tartines* laid thick with his cousin's farm's salted butter, and *galettes au sarrasin,* traditional buckwheat crepes, cooked in more butter still and filled with ham and eggs or roquefort cheese and walnuts. He had been a supremely masculine figure with a kind heart, deeply weathered smile, and joyous wife. Catherine had met him several times over the years during a few excursions she had made with Edmond to enjoy the seaside and do some sketching by the shore. Although a man of few words, his interactions were always warm and familial. He would want to take them to his favorite bar or cheese shop or to show them how the beach had changed in a storm. They would bring back a *Far Breton* or *charcuterie* proudly to his wife, Madame Valérie Gouyet, for lunch with the windows open to *rue de la Crosse*.   She nagged him about the dirt on his shoes and the way he smelled like gasoline and fish, or sometimes alcohol, but it was clear in her manner that she loved him. Her heart utterly belonged to him.   They ate every day like they were celebrating something and it was always delicious, even though Madame Gouyet would get upset if something had not been completely finished.   Even though she knew it was a flawed system, she showed love through her food. After lunch, they would then climb up above the house to the city walls for a walk and Jean-François would quickly leave them with *bises* when it was time to go back for the next ferry.

But when his wife had died five years ago, it made him sad and strange with Edmond. They each mourned her passing in different ways and Edmond found he could not stay at the family house without her there. He would take the train to Saint Malo to meet his father for lunch once a month, then every other month. They always had news to report, but never talked about feelings, never about the more romantic qualities of life anymore. Because emotion was Edmond's center, he could not risk talking about a subject that would be so sad. They experienced a lot of silence together.

And to Edmond's biggest regret, he had never brought Pascal with him, or even told his father about him. He was pretty sure his father knew he was gay. He never said it in those words to him but he had told his mother as a teenager and his father never pressed him about meeting girls and never made an issue of anything that might be considered 'questionable' about his identity. This was a term he was happy to to use to describe other people.

He was a man of a small place despite its visitors from elsewhere. He had inhabited Saint Malo since his birth in 1923. He had lived there through the war, just far enough from the Normandy bombings to feel safe until it was bombed in 1944 and much of it destroyed. But they rebuilt and the tourists continued to come and the town continued to feel medieval in only the way that made it a small community inside the walls. He always said that having tuberculosis had saved him; this was why he had not had to enlist in the war, though he would have liked to join the navy like his father. But it was also what ultimately killed him at the age of seventy-six. He had begun to have trouble breathing soon after his wife's death. Within two years, he could no longer work on the boat and used a respirator while he was sleeping. Last year he had begun to need the machine most of the time, but Catherine imagined it was also to take in some extra oxygen to make him slightly delusional and to not deal with the world that was there before him without the joy and companionship of his life companion. An oxygen machine was a poor replacement for Valérie.

And so he had died one day. Out by the rocks as the tide was coming in. Without his machine. Cut off from help.

Edmond was his only surviving close relative, so he kept the nondescript urn with the ashes in his flat now. There had been no funeral nor memorial service. Instead, he had simply slipped into a dark place, one that was hard for both Pascal and Catherine to watch and to be with. His feeling was more than sadness, it had to do with insecurity about the way he had left his relationship at the time of death.

And Edmond had never been completely honest with him. He had hidden part of his life and he would always regret it.

He would not let himself be helped and they imagined he felt quite alone and misunderstood. They were patient with him, careful with him. Walking on eggshells.

And for this reason, Catherine had not told him about the tumor. Instead, she had filled their encounters before her departure with a show she would do in June. These would be family portraits at a gallery on *rue de Seine* that she had shown at before. Portraits of everyday activities. Portraits that would also reflect herself. Knowing her family through the angle of color, experimentation with her sentiments, and a homage to their virtues.

As she reaches the warm cup to her lips, gazing out over her sunglasses, she sees Edmond arriving from a nearby side-street. Auburn hair that shines in the sun, bronzed skin from his daily meetings with clients on terraces. His face is lightly bearded, smooth-skinned, and wide-eyed, almost like an innocent doe. The undulations of his chest are exposed by a deep gray V-neck that hangs loose and low to his mid-hips. It is covered partially by his open black trench coat. His jeans are tight and dark with just the right amount of wear and a slight bootcut. The Italian black leather loafers with pointed toes complete his simple coolness. Although of average height, his leanness makes him long. He makes casual chic look effortless, but he still holds evident tension in his brow that has not yet been released.

He used to be a makeup artist to pay the bills while he also began to be an agent, making his connection slowly through the studios of the Marais. This is how they met, through an ad he had hung at a café. She wanted an agent to help her become a professional, to show her work while she continued to enjoy smaller sessions with students. The café is just around from the corner from his old makeup counter. It's where they had first met after he had helped her choose some makeup, which led to their conversation about art.

Edmond greets her with three kisses on her cheeks and slides into the seat next to hers. The soft hair on his face carresses hers. As he orders a half-pint of beer, he enters right into a relaxed conversation about an Indian artist, cigarettes, and a fascinating judo champion. He seems relaxed and even happy despite her worry about his wrinkled brow; perhaps it was just the sun. Easily their parlance twists until they turn to the subject of her art show in a few weeks time. She tries not to think of it as the last show for fear she will reveal her secret to him too early. He suggests it could be the beginning of something fresh…something familial and yet universal.

It feels like the time that she has to say something, something about this being her last show, about what it means to her. She begins, 'Edmond…I wanted to talk with you about something. I haven't been trying to keep a secret but….' He stops her with his hand, held firmly but gently in the air. He seems to know already. She questions him, 'You know?'

'Pascal told me last week.'

So he is pretending. His talk about the show is a diversion. She presses him to talk about it a little bit more, not sure exactly what to say besides the medical details, but he stops her again. '*Non, s'il te plait, Catherine.* Let's walk to lunch.'

He has no idea she even has a slight chance of survival. She has told no one and has nearly forgotten it herself. She wants to live as if she is dying. She does not wish to battle the invisible disease. It would be to pit herself against a black hole and inevitably plummet, disintegrate. Instead she fights the same battle we all do: the challenge not to fight and merely to live. The battles fall away from her now. Choice is not a struggle. She moves with deeper and deeper intuition with quick knowledge of what she wants and how she feels. But she can't explain this to him now. For him, death is absolute and he wants to escape it. He is battling the idea of mortality by trying to push it from his mind, and so he cannot look into the eyes of his friend who is facing its imminent arrival.

They get up and walk some of the same streets Catherine had just inhabited by herself. They are moving north but she is not sure of their destination. She waits for Edmond to break the silence. But they continue. Quiet minutes that seem endless.

Until he stops in front of his apartment building. He says he just has to go up for a moment, to get something he forgot. The wrinkle in that brow has deepened and he turns away before he finishes speaking. As he enters the courtyard, Catherine follows and catches the door to his building as it is about to close. She runs upstairs with the instinct that Edmond has retreated to his womb to suffer. She will not let him suffer alone; he needs a friend.

His door is still ajar and she pushes it open. She's never seen him cry before. He is bawling like a young child on the futon in his and Pascal's living room. Hearing her entry, he gets up slowly and approaches her with timidity, embracing her as if she might crumble before him. He holds pain in his eyes and looks away. He sits next to her on the futon, so as not to face the pain. To face a reflected pain that is in himself still from his father's death. He had made the mistake of thinking his father could not handle the truth when in fact the lack of truth hurt him. There were never full conversations between them. Instead they would talk about someone mutual, like one of the cousins at the farm or Catherine, or observe the progress of the French rugby team. They would talk about the house and the work that needed to be done on the floors.

And he had died. In the middle of all these evasive discussions.   He had died as they were separated by silence. Not the calm silence of understanding but that of anxious suffering. It was going through his mind at this moment and as he looked again at Catherine he felt guilty he was not thinking of her. But then he forced himself to and the tears came again; this is how they had finally come a moment ago after months of drought.

He has nothing to say to her in the confusion of his internal suffering.   They had once been so intimate, so carefree and now he has become a partial stranger. He tries to begin several times and then simply asks her to go.

He is sorry. 'I'm so sorry. Please forgive me. I don't know...*je suis désolé....*'

As she walks home, she passes people laughing together, clinking glasses, and suddenly does not feel so calmly solo and free. That human instinct of loneliness when we are alone creeps in and grabs her throat. She finds fingers tense and pulling on one another.

...

She takes the rest of the day in silence, like a Trappist Monk. She resists the temptation to call him or Pascal. She trusts Pascal, knows he will talk to Edmond, help to make it right eventually. But she worries, and she does not think mostly about his suffering but her own. *Alone, just myself here, I've left my family in America...*It is a hazy uncomfortable day and she will have trouble recalling later how exactly she filled up the rest of it, if she ate lunch, and if she cried for just a few moments or until nightfall.

As she hits the pillow finally, her mind wanders back to

Edmond. She wants to feel stronger than him. Feels as though she must be stronger than him, help him. Someday, he would move on from this inability to deal with her mortality, which was a reflection of his own, his parents', and Pascal's. He was angry. He was scared and confused. She already forgives him, but she misses him, too.

She pities herself and hates it.   Hates the the embarrassment, the weakness, the face in the mirror. She screams at it, pulls on her skin, falls on all fours to the cold tile.

It can't end like this between them. As she slowly picks herself up and wraps herself in a soft white robe, she decides to try again. They are family.

V

Camille et Auguste

The museums of Paris let its denizens jump between centuries and inhabit living spaces of another time, preserved by the graces of the French government that has seized an estate in at the moment of an artist's death within the country's boundaries or through the generous donation to the public. The acquisitions of the French museums, for their artistic value and scope, are often described as unparalleled. Living in Paris, one can travel just by entering a building for a few hours. Catherine feels like she has a time machine, where she can jump into portholes to experience others' lives. On several trips to one of her favorite parks, especially during Esmé's

Wednesday afternoons off from school, they used to enter the Victorian era through the *Musée Nissim de Comando*; although a twentieth century home, one that cultivated beautiful furniture from the nineteenth century.   Just a few blocks from her apartment, she could likewise visit the third century bath ruins at the Cluny Museum, and, on the other end of the spectrum, the Centre Pompidou is not far from her studio and always has rotating exhibits of twentieth century art.   But she really loves the museums that house so much work from a single individual - Picasso in the Marais, Dali in Montmartre, Monet in Giverny. Her favorite of these single artist museums is that of Auguste Rodin, infamous sculptor of the early twentieth century.   The modern master of marble and space, of delicate emotion in a substance equally useful for making monstrous columns of power with references to the origins of democratic civilization.

Just after this day's morning fog has lifted, Catherine meanders toward the back entrance of the *Musée Rodin*. With the intention of only paying a small tariff to enter the gardens, she has the urge at the cashier to pay the full price to re-experience the statues positioned all over Rodin's former home in every crevice.   There is so much detail to look at here.   So many angles of each sculpture to see.   Although she knows it well, she always finds new negative space to fill with ideas or reflection.

As she enters and moves away from the stairway, the pure whiteness of the marble always calms her.   Roaming the rooms, she alternates between focusing on the pure figures before her and pausing by a window to capture the gardens in the light of the day.

She often takes longest in viewing the sculptures she

remembers being made in the film *Camille Claudel*, the one about Rodin's protégée and lover. The sadness of the story is in the violation of her youth and personal creative genius, both of which Rodin treasured, manipulated, and took advantage of. This is the way the director tells the story at least. There was love in this narrative, but it was controlled and lopsided. She remembers watching it and feeling heartbroken for the young woman whose life seemed to be stolen away. Thomas had fallen asleep midway through it. She remembers this because she had turned to him at the end with tears wishing to share this moment, to discuss the injustice. Perhaps it is better left as desire rather than a disappointment, she now thinks. She had felt as if she wanted to shatter Rodin from the center, despite her immense admiration of his artistry. Alone, the thought had spiraled through her faster and faster with nowhere to escape and she had stayed awake half the night thinking about it. Grabbing her journal and writing down her thoughts at about three a.m. purged enough of her anger to allow her four hours of restless sleep that night.

The statue she now stops at is of Camille rolled up into a naked little ball held up airborn by a hulking masculine figure, like that of Auguste. It is as if he possessed her naked beauty like a basketball. Here the hand holds her up with monstrous proportion. Pride is speaking of the way man believes to create woman and control her, give her something to be dependent on. But it also shows an awareness of his inability to interact with her fully. She is closed to him. Is it because he cannot understand, or because he will not take the time to listen, to consider a different perspective? Her innocence is marked in her fetal position, smallness, and lack of a direct gaze.

Catherine feels so conflicted here, knowing that she herself would fall in love with this man, had fallen in love with a similar man in *Firenze*. Those first embraces in the sculpture room where Ludovico had helped her hands to mold a figure of a child. Their clothes stained forever with clay in this lustful lack of inhibitions. It had been after Thomas' death, but she still felt guilt. She had desired a lover before the accident. The wife she found out about later, but that did not stop her from inviting him over again. Esmé's presence in the apartment. Her infantile witness of their act. But she craved these encounters and the only way she could stop was by moving. She left Ludovico behind and never contacted him again. But she still loves him in absentia. His artistic way of seeing the world, his olive-toned Italian skin, his lack of inhibitions, his appreciation of her work and her body. He could never be her husband, but something was created between them, something she could still cherish.

She had also become his model, like Camille to Auguste, or like Marie-Thérèse Walter to Picasso, or another Camille to Monet. But like Camille Claudel she had her own talent that he never seemed to acknowledge.

'Ah...I cannot come to your show,' he had sighed into her ear, 'My wife invited some friends over.' He had started to kiss her neck, then continued, 'But come to mine next week, and Federico's, too. You will learn some things!'

After they had made love, he took out a cigarette by the studio window and turned back toward her, the sun behind making him a dark imposing figure. He motioned with his cigarette toward one of her paintings for the show, the one that was a simple sketch of one of his statues, 'This one is my favorite. Will you keep it or give it to your parents? I think next time you might be ready to sell something.'

He did not have to love her work, but could at least talk about it critically with her, like she saw him do with other students. She had come to Florence because she knew it was the place of masters and students, not necessarily the best contemporary art, but where she could improve her foundation. She was accepted to work in the professional school through photographs she had sent of her work, not herself. All she wanted was for her work to be taken seriously, and that was what Edmond had finally helped her to do in Paris. She gave up her ambitions to add sculpture to her repertoire, linking its work with losing control of herself, even though losing control is exactly what she liked about being in love with Ludovico. She is in control when she paints or sketches, even when she lets her intuition take over. At least she feels ownership of it; it's something that comes from within. In her lessons on sculpture and Italian romance, she always felt she were the muse, even when the clay was in her hands.

In the adjoining room, the light coming in from the window hits Claudel's most famous piece: *Sakountala*, also called *L'Abandon*. Her work is shown beside that of Rodin's, partly to show his influence and their relationship, but also to give her the display space she deserves. Sakountala was the heroine of a Hindu poet's work, or with the more generic title, she is simply a woman abandoning herself to the pleas of a man below her, one who seems to worship her. The woman is more powerful than in Rodin's sculpture but still vulnerable and in love with the man to whom she is eternally attached. The swooning energy line, the beauty of the negative space between them. The white marble is like that of antiquity even though they were chiseled in the beginning of the modern era. The whiteness of the marble is pure and innocent, unwrinkled and smoothed by the hands of God, it seems. And if God is the power within each of us to create beauty in the world, then this is exactly what had happened in the creation of this statue. Camille's delicate, strong fingers and Auguste's immense hands that are so powerful in their repeated representations in marble throughout the mansion. A few statues only contain hands. They echo the often replicated reaching hands in Michelangelo's Sistine Chapel that seem to contain the invisible energy of God between them, a spark...life.

Deperdieu had played Rodin in the film about Claudel and as she looks at this statue now, she feels the doubled presence of the sculptor and the actor. Two artists who perhaps had so much zeal for the artistry that they forgot to be gentlemen. She didn't exactly forgive it, but she could forgive the women who loved them for being blinded by their passion and ultimately getting hurt. It had happened to her with Ludovico, and, to some extent, it had happened to her with Thomas. His dual nature captivated her toward an understanding of this untamable beast that could never be relinquished.

She remembers her college dreams that she used to work toward at three in the morning in the campus studio that she was only now fully tackling, a few months before her death. What had happened to them along the way? Why was she still seeking success? He had made her into the tight little ball of a naked woman that Camille is in the

78

immortal sculpture. The film explains it so clearly. Camille! Camille, who wound up in a mental institution for thirty years before her death. She cannot help to think that if Camille's brother, who committed her, had died before her, or if Auguste had given her the credit she deserved that perhaps she would have been free. A disgusting thought enters her mind. Shamefully, she acknowledges, *I am free because Thomas died.* She pursues her dreams; she lives in Paris; she lets her daughter study philosophy and physics in America.

And what if he hadn't?

She realizes she is still somewhat trapped by him. The baggage of this guilt, combined with that from her first affair as widow, has turned her into a lifelong bachelorette and she is not sure that this is what she wants. Had she tricked herself into its intoxicating solitude? But it is as if she, or Thomas from the world beyond, has shut off a part in her brain that desires intimacy, or perhaps dependency. She rationalizes with emotion and beauty, much like Edmond, so it seems she would fall in love with many men along the way. Why doesn't she at least dream of these encounters? With her doctor or a waiter...the gallery owner or Esmé's friends' fathers...why don't these thoughts come to her mind? It seems she has come to Paris to make love with the city itself, and, to some extent, it is working.

She craves a bit of air and wanders into the gardens. Still before lunchtime, the visitors are few in comparison. Quite a few stand in front of The Thinking Man, *Le Penseur*. Others stroll back toward the disturbing sculpture of Ugolino and his sons in the middle of a pond. She thinks of Dante and Carpeaux as well. This grotesque subject of eating ones own children in desperation. Even if they are already dead. The topic has fascinated several artists. A woman with two young children walks by the statue and Catherine watches for their reaction. The mother does not seem to realize what is before them as they pause to take sips of water.

Did these artists find their children a burden? That is one theory. Some would say that Catherine being left with Esmé alone, in a foreign country, made her chances at being an artist and finding another husband extremely difficult. But she has been able to support her family, financially and emotionally. *I am happy alone.* She has never really missed having a lover. *Have I missed out?* Never really thought about it consciously before. But she has enjoyed her flirtations like a happily married woman would.

She has also continued to buy beautiful, albeit simple, lingerie, and continued to admire herself naked in the mirror. She spends at least fifteen minutes after each shower completely in the nude. Then, she carefully massages her body, especially her thighs and shoulders, both strong from swimming, with lotion made of cocoa or shea butter and always scented with vanilla. Performing this task, then airing herself out, even making some tea or turning on the news before getting dressed. Several times she has forgotten to completely close the blinds, but it does not bother her if someone has seen her. If it were cold in the flat, she would put on one of her soft robes, the short silky black one or the warmer white terry cloth robe. If she had nowhere to be, she could spend an hour in her robe, eating breakfast, drying her hair, looking out the window, taking care of her single flower, a miniature yellow rose. Sometimes she would day dream. That's how it goes most days. But once in a while without warning, she is decidedly unhappy. Lonely. She has been getting old. Even before the chemo treatments, her skin has changed. She cannot compete with the youth, the actresses in her neighborhood. Even her paintings now only sell to her friends. Her vision is not so hip. She looks at herself less often in the mirror.

She takes a seat on a bench with a view of the *Eve* sculpture and some orange roses. She decides to have a go at a day dream with some romance. To free its excitement. Maybe it is time to try, to go that direction in her dreams before the real world. This is where she would try out many things in the past. Sometimes if they failed in her dream, she would do it anyway.

She puts her sunglasses on and closes her eyes. Who can she think of in this way? Before anyone comes to mind, she opens her eyes again and looks to see who is around her. A guard passes by, smiles; the woman with the children is walking a different direction. Several others float around, but no one pays any attention to her. It is as if she is afraid they can see through to her thoughts, or her naked tumor. She doesn't want them to notice either one.

Who can it be? Not Doctor Caillot. He is too clinical, or too fatherly, even if he is only a few years older than she. The gallery owner? Too flashy. She can't imagine him taking off any of his clothes. What about Henri? She has not seen him since she got back and he would be coming for his lesson tomorrow. Henri, a silver-haired Parisian ten years her senior who comes to the studio once a week after his banking job. He had been coming to her studio for over a year now, and she learned of his diverse interests in Scandinavian culture, Greek and Latin literature, the NBA, and sailing, especially to North African ports on his brother-in-law's boat. They talked about many interests, but not about their families or personal histories. He always wore a business suit to the studio and changed into designer jeans and a thin cashmere sweater to paint in, worried about his comfort rather than where the paint might go on his clothes. 'Come what may!' he had said when she warned him the first time. His gray hair complements his beautiful green eyes with a sparkle caught in reflecting the silver of his hair and his stubble. A Latin scholar, a romantic, but also a realist when it came to his job, and, earlier, selecting his education as well. He had always wanted children but never found the right woman to settle down with. He didn't think it was worth settling for someone for the sake of companionship, since he had told her that 'love can take many forms.' He seemed to believe this was also the reason Catherine was alone, as if confiding in a kindred spirit.

She tries to think of him then. But it just feels strange and as if she is being watched. She goes back to the real world, opens her eyes and sees there are actually quite a few handsome men in the park. They are likely tourists, she guesses, not at work, maps or brochures in their hands. She should not worry so much about this trivial thing in her life; just look at where it had gotten Camille! If Camille had been free and had only her father as a protector in her life, all would have been well. All would be well without *un amant*. She decides right then not to let it take up what little time she has left in the world, possibly thrusting her into misery when she has been so happy. When it comes to men, she'll focus on talking with Pascal about how to get Edmond back in her life instead. She values his love more than any possible fling. The show did not matter, she pretty much knew what she still wanted to get done for it and could always talk with a few of her artist friends or the gallery owner - Gregoire, about it. Edmond weighed on her mind — how to help him? How to get him out of the trap he had made for himself? She fears this could even hurt his relationship with Pascal, one that she felt she was a part of, like an intertext created in their dissonant harmonies.

She exits the gardens under a spit of rainfall and heads down *rue de Varenne* a long time until she reaches *rue de la Chaisse* where she then weaves in zig zags between the Seine and *Boulevard St. Germain*. On *rue de Beaune* there are some strange little shops. She pauses at windows, making a tent between the glass and her tiny black umbrella. Antique shops cover all areas of household items: kitchen utensils, letter openers, porcelain tea cups, and gramaphones. One is particularly devoted to historical boardgames, pieces of art that take us through the lifetime of a king or the uprise of the Revolution. It seems more of an esoteric museum than a shop, although she imagines that Parisians with country homes may find a way to incorporate these historic games into family gatherings in the parlor or at least keep them on display so they may be discussed when tea is served. She wanders slowly by this window to the next shop, doing a sort of karaoke agility drill with her feet. Right next door is a storefront with tin boxes of all shapes and sizes. She browses the window at the scenes of Paris or children playing, and images of food that had been sold inside the box. Some images of the *Banania* man startle her.

To the right, as she walks along, are brilliant lavenders and fruits on the Provençal covers to the tins. As she moves to the second window after the door, she spots her favorite retro design, Théophile-Alexandre Steinlen's poster of *Le Chat Noir*. She enters the shop and leaves her umbrella at the door. '*Bonjour Madame!*' sings the shopkeeper, and Catherine gives her similar reply. She asks to see the box in the window. The woman smiles and removes it from the display, gingerly handing it to Catherine. On the edges, there are images of people dancing in *La Belle Époque*. There is much to examine in their costumes and happy faces. She takes her time. Turning it over. On the bottom, the price is marked on a small white sticker as forty francs.

She begins to place it down although already planning to purchase it, to look at a few more, when the shopkeeper makes her choice easier, '*Celle-ci est parfaite pour garder les lettres. Moi, j'ai le même chez moi.*' A beautiful idea and a fitting one. She has an old *Repetto* shoebox under her bed that is filled with letters. She could use the tin instead and keep it on her shelf. She would open it more often.

This careful craft was instilled in her by her parents during childhood. Her father's profession as a writer made him a fascinating read filled with creativity. At his desk, he would push his typewriter aside when artfully penning his letters to friends from his years at Williams College or to relatives in Colorado and England. Her mother had made sure every gift, including food, wine, or flowers brought to the house was acknowledged with a handwritten note as well. A chore as a child, it turned into a pleasure by the time she turned nineteen. Every year at Easter time, her mother would also write lengthy notes about the family to her relatives in Italy and several others they had known in Brookline who had moved to San Francisco, Huston, Dublin, and Toronto. Some of them wrote back, others never would. But she had continued to write, hoping they would benefit from its reception and maybe even one day get a reply or a visit in return. She enjoyed the process of writing the letter. It allowed her to think of them for a while and also reflect on her own life, the pride in her home and family, the little changes she wanted to make or resolutions she held. Her father now continued these letters, always at Easter. Her mom had said that way they would not get lost with all the others at Christmas, and she preferred sending floral or spring harbor notecards with lighthouses or Victorian front porches. Although her father preferred snow — images of it covering all the land, like the ending of Joyce's *The Dead*, he continued her tradition, occasionally sending Christmas cards as well when he inadvertently came across a wintry scene at the stationery shop in Harvard Square. He could not help climbing the creaky stairs to the balcony filled with traditional images of Noel and Kris Kringle. He always sent one to Catherine, too, and her favorite is one of Boston rooftops covered in snow, reminding her of a painting by Gustave Caillebotte of Paris' less frequent snow-covered roofs.

This card and all the others are in that shoebox. She has not looked through it in at least a year. She makes her purchase. '*Merci, au revoir!*' the shopkeeper sings as she exits, holding the door until she safely opens up her umbrella. Catherine catches a glimpse of the woman going to the display, to move some items around. Smiling as she does so, looking out at her latest happy customer one last time.

Catherine continues more quickly and directly back to her apartment. As she arrives and closes the door behind her, ready to get dry, she first shuffles under her bed in an acrobatic spiderman move and finds the black box of letter. She rests it on her bed next to the new tin, still in its white paper bag, while she finds something warmer and dry to wear: thick socks, a fresh scarf, and a wool sweater.

She then proceeds to move the letters one by one to the next box, reading some as she goes along. They are not particularly orderly in terms of date or who the sender was. She does not discern between them, categorize or hierarchize, and certainly does not throw any of them out.

She comes across one from Esmé last autumn:

> ...I've just found our favorite *Poulain* chocolate bars and *crème de marron* at a little shop in Medford called 'Chez Juliette'. I cannot wait to stick a spoonful of the chestnut cream in my yogurt tonight! I'm also going to use the chocolate wrappers to decorate my desk. It'll be part of a collage with my name and some photos of us and Grandpa and my friends back in Paris. I was feeling so homesick last week after you were here for parents' weekend. I'll go back for a wheel of *Reblochon* next week to make a *tartiflette* for my roommates. It's getting cold here and they've never tried it. They were shocked that something I love and miss is just potatoes, cheese, and bacon, but

I will open their eyes to it….Mom, did you feel lonely
when you went to college? I've made some friends
but it's not the same as before. I miss you, and
Natalie and Geoffrey, Edmond and Pascal, and the
fencing club. It just seems hard to find such
closeness, you know?….

She folds the stationery and puts it back in the envelope
and sees a more recent one from her:

…We learned about the physics of color in
photography today! I thought about your paints,
because we talked about how the light and paint
pigments work differently. Then in Italian class,
we've started to read Dante. Now I get why
Grandpa is obsessed with it. I really can't put it
down and kept reading it until 3 a.m. on Sunday….

Esmé used to tell her everything, but she had been
noticeably silent this time during her stay, avoiding the
subject of the tumor. But worse, avoiding creating more
loving memories with her mother that would only hurt to
look back on one day too soon.

Reading instead of speaking. Immersing instead of
opening. She was like her grandfather with the books.
Then there was one from him not too long ago as well:

…I've put up your painting of poplars near the
window to the back so they can add some color to the
evergreens. I love the pines, but this will mix it up

nicely. Some of those pines must be over a hundred years old. How did you have the idea to use purple highlights on the leaves? That's what your mother's hair looked like in the sun....

Scanning lower, she finds another one from her dad, the letter inside the snowy Boston rooftops back in 1989:

Dear Catie,

I got your very sweet letter. Please don't worry about me. Your mother is still a part of me here. I miss her, but life goes on; we must 'turn to [our] affairs,' like Frost tells us. I have several projects to work on now. Come home when you can, but I'm happy knowing you   have found joy in Paris! I know it would have been expensive for both you and Esmé to come for Christmas again after the funeral....I thought I would send you this clipping about the Gardner robbery; isn't it fascinating?...I've also included some interesting commentary in *The New Yorker* on the fall of the Berlin Wall. It is not that far away from you! What are they saying about it in Paris? It also makes me think of Frost and that 'Mending Wall' of his, but I guess in this case the wall did not make good neighbors...

He was always being so literary and she loves to read the weaving of his mind again and again in his epic letters.

Underneath the last there was a Christmas letter from a few years later from her sister. The card is signed simply with the names of the family:

> Merry Christmas! —Lawrence, Charlie, Jimmy, and Undine.

There was a Christmas form letter as well:

> …Charlie continues to get straight A's in school and recently won a math competition…Jimmy is the leading scorer on his T-ball team…Larry just got a promotion at work. He also went on a golf trip for a week with his three best friends from college. They had a marvelous time!….

She skimmed down the letter, but there was no news about Undine herself. There never was in these letters, nor when she visited her. Where had she lost herself along the way?

Another one from Undine catches her eye. One of the few she wrote out by hand:

> …I just don't know what to say, it's so tragic. I know he was your whole life. How can you go on?…

She received pity from her sister about Thomas' death on several occasions, but she felt like they could never really talk about it. It was like that was her one shot at the normal family life Undine had imagined for each of them. Without it, and especially with her more spontaneous moves to Florence and Paris and her artist lifestyle, they had drifted further apart.

A paisley print on cream stationery separates itself from the pile. It is her mother's favorite stationery. Her *Mama*, as she had called her, wrote often before her early death from a stroke that nobody had seen coming. Nobody could have seen it coming. It just happened one day while she was at home alone, cutting the garden shrubs in preparation for the first frost. Catherine holds the letter to her heart. She already knows what it says. She has read all the letters from her mother a hundred times.

This one, too, goes in the new box. She continues to relocate several others.

A few letters from Thomas, their early years, are held together with a rubber band. She puts them to the side instead of opening them up.

As she takes out a small stack, a photo falls to the floor that had apparently not made it to an album. She picks up and turns it over. It is of Henri, her student, by her side at her art opening last year - why is it in there? She looks on the back, Esmé's handwriting - '*Maman, que vous êtes beaux ensembles!*' She doesn't think she has ever seen this before. She flips it back over and lingers briefly before putting it back.

This and the rest of the letters get closed in the box. Rather than place it back under her bed, she puts it on the bookshelf next to her reading chair. It is both decorative there and a reminder of its contents, which she may pull out more regularly now.

She moves toward the little antique desk where she

keeps keys, several types of currency, trinkets without a home, and her stationery. The photo rests on a small pile of books and recent mail. She perches on the old wooden chair, opens several tiny drawers to remind herself of the items inside — her keys for the Brookline family home, several bracelets, a button she and Esmé had made at a fair, and her wedding ring. She takes this last item out of the felt black pouch. She never wears it anymore. If people ask, she says it's because of her painting; it would be ruined or at least get in the way. She tries it on. Still fits, perhaps a bit too loose. Another excuse not to wear it. She felt a fool wearing something that is now a fake promise, something she would have stopped before his death. In fact, she's angry she didn't get the chance to. Then she never would have to bear all this guilt, all this strange widow mourning when she really felt reborn and free! Free…but also tremendously guilty and sad. Sad for him, for Esmé. For his parents, who still write to her.

Had she wished him dead? Could she really have gone that far?

She is holding her cheeks and lets out a sigh. She gazes into the drawer again as if she is looking for something, realizing perhaps why she sat here in the first place. To write a letter.

She opens a lower drawer with the stationery and pulls out three sheets of olive *Vergé de France* paper, unsure if she will need them all. She takes out a fine black pen as well, then opens the cap and writes her greeting: 'Dear Edmond,' she pauses, then dates it in the top right corner: 'June 10, 1999.' She keeps her pen ready but holds it in the air as she perches on the chair and rests the other hand under her chin like *The Thinker*.

She waits for it to come to her and begins a long explanation of how good he was to his father and how he was her best friend, how she needs him now, how she misses him. She takes out two more sheets of paper. She talks about his relationship with Pascal, about the trips he had taken to see his father for years after his mother died. There were quite a few non-sequiturs but somehow she was trying to get to a point. Something to change the way he was thinking about her, no, about himself.

She impulsively crumples up the paper and pushes it to the corner of her desk. She takes a fresh page of olive paper and writes the same greeting and date at the top.

She sits. She thinks.

Retreats to the bed, face down in a starfish pose.

Suddenly, she scrambles up to the desk again and puts her pen to the middle of the page: 'I love you.' She underlines 'love' then underlines 'you.' She signs her name. This is something she feels is not always said with such clarity to friends. It is something he needs to hear.

She addresses and stamps an envelope, skips down to the nearest mailbox for its delivery, then does several errands with shop owners she knows by name before retreating into her apartment to avoid the damp evening and enjoy an endive salad with walnuts and avocado, a glass of red Bordeaux, and a French-dubbed version of *L'Avventura* on television before falling asleep quickly in the bed she warms with her body heat.

VI

Le Studio

Catherine likes to start her painting days with a reflective coffee at *La Palette* around the corner. Before she walks over to her studio in the Marais, she wakes up, focuses her energy on the day's subject, and then continues a wandering aesthetic investigation during the promenade. A cognitive map shows up on the canvas through colors and lines.

Today she arrives at 8:20, well before a modest-sized crowd of local artists or gallery owners and occasional celebrities and writers gather. The buzz shifts if the editor and her young children arrive for their *petit dejeuner* before school or if French President Chirac happens to show up with his small entourage, which happens once in a fortnight and always early. She first sat at this café because it was open early as she looked for a place to go for breakfast with Esmé the first day they had arrived in Paris. It is only a two minute walk from her apartment. She has come to find out that it was one of the famous haunts of Picasso and Hemingway. If she were pushed inside in extremes of cold weather or when they were cleaning or fixing something out front, like the awning, she would feel these artists' presence in the interior that was largely unchanged. Old oxidized mirrors and early twentieth century paintings hang on the walls by the antique wooden benches and chairs. When she comes here before spending a day painting, like today, she likes to imagine that she could channel the spirit of Picasso into her work. Not that she has the same style as he did, although perhaps somewhat like his early pieces held in the Barcelona museum, but she feels that his spirit is proud, talented, free, and eternal; traits she desires or, on days she feels confident, beholds. In fact, his career had covered nearly ninety years. It was as if painting and living were the same for him.

These days, artists of all kinds come to *La Palette*, including actors. Once, about a year ago, Gerard Deperdieu showed up, Rodin himself. She had seen other actors there before, and there were a few regulars, but he was the quintessential French actor of the era. Eminating from a young comedic actor in the eighties, he had many successes, including a few with the genius Claude Chabrol. Although he was now severely overweight, a bit ruddy in the face, and had stores of improper bar behavior that followed him in his wake, he was still incredibly alluring.

Actually he had never held model-like looks, but it was something about the method of his acting, the gentleness contained in his impressive mass of manhood, a density like no other, that made him so gracefully attractive. His looks had even allowed him to play a deformed figure on several occasions, twice a hunchback and once with an enlarged nose. But he remained sublime in those roles as well. He held something that surpassed physical expression.

She had a quick fantasy about dropping her fresh new cobalt blue paint, *no too messy*, then continued the fantasy with the drop of her coffee spoon, *more probable*. As the daydream continues, she hears the clank of metal on pavement, he shifts to pick it up, holding it ever so delicately between his thick fingertips, the same way he held love letters in *Cyrano de Bergerac*. She turns to him to say, *merci beaucoup*, in a perfect French accent . He begins small talk and is impressed by her French, wanting to meet later for cocktails at *Le Fumoir* on the other bank…

But not only does she know that this is silly, that the simple drop of a spoon would have never led to such an event, but also that she probably prefers the dream. The reality may be that he is not so gentle and refined. It's hard to know with good actors. If they ever made it to martinis, he would likely be more interested in talking about himself than asking questions, debating, admiring her and her life. However, maybe he really was so incredible in real life as well. *What if he were the perfect man*…but if that were the case he would also be loyal to his absent wife. She could dream about this fantasy on the *terrasse*, behind her sunglasses, and walk happily to her studio to move this muse into some aspect of her painting.

This morning she orders a *grand café crème* with a buttered *tartine*, wanting some sustenance for the enclosed morning before her. As she awaits her meal, she hears the advance of scooters, the opening of nearby windows, the hiss of the espresso machine. The sound of running water as the waiter takes care of the rose bushes. Small chatter in French and English take place on either side of her. Two tourists from the south, maybe Arles, a gallery owner and his visiting friend, or mistress, from Los Angeles.

Catherine's *crème* arrives and she focuses on the horizon as she holds the large cup with two hands just above her chin. Her eyes glaze behind brown angular sunglasses, moving toward thoughts instead on today's subject.

There are two paintings she is working on at the moment, going back and forth as she works with malleable oil paint, and allowing some to dry over time. The first is of her sister, before the children. She loves her sister's children but she loves *her* Undine more before them. It was as if her identity had been wiped away in an instant of the first's birth. No more photographs of herself, no more new hobbies, no more bed and breakfast excursions to Vermont with her girlfriends, where she would always take a day by herself to go horseback riding in the mountains. Catherine used to wish she could be invited on these or that she had her own girlfriends as carefree.

She knew the jealousy had flipped when Undine would ask her how she could go to gallery shows and leave Esmé with a babysitter or the neighbor so often when she was younger, or why she continued to live and paint in Paris once Esmé went to school in the states 'where the whole family is!' Even back when Thomas was alive, Undine had wondered why Catherine would try to work while they were in a foreign country, allowing a stranger to take care of their new baby when they did not need the meager salary from her teaching. Undine's Christmas card arrived each year with a picture of the children and a letter describing their achievements in school activities, just like the one she came across yesterday. Why not include what she was up to? She wished that Undine would share more of her own life with her, if there was anything left to share. Her husband used to encourage her to continue horseback riding lessons on Saturday mornings, but she wanted to drive the kids to T-ball and baseball practice. Study groups, CCD, soccer games, Spanish tutors, play-dates with the families her husband had approved for their pedigree, or in reality, their perceived wealth. They were turning into Tom and Daisy Buchanan, except that Undine actually cared about her children. This was a characteristic she could be proud of. She was an exceptionally loving mother and when Catherine is honest with herself, she wonders if she has been as generous.

So this image of her sister is like an eggshell memory. Se wants an effect that the painting is about to crack to allow her little spring chickens to come out. At that moment in a photograph from 1979, at the small party before she and Thomas had moved to Italy, she holds her chin up with her gorgeous cheekbones radiating in the light. Catherine is trying to get that youthful sparkle in her eyes just right.

She ponders this image, the colors of paint she will mix, the highlights with pure white she might add, and starts to break off pieces of her baguette to eat. The bread is only mediocre here, but the butter divine. They spread it on thick and its flavor is full, more like a salty cheese.

The other painting is of her daughter. The image is from a morning after swimming at a local municipal pool. She has a photograph. At their tiny breakfast table, she was engrossed, with her hair still wet, in a Judy Blume book while also biting into a *tarte aux pommes* leftover from the night before. The revealing young adult novel and *tarte* seem to hold equal importance for her and much less than the thought of drying her hair, although clearly chilled and wrapped in a plaid wrap that could show Catherine's clever technique of the contortions of the fabric around these tiny shoulders. She remembers that just after the photograph had been taken, Esmé dropped the tart on the ground. They both looked at it for a second then giggled, noting how much of a bookworm she was already becoming, 'just like Grandpa.' She ordered a second, but they gave it to her for free, noting how politely Esmé had both cleaned up the mess and excused herself to the patrons.

She finishes the *tartine* and lingers over the dregs of her coffee. She exchanges *Bonjour* and *bises* with a few people she knows from the neighborhood. Each one like her retreats to his own morning thoughts or reading. She is happy to be left alone and returns to think about the joyful task before her.

This morning Catherine wants to work on light. In both of their eyes and on her daughter's wet hair. It would sweep across to land on the tip of her nose and also on the glaze of the tart, as if the light is what would later cause a slight tip in balance, resulting in its drop to the pavement. Esmé's eyes, lost partly in the shadow, hold an unnatural shade of blue from the morning sun, not unlike today's but slightly later during the summer and a few hours later in the day, peaking through the imagined window outside of the frame.

A tall gray-haired man beside her rises. He swivels his hips around the tight spaces and leaves his empty dishes and re-folded newspaper on the small table. When he is out of view, she takes the newspaper for a quick peak before heading to work at the studio. Kosovo refugees. Serbia rebuilding. US troops enter Greece. Johnny Depp and Vanessa Paradis have a baby girl. A story on a man from Ikiria catches her eye: 'The Island Where People Forget to Die.' She reads on, intrigued. Stamatis Moraitis was in immigrant in Florida and had some kind of lung cancer with ten months to live. He returned to live with relatives in Ikiria, to enjoy life before he died. But this was twenty years ago. His cancer has disappeared.

Catherine puts the paper down. No use thinking of surreal solutions, as if *this* could be one at all. She extracts the ideas from her mind by staring up at the sun for an instant. Thinking of drug treatments and chemotherapy had only given her anxiety before. What has it accomplished? Deferring this knowledge is the easiest solution.

She feels ready for the walk, for the painting, and leaves the right amount of francs plus a few extra on the table before getting up and walking with brisk stride toward the studio. She gets up with shoulders back, a quick fix of her hair in her sunglasses before putting them on in slow motion as she faces toward the sun, which is trying to make its way through the risen fog. Today as she walks through *rue de Mazarine* and across *Pont Neuf*, the weather seems to shift, the clouds on the right bank have dropped from the sky as if this side wants to go back to bed. Soft wind blows through her loose hair and opens her trench coat like a kite as it almost takes off her scarf. She weaves in several angled roads between the *Louvre* and *Hotel de Ville* on the way to her studio. This route often changes; it is based on a feeling or a giving over to the flow of the wind. Even the first bridge she takes over changes. Today as she blows onto the side street called *rue Boucher*, she notices a large man moving toward her. Her natural radar keeps him in view and due to his size, she feels compelled to move her vision up from his jeans and unstriking blue sweater to his thick neck, his unmistakable French nose, his loose dirty blond hair just over his ears, and his brow, clearly in the state before the first caffeine of the day. He holds a motorcycle helmut in one hand as he stares at the space a few meters in front of him. Her vision refocuses on the features of his face since she realizes she has seen it before. Rasputin, Cyrano de Bergerac, Jean de Florette. Her eyes widen and mouth goes agape as she recognizes the iconic Gerard Deperdieu whom she had been thinking of just moments ago. He manages a small smile to acknowledge her recognition and continues forward, blending into the fog. Sometimes in this city of strange unexpected experiences, reality feels like a dream. It is a city of coincidences and *déja-vu*, or karma and chance. This may be why she does not feel all that surprised. She only lets herself turn to make sure it was him after he has already disappeared either in the fog or around the corner. Now she's not sure.

She continues to the studio with his presence in her mind.

.....

In the quiet solitude of the morning, she mixes her palette. Shades of dirty blonde for her sister's hair, creams and pinks for her skin, and a special blue for her eyes. These elements are already painted on the portrait, but need some saturation and dimension. She adds these slowly with a much smaller brush than before. Every hour or so, she gets up to walk around the room, to step back to see her work developing.

Around noon, a sculpting neighbor arrives and knocks on the window of her door, waves and smiles, and continues to his next-door studio.

She re-focuses, returns to the face in front of her that is also a reflection of herself. Smooth curls and highlights of hair are next. She is happy with the progress she is making.

She puts the portrait of Esmé in front of her as well now and adds layers, texture to the tart, her child-full cheeks, the towel around her shoulders. She is not as concerned with the texture of the towel itself as she is with its fullness and warmth, as if the viewer were being held by it as well. After another hour or so of these layers, before adding the important highlights she has planned, she steps back again. She only sees the reflection of Esmé's face as she turned without saying good-bye. Her pain and disappointment. She feels her body getting tense, gripping the palette knife harder before dropping it then smearing paint on her cheeks.

She decides she needs to see the sunlight for real again. She suddenly also realizes that she is getting very hungry.

After washing her hands, but leaving her brushes and palette on a small table by the canvases, she heads outside, only taking her scarf and small change purse with her. She walks over to *rue des Rosiers* for a falafel. There is no longer a long line at the window to *L'As du Falafel*, just eight people in front of her, so she realizes it must be after the normal lunch hour. A glance at another customer's watch confirms that it is well after two o'clock.

When she receives her *falafel special*, in a pita with tzatziki sauce and roasted eggplants, she takes it on a little walk slowly back toward the studio. Her mind is still on the portraits and she glances at the way the now present sun is affecting passerby on the street. What it does to their skin, their regards, the packages they carry. Even the way they tilt their bodies or move one way or the other in the street. It is a useful study, and an enjoyable one that she could practice for hours. But her focus is on the paintings now, and she is eager to get back to work.

.....

After several hours of adding details to her mom's hands, she's done, at least for today. She will let them sit and see what she thinks of them again tomorrow. She may need an extra day to distance herself, to let the paint dry, and start Esmé's face again. Tomorrow she also has a few children coming for a lesson after school, and she always likes to hear what they will say about it. They are always honest, sometimes brutally so.

She knows she has some time before Henri shows up for his lesson today, and she normally paints while he works as well, so she pulls out the canvas with the brown underpainting of a self-portrait. She wants this one to be abstract, channeling an acceptance of her life. But how can she do that when there are still large unsettled pieces? She thinks of the mother bear in *Blueberries for Sal*, the one she read to Esmé many nights, and ponders how to capture that selfless pride. But is she really were selfless, would she be here?

She sits down to look at it for a while.

Her mind drifts to Edmond - when will he receive the letter? She feels alone in that room all of a sudden. She thinks of her sister telling her how lonely she will be going back to Paris, *does she want to die alone?* Pushing, pushing those thoughts out of her mind, she goes back to her color wheel and mixes several shades of blue oils.

She starts to paint with a thick brush, fluidly tracing the underpainting and adding fresh details that come to her in mid-stroke. She lets herself get lost in it.

The moments of guilt, of sadness, of loneliness, and even self-pity, that she has been pushing aside repeatedly, burying deeper, now unconnected to particular moments or details, just emotion that spreads through her body. She had kept it at bay, successfully, to be happy, like most happy people do.

She wants to access this emotion for her painting and tries to reference a point - her husband's death? No, too complicated. The breakup with Ludovico? Perhaps. Esmé's departure for college. Well, that was more bittersweet.

All the while she is painting blue strokes, accessing different shades with her brush, greener highlights, violet-toned shadows. She stands at a different angle to find insight. The light from the window bounces to blind her.

And suddenly she is overwhelmed by emotion. She is not sure if it is sadness, loneliness, anger, or insecurity. She can't be sure if it is from the tumor she faces now or her memories. It is too unclear, too hopeless. She tries to paint through her tears, to find beauty in this breakdown, but it is no use. What is the beauty in lost love? In death?

Just as she is crumbling slowly to the floor, Henri walks in, still in his business suit from the bank, likely to say hello before he goes to change down the hall. He has walked in at a moment of weakness, of raw emotion. These moments are rare for her and she prefers them in private. She tries to wipe her face, only smearing blue paint on her cheek, accidentally emphasizing the turmoil within.

His smile quickly leaves his face. As she looks up, she expects to see a furled brow, a worried expression and questions, questions. So many questions she has endured these past several months! *How…why…when?*

But Henri has no questions for her. He reacts strangely, quietly to her honest breakdown. It is as if he accepts this fate of hers even though he does not know what it is, does not ask what is making her upset. It is almost as if he knew it were coming, as if that were the reason he came in before he changed. A few minutes later and she may have been able to compose herself again. At the moment he opened the door, she was finishing with her hands as paintbrushes, smearing the oils so that even the outline of her figure was lost in murky blue spirals containing her skin, her eyes, her shoulder blade, each decomposed in blueness. The paint is thick and tactile, like a Van Gogh, but the stroke was more contemplative and feminine. They were now lost in random spirals centered on nothing.

He walks toward her, saying her name softly, with concern, as she allows the blue to move from her hands to her jeans as she collapses to the cold tile. He moves to the floor as well, instinctively embraces her, filling himself - his suit - with paint, willingly. His suits are always carefully tailored, probably very expensive. But he doesn't seem to notice or care that this one is covered in blue paint, tears, and smearing makeup. 'Catherine, shh, shh.' He softly whispers these words to her as he comforts her, like a father with child.

Maybe this is what she had wanted from her own father. Maybe that's what had kept her from staying there. But she realizes as an adult, sometimes this is difficult to do. Denial is the only way for him to deal with his daughter's mortality.

…..

He stays with her as she cries, until the tears are done, but waits for no explanation. 'Let's get you home' is all he says.

They walk slowly and silently to her flat. After they crossed to the left bank, he tells her several stories from the day, including one about a boss who accidentally played a message from his mistress during a board meeting and another about finding two of his colleagues kissing in the elevator, as if he worked at a *lycée*.

'Ah, you are laughing now! That is always a cure, I find.'

She simply smiles in response.

'Just like in the studio, that is your visage when you are 'appy!'

She laughs again.

'Oh, now you are laughing because I cannot say my *h*! It is true, alas, but it's good to keep a bit of my French accent. You told me once that you liked it very much. I think I was saying, '*ip 'ip 'ooray!*'

She laughs again, then her face looks puzzled. 'I did?'

'Yes, stored away.' He points to his brain.

When they arrive at her place, not so far from his own, she gets into the elevator alone, insisting she will be alright. 'Thank you for understanding…for not asking….'

He allows her this space with a smile and what appears to be a small bow. 'Thank you for the lovely walk. *Merci beaucoup pour la promenade, Mademoiselle.*'

Henri exits the building to walk home alone, and she hears him whistling through her window as he leaves the courtyard. She stays by the window until the sound disappears, looks up once at the sky, and retreats. She takes a hot shower, combs out long wet hair, and then collapses in bed, still naked under her robe.

VII

La Touche

Catherine wakes before 6:00 a.m. with the sunrise. She did not fully close her blinds last night. There are still four hours before her massage with Pascal and she decides to wait to paint until after she has seen him. It should help her reset herself before facing the blue painting, in case that is what sparked her tears yesterday.

She takes her time getting dressed, eating some toast, and watching the news, before going to have a coffee at *La Palette* with Gregoire, the owner of the gallery where she is showing her work. They have known each other since Edmond arranged for her first show there many years ago, and they usually wait to cross paths at the café rather than setting up appointments, but they wanted to make sure everything was set for the June 21 show. She throws on white jeans, a black v-neck, ballet flats, and her trench coat for the morning dew.

He is already sitting there, reading *L'Équipe* and drinking a *noisette*. He gets up to exchange *bises* when he sees her. He calls inside to the waiter, *'Benjamin, un petit café,'* and turns to Catherine. *'Deux?'* She nods as he holds up two fingers in flagrant body language so Benjamin cannot miss him. 'It's so good to see you, darling.' He kisses her cheek again.

Catherine laughs and asks him about his weekend, which is always busy and filled with entertaining anecdotes.

They have already had coffee together once, *par hazard*, since she got back. He is fascinated with America and always has a lot of questions for her that remind her of why she also loves her other home. He wants to know about the Mexican restaurants, the latest sitcoms, the big flashy cars. He wants photographs and tastes, if possible. Once she brought him a whole box of Munchkins from Dunkin' Donuts. Another time, maple syrup. And, more courageously for a French man's palate, white wine from a vineyard in the Adirondacks. He loved it.

Today she is happy when they jump right in to the topic of her show. They quickly discuss how many paintings, the pricing, the business arrangements that have already been sorted out. They instead focus on the details for *vernissage* - the opening with wine and socializing. What kind of champagne to serve (*Canard du Chene*), the *amuses bouches* (cumin olives, little glasses of gazpacho, salmon *paté* and rabbit *rillettes* on toast, and avocado puree on thin slices of cucumber), and the music (something between jazz and funk; for this she knows a former student she is going to inquire with). He would handle it all besides the music - some water and fruit juice as well, a couple of servers, a real *fête*. It would be a big night. The summer solstice would also be the annual *Fête de la Musique* with music playing on the street on that longest day of the year. Several other galleries on *rue de Seine* were planning openings that night to profit from the *soirée*, even though it would be on a Monday this year and *vernissage* was typically a Thursday affair. And anyway, for people like Gregoire and Catherine, the day of the week makes no difference. A party could be on a Monday night as easily as a quiet evening at home with a book could be on a Saturday night. There were no rules about schedules and hours and they often ended up doing things they hadn't planned on.

'So is there anything else you're worried about, Catherine, dear?'

The question catches her off guard, as if he can see through her.

They remain a while to talk with another friend about his recent trip to Lubijiana before she leaves for the other side of the river - *La Rive Droite*.

She takes her time to walk back toward the Marais, this time bringing her sketchbook to stop at several places along the way — *Place Louis Philippe*, a quiet bench on *Ile St. Louis*, and another bench behind a church not too far from *Pont Henri IV*. At each point she takes out her sketchbook and charcoal pencils. She does several quick drawings of people who pass by. Young children on the way to school carrying too many books but walking lightly all the same; a delivery man with long orangoutang limbs and an Irish cap; an old couple holding hands and walking slowly. Her impressions make lines of vitality that capture a person in a moment of action and thought. She used to do this in Florence, to explore the different neighborhoods. If Esmé was not with her babysitter, she used to bring her along, attracting interesting grandmother faces to beam in at the stroller. In high school, she had done it, too, often going on excursions with her father. He would write what he saw; she would draw it. They would compare their versions and laugh over some silly features - warts, bums, and snobby expressions. Her mother had made an album of these paired sketches. Where is it now?

She starts a sketch from memory instead, of her mother. The image comes to her suddenly as the shape of many emotions that she attempts to capture before they can escape. She often thinks through her drawings, having found that words take longer for her to formulate, long enough that she may lose the thought, like the flash of unnatural colors before the sunset. The incarnation of her thought is in the image. Here, she captures an almost cartoon-like smile, plump cheeks, deep contours at her mother's eyes and chin, dyed-auburn hair pulled up in a bun almost on top of her head. This one she may actually use in the studio today.

The sky is clear blue. The air is still crisp. She places her pencils and sketchbook in a leather satchel, wraps her red scarf tighter, and continues, energized, toward her destination.

As she heads somewhat toward Pascal, she thinks back to the last time she has seen him. It was just before

Catherine had left for New England, she had gone to see Pascal for the same weekly massage. This was after a little good-bye lunch they had along with Edmond; they had told him the trip was to see her family and to help her dad with some things around the house. This was true, of course, and they felt they were really protecting him from a truth that might hurt too much, that might derail him even further.

On this last meeting with him a day later, just hours before her flight home, Pascal had left her with a Zen Koan. She lets the scene come back to her now; somehow it was the beginning of her turning point, so it remained etched in her mind, vivid to all the senses. He said it was something for her to ponder while she was away, and he wanted her to return with her answer. He said this with a knowing grin, knowing that the riddle of the explanation would seem impossible to solve.

'So,' he started as he began working on her right forearm, tight from holding her paintbrush, 'I was at the Buddhist Centre over in *Bois de Vincennes* the other day, and the monk told us this Koan. I thought of you. But I won't tell you why. Actually, I guess it's up to you. It meant something to me, but maybe it will mean something to you. I'm not sure…'

'Ok, get on with it then! I love your riddles you are always bringing me. I could use a bit of a diversion at the moment as well. It's no fun thinking about the riddle of life and death all the time.' She grinned when she said this as well, for they had had many conversations on the subject in the past. Well before her tumor. Not morbid conversations, philosophical ones, metaphysical ones, Buddhist ones, and personal ones. Actually, they had talked about most topics that people tend to talk about together and even other ones that most kept inside their own minds. She often wonders if they would have the same discussions face to face.

'Alright. So, once upon a time, the monks of the East and West in Japan were disputing about a cat.' As he said this, he pushed into her back, causing her to arch slightly as her spine stretched and she breathed out through the little hole in the massage table where her face was resting on a circle of white towels. 'So, Nansen - the head monk, so to speak - holds up the cat for them all to see and says, *Monks, if you can say a word of Zen, I will spare the cat. If you cannot, I will kill it!*' He made his best impression of an old Japanese man as he said this, a bit humorous, then switched to his most soothing low tone, 'However, no monk could answer with Zen. They were lost at how to save the cat. Nansen finally killed the cat. Although he was sad to do this, he had to prove his point to his disciples. In the evening, when Joshu - another elder monk - came back, Nansen told him of the incident. Joshu took off his sandal, put it on his head, and walked away. Nansen called to him, *If you had been there, I could have saved the cat!*' For this last part, he switched to the comic Japanese voice again and turned his hands into cat claws for a moment, but the pensive metaphysical tone of the rest of the story lingered in the room.

Catherine had not replied. 'So, this gives you something to think about on the plane. Maybe you can see what Esmé will say.' He continued in silence to realign her body and finished with a comforting soft massage that he knew she needed. He didn't need to explain it; it was the same one he had used right after Esmé had left for

112

college, the same on the days she felt stressed with a deadline for a gallery opening or after when not enough paintings had sold. The several times when she started to talk about Thomas. These thoughts floated into the air as he found a knot in her muscles and released it.

She thinks back to the cat. She wanted to have an answer ready when she walks in, but had not figured out the riddle. Esmé had just laughed and said, in an endearing way, that Pascal was always saying crazy stuff.

She's not sure about this riddle, but she focuses on the cat. She would like to jump the rooftops like a cat for the day. Out her window, the next windows angled hat seems within reach if she stretches and lunges with all her might. It's not a suicidal idea, but a desire to somehow make herself exterior to the living space that holds too many memories, sometimes. To be able to soak the most sun Paris had to offer. The frequent rain is beautiful, but occasionally she would desire the full sun available in plenty, like when they had all lived on the base in Napoli. Today's sun is an exception, one that often is true in June.

In fact, she is like a cat; her husband had always told her so. Has she told Pascal this? She enjoys solitude, but would cuddle up to him, wanting his touch, a petting. His laughter still usually followed with some needed human touch, but if he was tired from training or had his mind on his ambitions, which was increasingly the case in their time together as man and wife, he instead shrugged her off a bit until it was no longer fun for her to try. This is when she had started going to a weekly massage - always done in secret and with her own meager salary, knowing that Thomas would find it frivolous without realizing he could save them this weekly sum by kindly submitting to her request for his touch. Or without realizing how much happiness it gave her, nothing that saving for a fancy retirement house could give her. She could have explained the economics to him, and maybe he would have responded, but his touch would have been meaningless and even forced at that point. It needed to come unbidden. Ironically, the touch of the hand that she paid for seemed to care more than his. Maria, the masseuse in *Napoli*, a grandmother of fifteen and counting, was the only one she had talked with about her marriage problems at the time. In Florence, she had saved money by not having a masseuse, and decided that Ludovico's touch, until it lost its purity in her mind, was a fitting replacement. Looking back, she realizes another's touch could have helped her see more clearly, maybe not react so quickly to Ludovico's egoism.

Before she realizes it, she has arrived at Pascal's. She enters the waiting room where a secretary who handles clients for their small company greets her by her name, tells her that he's still with another client. He never really looks at the clock while he's working, finishing instead when his job is done, when the body is whole again.

Several moments later, he emerges from the back room. Pascal is striking to look at; he is tall with skin the color of chestnut cream and tattoos on his chest and forearms in black ink that are subtle beautiful designs of Chinese dragons. They reflect his training in the East. His short dreadlocks cover his head in uneven but well-coiffed randomness. Its contrast with his smooth angular face highlights his deep set piercing eyes. He looks a bit like Yannick Noah, the tennis hero turned feel-good singer. Pascal used to play judo and the muscle mass somewhat remains although it has been made leaner through yoga and a mainly vegetarian diet. He looks glowingly healthy, as usual, in a deep V-neck, like Edmond wears, and his loose fitting work pants. 'Catherine! *Ça va? Très bien de te voir!* '*Oui, ça va. Et toi?* It's so good to see you, too!' They exchange kisses and she goes ahead to change into loose cotton t-shirt and shorts that she has brought along. She lies on the table and waits, relaxed, for him to come in.

'Catherine, Catherine. I've missed talking with you. How is the family? Is Esmé knockin' them dead at school? What's her latest boyfriend like?' His accent in English holds a fascinating mix of his upbringing and ancestry. Born to two Tunisian parents in France in the sixties, who gave him a supremely French name in an attempt to allow him immediate assimilation, a decade later than she and Edmond. He had spent high school in Portsmouth, England due to the set up of his parents' import business of goods from their homeland. Once Pascal decided to move to Paris in his mid-twenties, his parents moved back to Tunisia to handle the export side of things. He and Edmond would visit them there about once a year. So he spoke French, British English, .and Tunisian Arabic fluently with the timbre of his voice reflecting all three accents in all three languages.

'Esmé is doing really well. It makes me feel good to see her so happy, but it's still so hard to leave her. I guess that's what I would do even if she were in France for university.' She pauses, then adds, 'I'm not sure how she feels about my coming back here.'

'Well, that's to be expected. She'll come around, and she'll be here for the summer, right?'

Catherine mumbles, 'Yeah.'

'What about Undine? I'm sure she had a thing or to to say about it!' He laughs a little as he starts erasing the damage of the plane trip in her legs last week. He knows all about her complicated relationship with her sister.

'Oh you know…she was not very supportive. But she made it a lot easier to leave. Every time I spoke with her, I got the feeling she was almost happy that my grand plan at being better than her, as she sees it, seems to have been spoiled with this tumor. Maybe I'm reading too much into it…'

'With someone else I would say you were. But with her track record, I don't think you're out of line. Don't worry, she still loves you. She just doesn't have control of her life anymore. She's taking it out on you.'

'It's too bad, she was so different that one time she came to Paris on her own. You remember?'

'*Bien sur*! She was the life of the party. I really thought she might go home with Gregoire that evening, or maybe one of the other gallery guys.' She had been different even when she wasn't drunk during that trip, like she was discovering herself again. She seemed so sad as she was leaving, crying at the airport. It wasn't because she would miss Catherine, who was clearly happy with her life in Paris, but because she would miss herself. That self from when she was younger that had been found for a short trip on her own. Even though she didn't much like French culture or museums, or really anything in particular about the city of Paris, she liked finding herself. She would never admit it, but it was true.

As Pascal moves in long circular sweeps over her hamstrings, he mentions how healthy her skin feels. 'I know you lost some weight from your treatments, but I can see you've been taking care of yourself.' It is true that she finds herself drawn to healthier food than before and many more vegetables and fruits. She craves vitamins, minerals, enzymes in their pure forms, so she can soak them up almost immediately. For some reason, she feels that after the brain tumor, it is still just as important to keep good health, good figure, good skin. Even more so.

Her sister Undine wondered when she stayed with them why she didn't just eat as much chocolate and ice cream and French fries as she wanted. Of course she ate those things at times, but the thought of waking up without a clear head, shiny hair, and nourished skin seemed as bad as just dying already, and she wasn't ready for that. Actually, her sister wondered other things, too. She thought Catherine should buy herself the fancy dresses and bags she often looked at in the windows. 'Why do you still live so simply? You might as well use up what you have and Esmé will continue to get the military money. We can go shopping while the kids are at school.' Undine had been named for her wavy hair, present at birth, but Catherine thought at these times the allusion to Edith Wharton's mock-heroine had suited her well.

It took everything Catherine had to keep the nugget of rage that was building in response to that comment from coming out. Instead, she responded simply that she preferred spending her time on other things and pushed the thoughts away so she wouldn't explode at her sister. Later, she revisited those thoughts while she was on a walk in the familiar forest behind her childhood home. She wanted to know why there was such rage, beyond some judging she was guilty of about silly materialism. She tried not to judge Undine, and realized this was not really the heart of the matter. Instead, it dawned on her just as she was noticing a new pine sapling that she was angry at her sister for only wanting to spend time with her to help her die. Or at least that's what it seemed like. She wouldn't take time out to call or be with her until she was dying. And what's more, she wanted to do the activities she found beneficial or fun rather than ask what Catherine might want to do in their time alone together. She had been invited for many meals at their family home in Newton, but it was always a group affair. One where Undine could place her pity on display: 'Don't get up, Catherine. You're our special guest,' and, 'Are you sure you should have more wine? Why don't I make you an herbal tea instead.' Could it be that her sister was even jealous of her? Not exactly of the brain tumor, but in the way she was able to seem so calm about it? Or maybe she had anger herself for one of her best friends leaving her. Although they had their differences, it was true that Catherine was the first one she would call in a crisis. Maybe they did not do a lot together like girlfriends would, but they were close, and Catherine still feels that hidden essence of Undine's being that she yearns to be closer to.

She feels Pascal's fingers digging hard into her shoulders, almost underneath the bones. 'Now, not to bring up a difficult topic,' he hesitates to go on, which is rare for him, 'but I told Edmond about your tumor. I thought it would be easier for you that way. Have you seen him yet?' So strange, she thinks to herself before responding. Why has Edmond kept their meeting to himself? Embarrassment? Anger? Self-pity?

But she has no reason to hide it from Pascal: 'I did. I'm

surprised he didn't tell you about it. It didn't go so well. I mean, we couldn't even really talk, I don't know...he just...' As she trails off, she feels his hands leave her body, then rest lightly on her hamstring without moving. He's struck as well, it seems. Usually he can think, talk, and massage simultaneously.

'He was so quiet yesterday.' He continues to rest his hands without movement, 'Yes, it makes sense,' he whispers, 'Please don't worry, you know it is still about his father. I'm not sure how to help him anymore... sometimes I just can't get through to him...' He sighs and begins working on her shoulders again. They both remain quiet for a few minutes until he asks how she has been feeling with the treatments.

'Maybe they helped, I'm not sure. I'm supposed to go see the doctor at some point to get more tests and see the progress, but I just feel so good, so healthy right now. Especially here, back in Paris. It seems silly to go to a doctor.' No more news until after the twenty-first, she decides.

'Makes sense to me,' he says simply. He moves away from the table briefly. Indochine's '*Tes Yeux Noirs*' begins playing lightly and Pascal takes two stones out from the heater near his CD player. She feels the movement of warm, smooth stone on her back. The sensation reminds her of childhood holidays at the pond near the ocean where she and Undine seemed to constantly be searching for the right rocks. There were different kinds of right rocks. There were the stones for skipping across the water; there were the mica layers like *millefeuilles* to use as paperweights; there were the large threatening rocks to build a fort; and, lastly, there were the smooth pebbles and sca glass to fill up a *Bon Maman* jam jar in the kitchen. The jars would slowly fill up the cabin over the three weeks of the holiday, often doubling for some other use, such as holding up some books or keeping newspapers from blowing off the deck.

The smooth rock of Swedish massage brings her comfort and happiness in this city. Maybe happiness is too strong a word. The French say *bonheur*, which literally translates to 'good hour,' and this seems more fitting. It is more like the rich goodness of life in the present rather than a manic happiness, which is often fleeting or, worse, fake. An hour for eternity.

Pascal's hands move over her body in deep, penetrating motions. He is not afraid to push hard since he knows it well. Pascal thinks massage is one way to purge bad thoughts – he lives by this credence. He is the only one she can fully talk to about some ideas and often only during her massage sessions. They rarely talk about energies and spiritual points outside of the massage office. She knows that even with Edmond, there is a sort of understanding and use of these teachings, but he has a hard time talking about it, often refuting some of the claims he has come to use in his own life.

Pascal had started as Edmond's masseuse as well. After discussions about art, politics, and food, they had finally decided to share a meal together. Their partnership is much more than lovers. They find *bonheur* together. They fit well. Still, Catherine knows these past few months have been tricky since Edmond is denying a part of himself to be free. It makes their relationship also constrained.

Catherine had met Edmond through Pascal. She had been going to him for massage a few months and they had become friends. He also knew she was looking for some help to show her work at the galleries. He set up a lunch for them to meet each other and to also set up this professional connection. The immediate click between the three of them seemed fated. This blip with Edmond now is simply a challenge for the three of them to become stronger and find new parts of themselves, to respond and make sense of it. At least this is what she hopes, what she must believe. As Pascal moves around scar tissue in her shoulders, several months of tension held within, the memory of her first encounter with Edmond comes back to her, as if popping out from tangled muscle fiber or cartilage.

After a normal Thursday morning massage, Pascal had led the way through the back streets of the Marais toward a street not far from *Hôtel de Ville*. They entered a small doorway to a two-room restaurant. The first room was filled with Harley Davidson paraphernalia, which she noticed only after wondering what the stack of nearly a dozen leather gloves on a wooden tray at the entrance were for. It was the middle of July. As she peered back outside, she realized they had just walked in next to a monster Harley Davidson, parked and glistening in the summer heat. It made her think at once of her cool Oregon aunt, her father's sister who had stayed near where they had grown up, who had found a new lease on life after a divorce and second husband with a passion for his bike and a desire to have children, although both were already in their forties at the time. It had taken her so much courage to leave her first husband, who had his own problems for which she was not responsible.

Sometimes Catherine wishes she had realized this about

Thomas early on. Her aunt's life could have been the harbinger she needed, but this had come when she was already living in Italy. Deep down she knows it is not her fault, all these problems she remembers, but somehow she holds herself responsible probably, because of his death. She is the only one left to answer for them. Sometimes she thinks she hadn't had the courage because her mother had died so soon after their marriage. It was as if she was cheating her mom of what her daughter's reality had become if she were to divorce him and start again. She had her mother's blessing before, and their marriage, because of this blessing, and because of her mother's celebration with them made a break in the marriage seem somehow like a loss of her maternal figure that she could never fully recover.

She tells herself to stop thinking about Thomas again. It is just weighing on her for no reason while she tries to enjoy the present. With another release of tension, she drifts back to the restaurant scene like a film playing back, selecting highlights. The inner room was like an old tiny farmhouse with exposed stones, paintings of animal life, and vintage posters in the style of Toulouse L'Autrec. The tiny blackboard provided a fresh daily menu offering some kind of meat next to vegetable and potato. Simple fare, beautifully executed. Both men had assured her she could not go wrong.

The round owner from Alsace came and suggested '*un carafe du vin rouge?*'. They agreed as he continued with a description of the special, rabbit with mustard sauce. They each ordered—*confit de canard, l'entrecôte de veau,* and *poulet rôti*. They decided to each try a little of each other's plates, Chinese style. Ordering for the table – although not typically done in France, seems like something that goes with their culture – to try many types of food in small doses. It is as if you can have six courses if each orders a different *entrée* and *plat*, and it gives a pretty look to the table, so many colors at once. Their food came with a large side of baked potatoes au gratin like she is used to after skiing in the Alps on the French side. A bit hearty for July, but since they were sharing it worked just fine with some mustard to cut the heavy cream. The wine with the meal and coffee after also help to digest.

As she sat happily consuming duck *confit* and too much table wine for a Thursday afternoon, their conversation turned to Edmond and Pascal's relationship. She asked how they met and did not expect brutal honesty. They had their priorities in order. Pascal said that when the couple had first met, Edmond was not taking care of his own needs. He was helping too many artists, too many friends who were looking for jobs. He was also giving his time too often to a depressed cousin or was on the train back and forth to Bretagne when he mother became ill. All this would have been fun if it hadn't been too much, overwhelming. He always seemed to be with somebody, helping them, and always exhausted, while Pascal spent a lot of time in solitude after work hours. Although Edmond's habits were kind, he reflected that he had to spend time on himself in order for their relationship to work. Pascal had constantly fought for evenings alone, just the two of them. He also felt like Edmond was not always at ease, as if his mind was preoccupied with the worries of other people in addition to his own. It made it hard for him to commit to their relationship, and it wasn't until his mother's anticipated death that Edmond was able first to grieve and then to live. It wasn't her death that set him free. On the contrary, she had cultivated in him a sense of how to live gracefully. In the wake of her departure, he reflected in the way she was able to stay happy until the end. Although her days became a short walk around the village or on the city walls, three small, but never simple, meals with her husband, a reading of the regional paper with the aid of her magnifying glasses, and an evening discussion with Edmond on the telephone, she enjoyed every second of them. She noticed everything, from the new red dress on display at the corner boutique to the way the flavors of the *salade turque* and *koftas* Edmond would bring her from *Chez Marianne* had the perfect complement of separated, flavorful Middle Eastern ingredients and an indistinguishable blend of flavor. When she died, he spent seven days at the edge of the world, the farthest west he could go in *Bretagne*, near *Douarnenez*, staring into the ocean from the cliffs in solitude.

Pascal had joined him on the seventh day, when Edmond cried in his arms upon his arrival at the rented cottage doorstep. They did not speak, not really, for hours, and then, all of a sudden, Edmond told him how he would change his life.

And since then they had been happy together. Each taking time out. Each throwing themselves wholly into their work, their passions, but also receding when they needed to think, sleep, or to spend time as a couple, alone.

Pascal had also brought Edmond to the Buddhist center where he went to meditate and listen to monks' teachings each week. Although Edmond would not go often, it allowed him to understand the way Pascal found his inner peace. Edmond went to the lectures in both French and

Japanese. Although he did not understand Japanese, beyond a few words from his travels there, he found the energy from the teacher during these séances to be peaceful and uplifting. The unfamiliar sounds actually helped him to meditate. Catherine had also attended occasional lectures with Pascal, usually when she felt a bit unsettled or had a friend or family member who seemed to be going through a hard time. She would come to the center and hope for an answer. Since the problem is now one that she was facing head on, it seems too strong to bring into the center. She would just feel lost, less sure of her beliefs in Buddhism.

She feels his hand on her neck, which means he is nearly finished. Just then she starts thinking of Edmond again. Edmond in the present. Why is he being so difficult? So selfish? Has he received her letter yet?

'Ut oh, somebody's thinking some bad thoughts! I can feel it. What's up?'

'Oh Edmond again. I'm just at a loss.'

'Ok, I understand, so am I,' he says calmly, 'Let me deal with him, or let him have some time and space to himself. That's probably all he needs,' he pauses before placing a large towel over her body for a final relaxing pat-down. 'So I asked you before how you were feeling but not really about how it's been since you came back. You happy with the decision?'

She does not need to reflect: 'It's really been amazing. I feel almost like I'm high all the time, like I have this hyperreal experience with the world. I don't know…it's hard to explain…everything just tastes so good and looks so interesting to me. The colors are supersaturated. My neighborhood buddies at the café are so vibrant. I just love being here. Even more than before.'

'That's so nice to hear. Really, I'm not surprised, but I'm happy my expectations were true.' She sits up and sees him beaming as if he's proud of her, almost like a father. Then his face shows he has just thought of something suddenly: 'I forgot to ask you about the Koan! Have you figured it out? Do you need a reminder?'

'Of course I remember it. But no, I haven't figured it out. Does that mean I'm not enlightened or something?' She says this lightheartedly.

He doesn't respond to the question and asks quite seriously now, 'Tell me, are you happy here? Have you found *le bonheur* in your return?' He is holding her shoulders lightly and since she continues to sit on the bench, they are eye to eye.

'Well…yes. Yes. That's what I've just told you, I guess.'

'*Exactement!* Then you've figured out the riddle.' His serious expression turns happy again and he waves as he leaves the room for her to change. She waits on the table some time before doing so, still thinking about the riddle, still confused. But she trusts Pascal. It makes her feel like she has done something very right at a crucial moment in her life. Like she has taken control. She feels an inner calm that is stronger than she has ever felt before and feels like she is dancing through the rest of the day, like Zen messages are spilling into her paintings and out from her fingers as she walks down the street.

…..

The next few days are filled with surprise encounters with old students, a discussion about the gallery opening with Gregoire over a tagine and couscous dinner, the completion of her blue self-portrait, although now with more of a violet and green complementary effect, and many small moments of discovery — new streets, clever anecdotes, the juxtaposition of flavors, and beautiful birds, storefronts, cars, forgotten memories, people.

And finally, she comes back to Esmé's portrait. The movement of the paint make her feel as if she is massaging her child's face. She is helping her release. Helping her to live, even when she's gone.

VIII

Le Régime

On this Sunday morning, she wanders over late to *La Palette* to eat the set breakfast of *tartine*, *café creme*, and fresh squeezed orange juice - *orange pressé*. Last night, she went out late for a drink up in Montmartre with some former students she had run into during the week, so she took advantage of the quiet to sleep in. After ordering and looking out at the other customers she doesn't recognize from behind her sunglasses, she hears the nearby church bells striking ten o'clock. Although she no longer agrees with much of the Catholic Church (or had she ever on many points?), she fondly recalls the infrequent Sunday visits to the church near their home in Brookline with her mother. Her father would stay at home to take advantage of the quiet house. It was a time when she could think freely without anything else to do. It was a similar feeling to going on a long car ride and looking out the window. She relished those moments, even as a child, pensive space for personal development. At the time, she just saw it as adult-like freedom. What used to go through her head now made her laugh: daydreaming over schoolgirl crushes, wondering what college would be like, thinking over the memories her parents had recounted to her of their childhoods in Italy and Buffalo, New York.

She now recalls eating her mother's Ratatouille that would fill the house with Mediterranean smells. Mediterranean food seemed to capture both her French and Italian ancestry. She felt drawn to each culture, feeling them in her blood. She thinks this is the reason she stayed in Italy when she finally had the freedom to go wherever she wanted. There was something still so raw about Italian culture, so much about enjoying food, love, the seaside, despite centuries of evolution from the Roman Empire. Her mother had instilled in her a need for the Italian way of life, especially fresh nourishment. She spent more money than many of her friends in America on produce, fish, and meats to ensure they were fresh and often organic. They delivered the best flavors and the best health benefits. She remembers one Christmas Eve when she and Undine were asked to continue walking in the sleet to countless butchers and grocery stores to find a local farm turkey, one with vegetarian feed and humane treatment. Although the girls had complained and rolled their eyes at the time, Catherine now thanks her mother for the food that they ate and for these impressions that have shaped her.

Today, Catherine will go to the *Marché Raspail*, feeling ready to indulge in these senses once again after so much difficulty during her chemotherapy sessions and the Temozolomide treatment. At the time, she would not have been able to stomach the spices and fats on the grills, the odor of cheese, probably even some of the herbs. The weakness she had felt was nearly unbearable. The hours in the bathroom feeling so much confusion about wanting to live and fighting her death while punishing herself. There were times of private rage, scratches on her back, a broken plate, a wet pillow. She hid them from her father to protect him.

She is so happy to be back on this Sunday journey without fear of sickness. When she doesn't feel sick, she stops feeling death approaching. Instead, a flood of the hypersensory experience triggers memories that multiply the hour toward immortality. This market had the best produce, and Catherine had taken her mother there in the one trip to Paris. The way she soaked up everything while she walked slowly through the stalls made Catherine feel like her mother had left a part of herself there, and she always felt her presence when she returned.

On her twenty minute walk over to the market, Catherine takes in the other smells of Paris. She smells the roasted chicken churning at the butcher as she passes by. The delicious blend of North African spices around the next corner, where tagines and falafels were being prepared for the lunch crowd. Most of the shops and restaurants are closed, however, in Sunday tradition, to also give the workers the days to spend with their families and encourage all Parisians to delight in simple activities of visiting family and friends, eating a luxurious meal - in quality and time, and walking leisurely through the parks. In a line of closed bars and cafes on a small side street near *rue de Rennes*, she inhales the essence of wine, perfume, and cigarettes from the night before.

She walks over a grate and catches a scent that she finds unique to Paris but has such difficulty describing to others. It is the sweet wood burning exhaust from the metros. She doesn't know where it comes from but is present in at least all of the old metro stations and often when crossing a grate. She welcomes it and breathes it in, although it is likely mildly toxic. Toxic smells still hold valuable memories after all. She remembers how her father would always want to sit where they could smell the exhaust of the ferry on their occasional summer day trips to Nantucket Island. He would think of his own father's speed boat on Lake Erie and the exhaust it would release into the crisp summer air. This became an olfactory nostalgia he welcomed in their annual Cape Cod crossing.

Finally, she senses the sweet smell of fruit and vegetable from the *Marché Raspail* a block away. It looks like a tiny fairground with all the trucks and plastic awnings that provide ephemeral space for selling organic goods. It is well known as the best quality market in Paris by locals, tourists, and even celebrities. One day while buying a kilogram each of white asparagus and Renée Claude plums, she caught a whiff of beautiful perfume on an older sophisticated looking woman next to her. There was an incredibly feminine and elegant air about her that made Catherine catch a glance of her visage. Behind a large pair of Dior sunglasses were the unmistakable eyes of Catherine Deneuve, and when she noticed she was being admired, she smiled and winked, pulling the lapel of her trench coat up a bit higher. Catherine smiled back at her alter ego with a slight nod of greeting but turned quickly away so as not to attract attention. This was not only an effect for Madame Deneuve but also for herself. She enjoyed the secrecy of her intimacy with the star of *Le Dernier Metro,* alongside Deperdieu, *Belle de Jour* and so many other films and lingered just long enough after her purchase to delight that Catherine Deneuve also bought many Renée Claudes, perhaps by her influence. She wonders if other people, maybe even this movie star, think *she* might be famous. She has no desire to really have fame, even though she appreciates success of her artwork, but the idea of an aura about her is enticing. The aura of Madame Deneuve as she chooses her vegetables, as she walks in the fog. If she, too, has an aura, does it mean she is living the way one is *supposed* to? One *aspires* to? She almost wants to ask her namesake these questions and scans the customers for a possible match.

But today there is no sight of the famous woman. A Japanese couple on her left is taking photographs of the cheese. A young Moroccan man in front of her is attempting to sell handfuls of flowers for the wellbeing of his family.

Today the herbs table is especially colorful in all shades of green with an unexpected purple accent. Sprouts of *radis violets* catches her eye. The frizzy haired round seller tells her they are a bit spicy and of course add beautiful color to one's lunch plate. The rolling Arabic accent enjoys explaining the varying flavors and offers a taste of sunflower sprouts growing in a wooden box next to the scale. Her cheeky smile suggests the knowledge that anyone who tastes it will buy, and of course this works for the benefit of both women involved.

Catherine walks like a tourist another twenty meters before catching sight of a smooth and leathery coffee colored skin on the handsome young face at the Middle Eastern array. The tabboulis, quiches, and crinkles around his eyes enthrall her to speak with him. His energy radiates in the way he spreads his fingers and dances with every joint to explain the ingredients in his products. She would welcome their movement on her own skin, but settles on tasting what he has instead made especially for her to eat.

As she courageously tastes a *caviar des aubergines aux pimentes*, the spicy element would not have been tolerated during the chemo, she feels the perfect consistency of slow roasted eggplant slide over her tongue and she is able to taste all the simple flavors. She realizes that tears are streaming down her face behind the sunglasses. They are not from the heat of the *pimentes*, but from the joy of enjoying this food. She discretely wipes the tears away, but they continue as he ties the bag of hummus and olives for her with a proud flagrancy.

She walks up and down the aisles twice before buying anything else. She watches where the other locals buy, those who know the vendors from coming with their mothers as children, and smells and takes in the welcomed imperfect colors, unlike the neat rows of one-sized, always-the-same-color produce in the American supermarkets the past few months. It made it easier to eat bland food but she had to go to expensive specialty shops to find food to cook for her father. That had been short-lived anyway, since it, too, turned her stomach. Even in the French grocery stores, though, she could find tomatoes on the vine and eggs from vegetarian fed chicken. In the future, there must be a revolt against the factory farming, the antibiotics, the hormones, those things she would not have been aware of if it hadn't been for her mother's often annoying insistence and the revelation that everyday foods could be different in what she experienced in Europe. And Raspail was then the best of the Continent. Apricots here vary from cherry-red to peachy-yellow in tone. Heirloom tomatoes wrinkled and warted with a rainbow of green-white-red, the Italian flag, contained in each massive fruit. The berries come by the box – about a kilo in each – and the same price as a tiny bowl of fruit salad at a restaurant. You have to get what's in season, not everyone likes this. But that is what is sustainable, delicious, natural.

She purchases a few vegetables and fruits for her lunch, then finally arrives at one of the *fromageries*. The man she likes, the one with the neatly trimmed mustache, cuts generous slices of unpasteurized cheese for her to try. She tastes willingly and deeply, inhaling before biting in, and asking if there is some stronger but still as soft and flaky as the *chèvre* she has just tasted. He takes out what he calls a *pyramide* of cheese, slightly charcoal colored at the corners, that smells like a combination of hazelnuts, mold, and fresh dirt masking sweet fermented dairy. He takes a fresh one out of the glass display and holds it gingerly at the corners with his thick hands before placing it on smooth white paper, folding up the sides and twisting the corners. *Avec ceci?* She can never say no to this question and takes a wedge of the blue from Auvergne that he recommends.

She reasons that she has a guest for lunch and would like to offer her a variety.

She begins the return to her apartment with treats in her canvas bags that she pauses to smell or peer in at every now and then. She pulls out an apple for the man who inhabits the edge of the sidewalk near her apartment. *'Merci beaucoup, Madame. Merci. Bonne journée à vous!'* She holds the bag open after she passes to make a mental picture of the fresh produce. The colors swirl in her brain and she plans out how to prepare the lunch for her and Cecilia, her neighbor. They often have lunch together after the Raspail market on Sundays. Cecilia's sense of taste and smell were always especially keen. Her remarks about the food she would find each week would always be a surprise. She also had an acute sensory memory. She would compare a particular forest mushroom or white asparagus to one she had tried as a child or one she and Catherine had tried together years before.

The lunches were meant to be in English to help Cecilia learn the language she had always wanted to access, but often when they talked of the food they both somehow felt the need to revert to Italian or French. Cecilia, like Catherine's mother, had also been born in Italy. She had moved to Paris after the Germans had left with her French husband who had been an officer in the war, and later died from complications with shrapnel embedded in his neck, but luckily after they had had two healthy children who had both moved since to London for work. Cecilia tried to learn English to communicate when she visited them, to relate differently to her three grandchildren, but the memories of her family and her experiences spoke in Romance languages, and often the translations were elusive at best.

Today is a treat for many reasons: not only does she get to enjoy what would be a warm afternoon with her old friend but she also had been away from the wonders of this market for months and she is finally able to appreciate strong flavors and odors that were so sickening during the chemo treatments. The cooking and eating would be even better than the purchasing. But before she gets home, she starts to think about how far she has come already, how perhaps Pascal is right

The endless tests her sister had urged her to go through in the United States all arrived at the same conclusion: she had a Glioblastoma multiforme, the most common and aggressive type of brain tumor, and one that most would die from within a year. She thought it sounded like globalization, from which she also has a fear, something taking over the world invisibly. The tests had concluded that some chemotherapy treatment along with the medicine would prolong her life by six months, at least that's what the statistics said; this seemed like enough bought time for the pain, annoyance, and discomfort of the therapy sessions. Six months might get her to a point where Esmé did not withdraw from her anymore, where her father did not retreat to cry about her or the memory of her mother whenever they had a nice moment together, and where Edmond would come back to her. What else could happen in six months? It now seemed like a good decision since her first ten days back in Paris already felt like another lifetime.

The worst part of the therapy had been the trouble she had with food, the aversion to strong flavors or rich meals and the difficulty of digestion. It wasn't only that she couldn't enjoy certain foods and felt sick at times, it was also the way people reacted to her eating and her body. Like many cancer patients, she lost a significant amount of weight on her already slender frame. The change was obvious, and many people had opinions about it that they made her aware of. Advice came as an influx, too, and although she would have liked to accept people's help as kind and generous, it often felt intrusive and ungrounded. Judgmental and violating.

She remembers the first morning after the chemo treatment when she tried to have an omelette. The richness, even without meat, was just too much for her system, and she only managed a few bites before expelling the small amount that had made it into her stomach.

It was the first of strange mornings when she had no appetite, drinking only tea or black coffee. Unlike when she was pregnant with Esmé, it was unfortunately not a side effect of something magical happening in her body.

She used to think those who did not eat had no *raison d'être*, their body not wanting for sustenance, their dreams too sedentary to work up an appetite. She tried toast or rice, and it seemed to work ok until she would try something more ambitious - adding butter, cheese, or chocolate on top - and everything would come out in one great thick waterfall. *Hopefully the more sick you feel, the more it is working*, she thought. She tried to remind herself why she was doing this and thought of her painting, her father and daughter, walking her favorite streets, another winter's snow – reasons to live – even if it were a long shot. In this way she could trick herself into thinking the thin gauntness was a positive move or at least a gamble on her health.

She did not lose a noticeable amount of hair and only her very close friends and relatives knew of the brain tumor, about a dozen people in total. She had often taken extended trips to stay with her father and be close to Esmé at school. With her flexible schedule as an artist, there were never many questions about why she was around this time. She also had a relationship with a few galleries on Newbury Street in Boston that would either show her work or connect with her other artist friends in Paris. She did a bit of consulting for them, not for much money but to stay social in the lonely world of her work. Some artists wanted complete solitude; she relished these times, but craved interaction, too.

During this time of questioning, uncertainty, or rather the absolute certainty of mortality, she felt the need even more to reach out to this network on the most posh street in Boston, incognito as a person free from disease. She would take the slow green line train from her father's home in Brookline. Although driving would take her just fifteen minutes, with parking, she preferred the lazy path that allowed time to read or be a hidden voyeur, watching, and sometimes sketching, other public transport customers or people walking on the streets. The fifty-minute ride always had some revelation or moment of secret enjoyment when she would smile to herself or exchange a knowing look with another individual, often a child.

About two months into her return, enough time for her to lose a considerable amount of weight on her small frame, she was meeting up with some old friends from college on one of these trips to Newbury street. She had just re-balanced the way she thought about the chemo and her tumor, and felt she could handle a purely social trip.

One of them now ran a posh gallery, though she said it was like being a businessman and complained about it all the time, and the other was a primary school art teacher. Both had been friends from the art program often spending long nights painting together, bonding over many ruined clothes, ambitious projects, and late night secret-spilling-sessions. At the end of the semester with deadlines their professor would sometimes show up with beers for everyone. It helped them make these projects the priority in their finals, using only any extra time to study for tests or write papers. Professor Friedrich was a friendly guy – so much so that while Catherine was at school she knew of three affairs he had with students; the first two were with girls in her class, seduced in a swirl of early morning color in the studio, the third a guy in the year ahead. In any case, he had inspired all three of the women enjoying a bottle of Champagne together to enter the art world professionally in some capacity. Catherine had suggested Champagne, the others said it was too much, but she said it was her treat. Linda, the gallery owner, was 'famished' and also ordered some bread with cheese and olives; Janice had chocolate cake ('since they seemed to be celebrating something') and then looked at Catherine with concerned tilted eyes. 'Why don't you get something, honey? *You* need to eat.' With that, Linda gave a disapproving look at Catherine's figure and glanced over at Janice who silently concurred.

Maybe she should have appreciated their concern. But it didn't feel that way. It was interesting, annoying; it sounded angry. Catherine would not tell them about the chemo, especially now, but even if there had not been any, had they any right to…

She wouldn't bother to respond that both of them would stand to lose a little, that perhaps salad would have been a better choice for Janice. There was nothing wrong with chocolate cake, but they each seemed a bit lazy, always denying, always pretending to diet. Always complaining about it. They just didn't take care of themselves sufficiently in many ways. It wasn't just their food choices. One had her roots showing and wore tennis shoes all the time, the other clearly had tanned herself to oblivion. She wanted to help but she knew they were jealous of her – her artistic success, her life in Paris, her natural (and now unnatural) thinness – even though they knew her husband was dead. Would they still be jealous if they knew about the tumor?

It would be a low blow to bring it up now. It would just make them feel guilty about what they said. Or, at least, it would make for an awkward situation and she preferred to try to recapture a relaxed, pleasurable afternoon.

She sipped her champagne, laughed, changed the subject. Had they heard about their friend who had become a designer for Chanel or the other one whose husband left her when she was pregnant with her fourth child or the other who had quit her job at a bank and moved to Colorado to work as a ski instructor…the stories of others went on like this.

As their food came, and she uncomfortably abstained, noting their disapproving eyes especially after they offered her bites that she denied. It made her feel guilty, like she was hurting them by not eating, even though she knew it would really hurt herself.

She would never willingly hurt herself by eating or denying food. She had seen the effects of this on her sister in high school, not because of some internal desire to be model-thin but because of external pressures from her shallow friends. They gave up sports and music for getting skinny and going to parties. Rather than soccer and flute practice, free time became shopping and watching boyfriends at hockey games. Undine was always the pretty one, that was her identity in the family. A family friend had come over when Catherine was ten, her sister eight, and told her how pretty her sister was, asking for confirmation. She agreed, she knew it innately, but it somehow seemed wrong for both of them to pin her with this identity, simultaneously empowering and inhibiting. In addition to the picky eating Undine developed, her sister smoked to defer hunger; she had become a heavy smoker until expecting her first child, then went on the patch and eventually quit. Catherine was a social smoker, although since coming back to Paris, she hasn't had the desire to smoke again.

She asked for a cigarette then from two men smoking nearby on the Newbury Street terrace to the horror of her friends. 'Haven't you given up smoking yet? It's 1999!' Catherine cannot imagine what they would say if they had known of her cancer at the time. More than reprimanding, they may have violently grabbed the fag from her lips. They would fling it as far as they could from the table, dramatically. No doubt it would hit one of the hundreds of baby strollers passing by and cause an embarrassing altercation.

Catherine had laughed at this last thought, out loud. She recalls it now and laughs again on an empty side street. Her friends, of course, thought she was laughing at *not* smoking, at their safe lives, from the perspective of her snobby Parisian *borrowed* identity. But what they did not realize at the time, and never would, is that her snobbiness is actually confidence and pride, like many other misunderstood French, her identity is real, made up of pieces of different cultures and from within, her own cultivated desires. She does not pretend or try on. She just *is*.

Although within the five seconds that she paused to respond, all sorts of nasty comebacks danced in radiated beams from her tumor, in the sixth second, she had luckily recalled Pascal's inspirational truth for moments like this: 'we are all victims of victims.' Her mood turned to pity, common understanding that all three of them were tackling the game of life in their own ways.   And in the seventh second, she said simply, 'This champagne is too brilliant on its own and I'm dining with my dad and Esmé later, so a smoke will have to do. Esmé brought us some fresh seafood on her way home at the fresh market.' It was all actually true, even though an excuse, and one that she did not wish to have to make.   It probably still sounded defensive, she thought, too much information. She realized her explanation was more to make herself feel better both about the comment and the reality of her slight, now childlike figure.

She focused on the taste and texture of the champagne to gather back her composure and then began a series of questions about their lives, which they did not reciprocate. Maybe she would have told them about her tumor, her treatments, had they been more curious about her life. What a sad friendship jealousy creates.

She had waited instead, and reconsidered that she had judged them too harshly.   She had called Linda, the stronger personality, to meet her for coffee one afternoon the next week. Catherine quickly moved the conversation toward the brain tumor, wanting to get it over with quickly, and hoping that the honesty would be appreciated by her friend of so many years. Linda responded with shock, horror, hugs, petting Catherine's head, 'You poor dear. Oh my, oh my...' she recomposed herself, 'You must tell me what I can *do* to help. I feel so helpless...' Catherine assured her that just being a good listener and friend was good enough. That the best she could do is treat her like normal. Linda assured her they would have a fun, extravagant outing with Janice later in the week before she had to go back to work.

In the coming days, Catherine first waited for her to call, then decided to call herself. She left a brief message, saying when she was available, asking her to call back. Linda had called two days later. First she made several excuses before blurting out: 'Look, I'm really sorry...I just can't take being around somebody who's *dying*. It just scares me. It's just...I'm sorry, I just can't do it or maybe I need a little time. Please forgive me. You *know* I love you!' Catherine was surprised, to say the least, but said she understood, hoping it would change after Linda slept on it. Then, all of a sudden, Linda had said in a calculated tone, 'Hey, I don't think you should tell Janice about this tumor. I think it's pretty hard to take, you know? I mean she's got young kids at home,' she paused a moment to think of a closing statement, 'Good luck with everything....' At least it made it even easier to come back to Paris.

This awkwardness and jealousy is completely absent

from her relationship with Cecilia and she cannot wait to share the beautiful food she has found at the market this morning. Cecilia who told her that aging is a gift.

Upon arriving at home, she drops the bags in the kitchen and turns on some opera music. She then puts on her navy and white striped apron and proceeds to make a fresh tomato salad with herbs and sprouts, bruschetta with olive tapenade and hummus spreads, and spicy marinated sardines. She takes cold-pressed olive oil and Modena balsamic vinegar to pour over the tomatoes; it streams over them and pools into beads that continue to dance together, but maintain their distinctions, as she moves it to the table. Then she prepares a cheese plate and green salad for after the meal so that they can come to room temperature and expose all sides of their flavors. Lastly, she sets the table with white dishes that show off the colors of the food, cloth napkins from Marseilles, heavy silver utensils - the same she uses everyday, and four small wine glasses for water and a rosé from Provence that Cecilia has already mentioned she will bring.

With lunch spread on the table, she takes a few minutes to relax at her armchair, browsing through a design magazine and sometimes humming along to the music.

In time, she hears Cecilia walking over and gets up before she rings the bell.

'*Bonjour*! It is so good to see you!'

'You, too, my dear. You sound wonderful! Here is the wine I promised, from Jérome at the wineshop on *rue de Cherche-midi*, and some Stilton with cranberry that Lucie brought over last week.' Her old Italian neighbor wears a bright yellow dress over her tiny frame; it almost makes her white hair look blond again. She has on bright red lipstick and her gold cross fits perfectly in the scoop neck of the dress. The wine has a glass stopper instead of a cork; its color is that of raspberry vinegar. She can smell the cheese through its paper wrapper and as she places it on a serving plate the edges crack open slightly like fault lines since it has been guarded at room temperature to open the flavors.

They move directly to the table where Catherine pours the wine and they begin by talking about family - Cecilia's grandchildren, one of whom came on the visit with his mother, and Catherine's daughter especially. They first cover the last few months quickly before moving toward particular anecdotes, funny or touching, as they begin to enjoy their meal.

As Catherine pours them each a second glass of wine, she starts to feel compelled to be honest with her friend and warn her about the cancer. 'There's something I should tell you...' she pauses, looking for the right words, which she never found easy to do those handful of times that it was necessary. But she stops searching when she hears her friend's voice cut in.

'Catherine, although I don't always like to do it, I don't try to pry, you know I can hear everything that goes on in this building. You don't need to tell me anything, unless you think it would help to talk about it.' She reaches her hand across the table and Catherine takes it. Cecilia places her free hand on top to hold Catherine's soft fingers warmly, with movements that trace the empty space between her bones. 'I can tell you are happy. That feeling is real! Don't let them tell you it's not true,' she pauses and looks at the Catherine's palm as she turns over her hand slowly.

Then she lets her eyes move upwards with her face angled down, as if she is about to tell a secret, 'You know, the doctor told me last month that maybe I'm starting to lose my marbles.'

'But, no! Cecilia, you're so youthful. It's not true.'

'Well, I think he's right. I mean, my sharpness has declined a bit. When Stefano was alive, we used to have fantastic debates and push each other to be more intelligent. Although I always outwitted him and solved his most difficult law puzzles at work!' She gives Catherine a little wink. 'Well, we used to have great sex, too. Not all the time; he was so busy at work and me with the children. But when we had the opportunity, it made me feel so alive,' Catherine wonders what this has to do with the topic but listens intently to this woman that she admires. 'So, I asked my doctor if he thought it would be safe for me to have sex.'

Catherine's serious, anxious face warms into an unconscious grin, 'Did you mean with *him?*'

'Well, no, but now that you mention it…' she winks, 'I was thinking more one of these fine older gentlemen in the neighborhood. You know they have Viagra to help them these days. Alfred or Mario. Maybe Gregoire. He flirts with me during *apero* sometimes and his stories are so lovely and animated. Even when he talks about the German Occupation, he finds these beautiful people and moments.' It is almost too much for Catherine, who thinks of Cecilia as a cross between her mother, an older sister, and a best friend, but she appreciates this honest conversation that seems to be missing from so many interactions she has had lately.

'So what did the doctor say?'

146

'Oh, that's when he thought I was going a bit crazy, I think. He kind of started to talk to me like a child, but kindly. Although he did say it would be alright for my health. So, now I'm really looking forward to your art opening! Good opportunity.' She gives another wink and smiles in anticipation. 'And speaking of, have you been hearing that racket upstairs? Nicolas is really getting around these days. I don't even need to listen to movies anymore when I can hear their nights together. I mean, I don't really have a choice. Did you hear when he had a high-pitched American in there for apero and a raspy French girl after the *boites* closed? My, my. Times have changed!'

They recount several evenings that they each heard over the past week and try to identify if each one was with a different woman or not. They hypothesize about his life, since they only know him by chance greetings on the stairs.

They have moved onto stories about themselves when they were his age as they move onto the cheese course and toward the end of the bottle. As they finish, Cecilia's favorite aria from Aida comes on and she gets up to dance around the room encouraging Catherine to join her. They curtsy to each other at the end, Cecilia thanks her for a splendid afternoon and says she is sleepy now and will take a nap. She offers to help clean up first but Catherine refuses and instead escorts her to her own apartment, even though she is capable of doing so herself.

Cecilia kisses her on the cheek, '*Bella*, take care of yourself. I didn't mean to talk about myself so much...it's just that I've realized we're *all* going to die, so why keep worrying about it? I mean, go to the doctor, do what they say, usually, but don't feel guilty to just live your life!' She kisses her again.

They look each other in the eye for a quiet moment.

'I wish us many happy lunches and I wish you many handsome suitors. Ciao Cecilia.' They part gracefully with the buzz of their time together making a sort of cloud to take them through this Sunday with human comfort and stimulation.

Catherine spends the rest of the day cleaning and singing, then walking in the late sunny sky before writing a letter to Esmé and reading in bed. Another good day in Paris lets her sleep soundly until sunrise.

IX

Davide

It is a rainy evening later in the week. Catherine is
entering the *Comédie Française*, the majestical theatre that
sits next to the *Petit Palais*. She enters alone in casual attire
- jeans and a black t-shirt, but a smart long trench coat,
small brown crocodile handbag, and stiletto heels give her
just the right touch of elegance. After a fulfilling day at
her studio, she walked home under the rainfall for the sole
purpose to find these accessories.

As she gives the doorman her ticket, she looks up at the
insignia that is over three hundred years old. The date,
marked 1680, is still a hundred years before the French
Revolution. New England was still a colony at the time as

well, although Brookline was already a hamlet in 1638 and would be a town by 1705. The emblem creates an aura as she enters; a duplicity of time overcomes her.

Rebecca, an American artist friend, was supposed to come with her tonight and had been the one to buy the tickets. She was fortunate to have friends like that, those who were often seeking something inspiring, beautiful, or new in the city. Unfortunately, Rebecca called earlier to say she was ill. She is one of those friends you can count on for cancelations. Catherine admires Rebecca's work, enjoys their exchanges, so indulges her eccentricities. It was too late to call someone else to accompany her, having already been late when she called added to the fact that the message was not heard until Catherine stopped by her apartment in the evening. She used to get annoyed at last minute cancelations like this, especially because it always seemed to be the same people canceling on her. But now she realizes sometimes, even if you're not really sick, you're not in the mood - the rain, perhaps some melancholia or even anxiety - and it's not good for anyone that you go out from your cocoon.

So she is at the theatre alone and instead of rushing in at the last minute like most people would do by themselves, she gets there forty minutes early to enjoy a glass of champagne, *une coupe*. Actually, just seeking the taste rather than the alcohol, she orders a *coupette* once she arrives at the bar overlooking the street through impressive, open windows. She takes her half-filled glass to stand at a small table near a window and begins watching the street, but tires quickly of the tops of umbrellas passing by. So, instead, she turns toward the room in front of her, where there is a lot to see.

Mismatched couples, overdressed tourists, a jovial group of old ladies. She admires them all.

Her eyes wander down to the playbill that she has placed haphazardly on the table. She had forgotten what tonight's show would be: Voltaire's "Socrates," a satire on organized religion and governmental authority. She has read it long ago and can't remember much about it, but she knows that Voltaire always amuses her and the actors here are the best. She had agreed to the tickets without much thought of what they were going to see.

She realizes, however, that this was a good choice. Not only does she find Voltaire's humor witty and entertaining, and easier to understand than contemporary French humor as a foreigner, but she also enjoys politics. It doesn't seem to go much with her lifestyle; she doesn't have much to do with organizations and national agendas, especially as an expatriate, but she feels moved by certain political causes. She also finds the nature of political debate to be intriguing — like a verbal dance. She especially pays attention when they talk about foreign relations in American politics, knowing full well how Americans and the country herself can be perceived abroad.

Growing up, her family did not seem to have much to do with politics. Her father's writing often had a liberal angle, but when he talked about issues like equality and the environment, he did not make them political — they were moral principles, scientific facts, acts of kindness. Her mother wouldn't touch politics with a three meter breadstick, as she used to say. All she would do is complain about Italian politicians and how untrustworthy they were. Her political leaders were the Pope and his

Cardinals. She did not always agree with him, but she thought that he was basically in favor of goodness in the world and that he was stable. Those were two things she could not say for the government in Italy. She stopped even reading about the elections because it made her turn red and angry. In fact, Catherine only remembers her becoming angry when reading about Italian scandals; it made her feel shameful about the home she loved so much.

However, her mother who had abandoned any allegiance Italian politicians had loved Kennedy, had loved him as much as her father had loved Martin Luther King, Jr. She grew up visiting their museums or watching her parents read their biographies and quoting the most poignant passages. Her mother didn't do much of the reading, preferring *Life* magazine or television. Even just the image of JFK made her swoon or tear up. These two figures idolized by her parents seem above the political for Catherine now, more like the Pope in the way they had each been immortalized through their grotesque assassinations.

Catherine instead came to think about politics in terms of Democracy and strategy, her power as a voter and citizen. The ideas came first from Thomas, who had been studying government when they met, even though he later switched to pre-medicine. They were both students at a small liberal arts school in Lexington, Virginia brought together by the fact they were both New Englanders and both early morning swimmers: he for an extra session to aid in his soccer practice and she for the love of the water's massage-like circulatory properties. A way to wake up, fully. She had competed with her local YMCA and then on the high school team, but once she got to college, she decided to simply make it a pleasure. The team practices and competitions would not fit well into her artistic ambitions, for which she never knew when creativity would strike. Thomas had been a terrible swimmer, often resorting to the kickboard out of frustration rather than as a reason to focus on his leg muscles. She offered a suggestion after noticing the furled brow after his first few laps one day; this facial expression did not match the sentiment that a morning swim should offer and it bothered her to see another suffer so. Swimming was one way she would find her calm. She asked him to try something for her, a few easy drills: skulling - a movement that turned his hands into fins - and dolphin kicking on alternating sides. He taught her pool running in return, which she quickly abandoned save situations when she wanted to have a chat with someone else in the pool. The idea of swimming in one place was like using a treadmill in a gym for her. Unless the purpose was to recuperate from an injury, she saw no use for it. Although she reasoned that if you were swimming outside, you could also look at the view. This was something she did when she took Esmé to the Italian lakes, the ones her mother had always described, reverting to the old language she never spoke: '...*azzurro come un fiore di campo...Minerali freschi rotolano su di me ed io potrei anche morire li, in quel momento...*'. As if she could die at that moment in that beautiful lake and have no regret.

In just two weeks after her intervention, Catherine noticed a great difference in Thomas's stroke and this was the second time she approached to speak with him. It made her happy to be able to help him improve; she had a natural tendency to do such and it is probably what led to her teaching career that mixed nicely with her artistry. She had no idea he was a scholarship player and felt flattered when she later found out that she had a hand in coaching such a refined athlete. As the spoke this time out of the water, she was struck not so much by his physical strength but by the beauty of his body, even when the movement in water had been awkward at best. He invited her to see a game. It sounded like he had been rehearsing as the inner dialogue spilled out like water spouting out a dolphin's blowhole: 'So, I have a home game this weekend. I thought because you have helped me so much in the pool, you might like to see if it's actually working on the field. Anyway, we're playing a good team, Seton Hall, so it should be exciting. What do you think? You could bring some of your friends. But if you're busy, it's ok…'.

She smiled at his obviousness and agreed, though it was something not usually done with her artist friends but still more acceptable than going to an American football or lacrosse game, the big sports of the school. Instead of bringing friends, she brought her camera. This was for two reasons: to make the game an artistically captured experience and, more importantly, to use as an apparatus behind which she could hide herself and avoid conversation with strangers. She did not want to look like a girl going after a guy on the field, or a girl looking for a guy in the stands. The camera added to her identity as an artist, one she was quite comfortable sharing with the public. The photographs she captured from that first match and many others in that season, her sophomore year, and the ensuing years until their graduation, are etched in her memory. She would always go alone, even when his parents would come for a match. The drove down from Connecticut, often to also visit an aunt and her family in Baltimore on the way. At those times, she would sometimes join the family for lunch after the game. She enjoyed this form of artistry and often lost track of what was happening in the game, often celebrating, instead of a goal or save, the capture of a unique position that would arrive in reaching for the ball or blocking an opponent.

It was this form that first attracted herself to him, this intrigue by the movement and shaping of his body. She thinks of it in comparison to the bodies she may see before her tonight. The actors here have no inhibitions, at least not on the stage. Their souls, their bodies, belong to the audience, much like the soccer players who save their best moves for the games. For this reason, the actors get naked on stage without thinking of it as exposure. It is nudity in a raw, emotive sense. Perhaps it is different during rehearsal, but here, it is clear in the way they move that they do not even think about the way we will judge their bodies or the way to show them least offensively to the audience. Or they have rehearsed so well that it seems so. She remembers some of the actors over the years who had incredible lines of strength that connected through their tendons and spines. She wished she could photograph, or better still - paint, them during their performances.

However, the most captivating naked man she had ever seen, she saw from the bizarre angle of looking straight up toward the heavens at the line of his immense body. Michelangelo's *Davide*, as the people of *Firenze* call him, remains to this day the most beautiful figure. She had first scene the replica statue on the hillside from afar, but she realized that everything lined up better and added to the intense aura by standing under the original in the Accademia Gallery. The strange part of this idolatry she felt for his perfection is that if you actually see his proportions from head on, you see quite clearly that the arms are much too long, the head too large, and the legs are little squat troll stumps. But Michelangelo's genius took this all into account without the aid of a computer or even any use of mathematical perspective. Instead he just *knew*. His artistic mind carefully considered that we would be standing at *Davide*'s foot level, his massive domineering, yet beautiful foot, and look up the line of his naked limbs and the undulations of the perfect buttocks, and if our eyes happened to go any further, they would arrive finally at what appeared to be perfectly proportioned shoulders and head. And they absolutely are that way, when you take into account the direction of one's eye.

In the same way, Thomas was a *trompe l'oeil*. Not in the form of his body, but in the nature of his heart. He always seemed open, generous, but it seemed to her later after just a year of marriage, that this generosity was more out of narcissism. True, we are all egotistical, we all want attention, to be acknowledged, to be praised, and we deserve it. But for Thomas, it went beyond this. His open heart was a calculated form of creating connections for the future of his political career. It was the same reason he had joined the military. Not to do something for his country or pay for his education, which was the reason for so many Americans, but quite simply to make important political connections and have 'validity' when he would later work on his future as an ambassador.

She acknowledges now this is likely way too harsh a judgment. But she also knows why she sometimes feels this way. We are often victims of our traumas and fears, she thinks. That's what Pascal has taught her. It was one day when she was seven months pregnant; she had been driving home on the base from a friend's dinner where everyone except her had drunk the typical one bottle of wine per person minimum. She began discussing her plans to exhibit her recent paintings of the streets of Naples, possibly in New York or Paris, asking him if he thought it a good idea. Then, with a jovial grin, he said without pause, 'Of course it is, honey! You might as well have fun with it now. It will make you an even more attractive ambassador's wife later on.'

She would have to stand by his side, support him. To smile for the media, the other diplomats. She had grown into beauty, a lean expression of confidence and vitality. Not the pedestal beauty that he did not realize he really wanted; hers would disappear quickly on a campaign trail. Under lights, next to glamour. Curvaceous figures, made-up faces. But he had no idea. He said it was 'important,' he was 'lucky' that she was 'so good looking and could easily lose her pregnancy weight through swimming,' as she had planned to do and did do eventually after Esmé's birth, but it took long enough that Thomas began grimacing whenever she took dessert. When she finally succeeded, he was 'proud of her' for it.

These comments ripped through her core.

Quietly, her anger started to race through her mind. He had no right to decide her life for her. She had been admitted to college based on her artistic talent and her grades, not on her looks, not for what her assets as a swimmer to their team could have been. In the time after college, they had been apart. He joined the military right away; he had wanted to go to medical school through the army, but his grades were not strong enough. He was smart, but he focused more on his sport and his network in college. He decided he could work his way up and perhaps do something with medicine in the military as well. He began an officer training program and focused on emergency response unit training, having found a live for skydiving during an optional training day. Even if he could not be the doctor sailing into a danger zone to help a fellow officer in need, he could work on these types of honorable missions. 'Thomas is a man of great honor,' even her father, who is adamantly against the military, had once said.

At the same time that Thomas was embarking on this admirable career, she had received a scholarship for an MFA program in New York. They were 'impressed' by her large canvas of a May '68 demonstration in Paris and another of the busing riots in Boston, but they had been 'captivated' by her three self-portraits, showing 'fierce rawness of emotion and independence.' She had her own ambitions unrelated to his military politics and had never imagined herself as a trophy wife. She thought the statement might feel flattering for some women, but not even an ounce of her body felt this statement as a compliment. She wanted it to shrink to skeletal form. The pregnancy fat made her feel more on display, more obvious.

She began to redden, without immediate verbal reaction. It was building. She felt her grip on the steering wheel tighten and her teeth clench until she could not see the road before her as clearly as she would have liked. Even though they were only two blocks away from home, on the base, she pulled over and let out a deep scream as her knuckles turned white on the steering wheel. These actions confused and frightened him. He had no idea why she was upset. 'Honey, your hormones are acting up. Don't worry…there, there…' He was assuming it had something to do with her pregnancy and began to ask if she felt ok, if the baby was alright.

She quite simply stated, 'I will not quit my work for you.' But the statement was loaded with her studies of art, all the ambitions she had discussed with her mother to help children with their own artistic experession, her feeling of independence that she had always guarded. Her head was spinning, she paused for five minutes to calm herself and drove home safely before staying awake the remainder of the night in worried anticipation. She could run away. She could escape. But what about their daughter? What about her loneliness?

Catherine shakes herself out of the memory. These places deep in her mind are haunting her more and more. She turns toward the chilly open window, looking again down at the umbrellas passing underneath. She spots a couple huddled under one, enjoying the need to be forced closer together. Her fingers run along the stem of her champagne glass.

She still loved something about him, his *esprit de vivre,* and loves it in memory, too. But Catherine and Thomas had a fundamental difference that changed the way they saw ambition. His need to fulfill a sort of ambition or legacy made him take the path to early death.

It's always about one's father. Their mothers had been alike in death. So giving, both working at primary schools, not because they couldn't do something more important with their lives, but because that was the most important thing they each found to do. Her mother had taught first grade at the Catholic school every year since she herself had entered school, the public one next door. Thirty years and six-hundred students. His mother was the secretary at a small school in Stamford, Connecticut. Everyone knew that Mrs. James actually ran the school, like most school secretaries. Her heart was big and her voice was firm. There was no question of her ability to keep order to ensure the safety and accountability of every student and teacher in that brick building.

But their fathers are different. Hers had been in charge of a large publishing company in Boston and is still given manuscripts to this day so that he may find the right book to publish at the right time. He now does this work pro bono, for the love of the written word. And he writes himself, for the ability to find an ellipsis, a gap, in his daily experience of reality and his inner being. Here in this space, with his pen in his moleskin journal or his fingers at his typewriter, he plays with words to understand the world and to better enjoy his existence in it. This is where he had turned after his wife's death from a stroke thirteen years ago. He was more accustomed to being on the receiving side of words written on page, and then began to create the words himself, for the sole purpose of the experience of writing them. And it was different than thinking, speaking, conversing. It is a way to use the intricacies of the written word to assert one's identity. Catherine learned from him to do this with paint. Colors as her letters blend to create language at once personal and universal, reflecting her inner being and the world she experiences. She watches the endless stream of bubbles surfacing in her glass and makes a silent toast to her dad.

Thomas's father also has outlived his mother; they both appear a bit lost without their women who would be cooking for them at this common age of seventy-six. Food was the language of their wives, like many other Italian women before them.

She remembers his mother, being of a second generation in America, had focused on traditional Greek fare, like moussaka and lamb with Mediterranean spices. His father was always pleased with the food, but he wasn't pleased with his unrealized ambitions, and it showed in his everyday life. Without a college degree, he had been limited by what he could do, and after having a motorcycle accident as a teenager, he could not join the military. So he became a delivery man, and while it's true that he worked good hours and was his own boss, the job was not good enough that he could retire. As far as she knows, he is still driving the truck. But she prefers to stay out of touch now that Thomas is dead. He was so hard on Thomas to make something of himself, and we all want to please our fathers.

Catherine mistakenly thought for a while that being an artist without any fame and a teacher was not enough for her successful father. She kept chasing some form of what she thought he wanted mixed with what she wanted for herself, which is maybe why she had married her husband. If she could at least marry someone who would seek his ambitions, her father could happily take pride in his daughter's husband and her choice in him. But after his death, her father had understood the most that Catherine was set free. Simple glances or metaphors in his writing told her so.

The White Night

She hears the bells beckoning them into the theatre. It is just the first of a few times they will do this, so she does not rush to get up. She turns back toward the open room that is starting to empty out. In a brief moment she decides to get up, leaving a last sip in the glass, wanting to take in the splendor of the theatre before the lights are dimmed.

As she hands her ticket to the usher on the first balcony, he asks if she is alone. Yes. She wonders why he needs to point this out, but then asks her to go downstairs to see his friend working below.

She heads down the red carpeted staircase and finds the user below, a distinguished looking young man, and tells him what the other had said. '*Ah, oui!*' he says, as if expecting her to arrive like a guest of honor. '*S'il vous plait, Madame*, right this way.' He leads her to an empty seat ten rows from the stage. Never before has she been so close! She has been moved lower down before when the seats are not filled, but to be placed in the most expensive seats is a first. Apparently they were looking for the first solo ticket holder in the balconies they could find.

On this lucky evening, she looks at the theatre from a different angle, and as the show starts, she relishes the closeness to the actors. She can see every muscle of movement on their faces. As expected, several do get naked at one point and she feels as if she is at an artist's live model session. She wants to sketch them as they move, then pose, across the stage. She traces what would be their outlines on her program sitting on her lap.

As the play finishes, she is left with a feeling of inspiration: for democracy, for artistry. It protects her from the cold and the rain as she walks home by herself.

In another world yet fully conscious of the wet city around her. A centuries-old masterpiece that would never be finished.

X

Piscine Joséphine Baker

Summer seems to have arrived overnight. Parisian black rotates to white, and toes are let out to wiggle in the freedom of sandals.

The day is hot. The kind that makes people cranky, that causes fights on the metro. Most of the city is not designed for this rare heat. Although every year, the mayor attempts to turn the banks of the Seine into a beach - *Paris Plage* - because it's easier to sweat in a bathing suit on the sand. There are other escapes, luckily, because none of the special festivities begin until July. Swimming pools are hidden in every neighborhood of the city.

At first, the continued flow of vitamin D formation as

her skin, healthy now from all the fresh vegetables, and pharmacy creams form a threshold between this sky of full sun and her inner secrets. The heat is stronger than predicted. The sun's rays seem to see through her and the rest of the passersby. She can see which ones are satisfied, which are frustrated, and guilty. She feels the judgment of this sun, too, and she covers herself in sunglasses and hat as if to hide from its enhanced vision.

She crosses to the shady side of *Quai Saint-Bernard* after exiting the sculpture park, staying several lengths behind a couple with their young daughter with perfect black braids atop her head, who reminds her of Esmé's best friend in Florence. Her walk is like a dance, a brilliant blue cotton dress becomes a tutu, she glances back to see who's watching and Catherine acknowledges with a smile. The girl giggles and becomes shy - turning swiftly back to her *maman.* Catherine speeds up her walk to pass and has most of the large sidewalk before her to herself. With her light sundress on and her hair tied up, the heat already doesn't feel so bad. The breeze is free on the open road by the river and lifts up under her dress, probably exposing her little black bikini stretched over her bottom to drivers, but she doesn't even think about this.

Over the years, Catherine had made trips to all different kinds of pools, all over the city. Even before, she had relationships with the pools in Brookline, on her college campus, and on the base. She had made her one true friend in Naples at that base pool, a lifeguard with whom she would often chat before and after her swim, if the air were warm enough. It's funny how sometimes your best friends can be the ones you see *par hazard* - those people you just happen to run into often and who share some sort of view.   It's the building of connections through little everyday things. With Giuliana at the pool, it was often a word about swimming, then another about their children (Giuliana also had a baby), or sometimes about their favorite films and restaurants.

In Paris, the municipal pools are each unique. They are spread over the different arrondissements.   Their hours vary, the lengths of the pools, the way the lockers work. But what is always the same is the price, which is very low, and the welcoming of anybody who wants to swim.

As she walks in the cool shade, a similar effect to jumping in the pool, she thinks back to her favorites over the years. She has gone most frequently to the one in St. Germain des Pres for its proximity. She knows the kinks of the place well, from its entrance inside a shopping mall and then down the stairs, to the large red plastic hangers attached to boxes on which she hangs her clothes and purse, returning it to the worker like a coat check, to the trip down again through the showers and into the always crowded pool. Rather than separate lanes by speed, these lanes are marked by the type of stroke. She had found that rather strange to start, preferring often to switch between strokes. She realized, however, that this was not strictly enforced and that she could sneak in a length of crawl in the breaststroke lane without a complaint. Typically she would wait for a slower breaststroker and use the crawl as an excuse to pass quickly, before another oncoming swimmer approached. In fact, she enjoyed this crazy, crowded experience, often forgetting how long she had been in the pool or to think of anything else than these strategic passes and not getting hit head on.

Although she likes this pool, sometimes it is necessary to

visit another one, due to pool strikes, maintenance, or changes in the hours it is open. One of her favorites she has visited, besides the one she is about to go to. The best in summer is the one in the *Quartier Latin*, the *Piscine Pontoise*. This pool is especially old fashioned, dating back to the thirties. The pool sits in the center of an arena. On the balcony above are the individual changing rooms with circular windows, cutouts in the wood, to view the pool below as if through a lens. The room, when you are finished and have entered a different era, becomes your locker — the *entire* room. And there is no automated system to lock or even a key or code to take with you. Instead, you fetch the man or woman roaming the balcony with his own set of keys. He locks it for you, remembers your face, and obliges the opening when you return. The waiting time to open the locker gives everyone a few moments extended to be seen in their wet bathing suit and to watch the scene before them, one which is often lost as one swims in the water. She has spent many moments in these pools, none of them wasted time. She would do it all again if she might have the option to re-use these uncountable hours.

As she approaches the pool, she notes the long line but happily decides to wait while others turn back, not able to rest under the hot sun. She observes the Seine and the open solarium at the pool, then takes out the book she has been re-reading, *Bonjour Tristesse*.

Some time later - she has no watch - she is let in along with ten or so others in front of her. She enters the co-ed changing area, takes a locker, rinses off in the shower, and goes out to find a space for her book, towel, and sandals. There are many people lounging in the sun. But the first destination for her body is the pool.

She glides in smoothly, bends her knees, submerges her head, and pushes off down the lane. The density of limbs in the water doesn't bother her; she's not worried about speed. However, at this moment, she has a free shot in front of her, so she grabs it. She goes as long as she can without breathing, counting strokes — fourteen. The next breath is deep and desperate, moving to often unused parts of her lungs, and she finishes the length of the pool with it. There is a cluster at the end of the lane, so she turns slowly without pushing off the wall and switches to breast stroke. She lingers in the glide phase, head down, legs held tightly together. As she advances she comes up on a slower woman and stays behind to watch the way her legs move; they are round and soft, their density seems to merge with the water like submerged waves. In a long breathing phase, her head drifts to the right to reveal an athletic looking man, muscular legs, a simple black Speedo. His legs remind her of Thomas' - impressive in Herculean beauty - their strength holding latent energy, possibilities, that could be channeled toward graceful movements lasting decades. Or sharp moments of violence. She was drawn to him, but he was dangerous for her. This man to her right moves smoothly in the water, unlike Thomas. She wonders if it is also a sign of his finesse in manners or just a pretty shell around a rough man.

Suddenly, another swimmer - a young woman with strong shoulders - attempts a long pass around Catherine and the *Odalisque* in front of her before reaching the wall. The eager athlete just barely avoids an oncoming backstroker, flailing in inexperience or just a lack of kinesthetic intelligence.   However, disaster is avoided. Everyone moves a little on the edge in this tiny twenty-five meter pool.

Catherine continues for ten laps, then takes a break to lie in the open sun.   Even in the winter, one can lie under the rooftop, then closed with glass, and feel the sun's warmth come through.   But when the sun is direct, her body feels different, creating vitamins from its energy; the sun becomes a part of her.

If she were at the beach, she would expose her breasts as well.   But at the pool she keeps her top on.   She thinks it's a rule but she's not sure.   A few women lie face down with the backs of their tops untied.   With mixed international families in close proximity and lap swimming, it just makes sense.   You would never want to do this where you were the spectacle.   Once her back is warmed, she flips over and sits up to view the Seine, on which she floats.   The whole pool floats.   Tourist boats pass by and she also looks at the building across the river. It has many vines covering its side and balconies up high. She misses the standard courtyard balcony she had in Florence.   Gazing at the closed and open windows there, she briefly imagines what it would be like to live there as she often does in looking at buildings throughout the city. Borrowed flashes of another life.

She begins to look around at the patrons from behind her sunglasses and to listen to their conversations, much easier to accomplish with her swim cap lying by her side. She notes the large group of Italians talking about football and what monument they want to visit next - they are all extremes, either skinny energetic bodies, or round indulgent curves lying like happy seals in the sun. Nearby, she sees a single man, pretending to read the newspaper, but he, like she, is looking around at the exposed swimmers. They do not acknowledge catching each other's eyes. A woman with her young child enjoys a magazine and moves the stroller back and forth with her other hand. Two teenagers, just recently free for the summer holidays, talk nonstop about one's boyfriend and the other's crush, analyzing their behaviors and wondering about their motivations. Feeling distraught but enjoying it all the same.

There are other teens out from school as well. Noticing the muscular youth around her, she thinks again of Thomas' strength. He had never hit her, but his existence alongside her was violent. Violence is a latent contradiction; it is a power play of frustration. Their talk was either reserved or aggressive. No restraint was present, and this is why she had resolved to leave him.

That had been just before the accident. She had been a coward, and for this, she was doomed to an eternity of living in the in between, a sort of inner violence all her own. Between feelings about her husband, between an identity as a widow or bachelorette, between feelings of guilt for wanting him to be gone. The wish had been granted.

To hide her tears, she jumps into the water again. Seeking a release, a cleanse. Years of guilt and feeling she has done something wrong, but not able to pinpoint exactly what that is, as if she doesn't want to go to that spot that could be so painful. She wants the water to grant forgiveness.

It doesn't give her that, but it does slip away these thoughts for the time being. Her tears are quickly dissolved in the chlorinated water. Another ten laps and she loses herself. She continues to swim as she becomes a part of the water. Invisible.

She becomes a whale, holding her breath for long stretches of time, opening her round eyes under the water, trying out another world, another home. They used to go on whale watch boats from Gloucestor when she was a kid; she loved to see the whales but always got scared when everyone moved to one side and rocked the boat. Her mother would find her on the other side, often missing the whale, and together they would look at something interesting on the other side that everyone else was missing. Once, on the other side, they had seen a lone unspotted humpback who looked back at them with those curious eyes.

She experiments and spins in the water with her body. At the end of the last lap, she emerges like a whale jumping from the ocean, like they do to show-off to the audience on boats. She, too, leaves a white foamy wake, like that of a whale after she dives, that lingers until the next swimmer cuts through it. Everything around her is white noise and only the triumphant music from Kieslowski's *Bleu* resounds in her head.

. . . . .

On the way home, she thinks of the namesake of this pool, Josephine Baker - American, beautiful, bold, now with an accent to mark the way the French had adopted her as one of their own, and the way she had adopted them. She was American but moved to France, loved them, and they loved her back, not only her husbands but the citizens themselves. She gave herself to them completely, especially during the war. She became their spy - angered by the Nazis' personal attack on herself as an African-American and her husband at the time, a Jewish man. She moved secrets in invisible ink on sheets of music. She outwitted them, and for this, she earned herself the French military's esteemed *Croix de Guerre*. She became a hero, later, too, by Martin Luther King's side. She was fearless, she embraced her own identity independent of race, gender, and nation but also because of all them, playing with what they are. She thinks of Fitzgerald's Jordan Baker, too, who was modeled after her and her contradictions, not to be confused with violent internal conflicts. These contradictions were conscious parts of their identities, postmodern predecessors before there was a name for it. Not the struggling schizophrenic self, but the powerful breakdown of society's dichotomies to become exactly who they wanted to be. These characters may not be perfect, but we immortalize them rightly for their important presence in the world. They have something to teach us, to whisper to us through their aura as we read books, hear their music, visit their namesakes.

Impulsively, Catherine steps into her salon on the way home and decides to get her hair cut short for the first time in her life. Not crewcut short, still long enough to tuck behind her ears. But she has always been the artist with long flowing hair. Sometimes she would add bangs or layers, but it stayed pretty much the same length as far as anyone could tell.

As the first big chunk from a ponytail falls, it feels like the weight of some of that guilt flying away, those dead hairs of experience drop to the floor. Her head is free, light. The hairdresser, not her usual one, then continues to clip and snip into a still feminine and more textured look. Other women admire her in the salon. No one is looking at her like something is wrong with her, like she is crazy to chop it all off. Instead, she embodies vitality, freedom, confidence. She wonders what Thomas would have thought.

'Have you done this style before? It's perfect on you!'

'Thanks. I'm not sure…I don't know if it looks like me anymore.'

'You look like a young *mademoiselle*.'

She's still not sure. Perhaps her impulse was just a reflection of inner violence. Is it self-harm or celebration? The line seems so unclear. The action feels like exposure.

She steps out onto the street in her sundress and new hairstyle, continuing her walk and looking in every shop window she passes by. The day is still hot in the late afternoon and her walk quickly makes her sweat again. She can't bring herself to move toward a closed stuffy space, like her apartment or studio. She can't imagine getting much good work done today, which is why she went to the pool in the first place, so she heads where many people have been going all day long, *Berthilion* Ice Cream shop on *Île St. Louis*.

She has already gone into Saint Germain des Près to get her haircut, so now returns in the opposite direction but on different streets. She cuts back behind Notre Dame and over *Pont Saint Louis*, down *rue Quai d'Orléans* and *rue des Deux Ponts* toward Berthillon. The line is long, and probably has been since they opened at ten in the morning. It has been on many days since its opening in the post war renewal of 1954, when sugar and cream and money for treats were plentiful again. She doesn't mind this second long line of the day, she takes out her hat and her book again to wait.

Her mind drifts between the the pages of the story about losing innocence, reading Anne's character so much differently from the start since she already knows about her tragic ending, and to the hum of the people in line around her.

The others in front of her continuously discuss which flavors they want to get. The masses of tourists have not arrived. The line is mostly Parisians since the school holidays have not started yet abroad. Catherine stands out in the line of neutral Parisian tones in her orange dress and retro red pool bag. When she arrives at the counter, she sees a man who is happy to make so many smiles today. She says she will take three scoops, which makes him smile some more, and starts with her habit of salted caramel and dark chocolate, asking him to suggest a third fruit sorbet. He recommends the apricots, which are in season. It is also a new flavor for her. The coloring is magnificent as if she is looking at a Tahitian painting by Gauguin.

The only problem with this decision to eat ice cream today is that it melts fast as she eats it on a shaded bench behind Notre Dame cathedral. It is so sweet and so cold. She takes time to close her eyes and feel the cool flavors move through her belly. The evening breeze makes soft sounds that mix with the distant noises of children playing, an accordion, and picnickers on the banks of the Seine. Her eyes open, fluttering lightly in the wind. Her hands rise slowly and fingertips push through her hair and up to the sky before pushing herself off the bench. She moves forward to begin the sequence of side streets and bridges over the two islands that she likes best. As she finally crosses the second bridge, Notre Dame starts to strike eight.

She arrives home, she collapses into bed well before the next chiming can commence, the sun still high in the summer sky. After lying motionless a few moments, she grabs the book from her bag to finish it in bed. Sleep comes forty pages later, as language runs through her eyes to her brain but doesn't register. The words wash over her like an emotion and beckon her to rest. It is a welcomed sleep; she accepts it and it takes her for a long peaceful night.

XI

L'Odéon

The many cinemas in Paris are always showing retrospectives or seconds, interesting thematic decisions from the directors of theses institutions that have been mostly turned into mere spaces of advertising in the States. Catherine has a desire this afternoon to just escape from daily life and sit in the cinema for a few hours. To enter another world with the other strangers who make up the audience.

In perusing the offerings in Pariscope, she sees something brilliant. A double feature of the Brooklyn pairing created by Paul Auster and Wayne Wang in 1992: *Smoke* and *Blue in the Face*. She went to the same double feature upon the release of the second film and is now quite happy to go back to something she knows she will like.

After a short walk to the theatre from her apartment, where she stopped to change out of her painting clothes and have a quick lunch, she buys the cheap afternoon tickets and does a small circle - a *giro*, as the Italians said - around the neighborhood in the fifteen minutes before the show starts. She knows these streets well, and so allows her mind to drift to the subject of the film she is about to see.

Auster, as an author, and Wang, as a filmmaker, seem to utilize the titling and framing devices that she finds helpful in artistry. But additionally, Auster talks explicitly of ontology in his novels and channels it in these films. She wants to consider this melancholic optimism that resonates so well with the French—with whom the translations of his books are even more popular than with Americans.

She remembers reading about this joint project, which came from a Christmas story that Mr. Auster printed in the *New York Times* back in 1990. She also remembers reading this story, just like Mr. Wang had in San Francisco, on Christmas Day. She and Esmé, who was ten at the time, had gone to spend the holidays at her father's house in Brookline. It was the first year she had been home for Christmas without her mother. One of her favorite memories with her mother was that they always used to make an elaborate *bûche de Noël* together on Christmas Eve, modeled after the classic one Julia Child had taught Americans on PBS. Undine used to help when she was a kid, but had sworn off desserts in her teenage years and although she would now happily eat the cake, she always felt too busy to take time like this, time that wasn't necessary. For Catherine, it belongs in the category of life's needs.

The show often aired again around Christmas time, to give them a refresher about their technique and provide some entertainment as well. This year, she was lucky that it had aired again, so she was better prepared to teach Esmé how to make one. Because the show had aired on Christmas Eve, they decided to instead make the French yule log in the morning, after they had opened presents and eaten a breakfast together of omelets and fried tomatoes. As she let Esmé do a longer round of mixing, by hand, to make sure the cake batter was silky smooth, she took a glance at the paper, which she had been reading in small segments throughout the morning. This is when she came across "Auggie Wren's Christmas Story," which became *Smoke*, or at least its starting point. The story is a *mise-en-abyme* in the film. It is written by a character within the story and then repeated as a black and white short film at the end, still as part of the larger narrative. She found it so beautiful that a lonely man and a blind elderly woman, two strangers brought together by a lost wallet, would pretend to be relatives to share Christmas dinner together one day. The story suggests the woman dies soon after, and at the time, she could not help but to think of her mother, who used to welcome anyone into the house as family. The story lets the woman live on, in a way, and she realized then that her mother is living on through herself and now Esmé, too. She can't help but wonder if she shares enough of these little moments with her daughter — they lived just as two for a long time, but now that she is away, would she forget about the memories? Even worse, does she want to forget, knowing it might be painful? She realizes now this could be why Esmé has seemed so distant, even when she was geographically near.

Is the anticipation of her death keeping them apart? Worse than fighting, those quiet disappearances frighten Catherine. She knows they have a good relationship, but she doesn't want it to be over simply because she will die someday. She wonders if Esmé will even come to Paris this summer like she promised to do, she wonders if they will be making the yule log at Christmas again, she wonders if her daughter thinks of her from across the Atlantic...

Her circle is complete and the show will start in just a moment. She enters the theatre and picks a spot quite close to the screen where she feels the full effect of its grandiosity before her.

As *Smoke* begins, she is transported immediately to the setting before her — that corner Cigar shop in Brooklyn where so many characters find out how to live their lives, simply but happily. Characters come to terms with loss. Harmonies are created between racial divides. This is something Wang repeatedly does well. She jumps into the story through hurdles created in the *mise-en-abyme* of the initial discussion about Sir Walter Raleigh's weighing of smoke. The smoke becomes a metaphor for the grayness they are all able to embrace, the lack of definite answers, the feeling of death around them.

There is a ten minute intermission after *Smoke* and she gets up just to stretch her legs before reclining again into the red velvet seat. *Blue in the Face* is immediately funnier, more direct and she easily enjoys and loses herself in the opening monologue from Lou Reed. This film is part documentary with all sorts of cameos from the likes of Madonna, RuPaul, and Michael J. Fox. Their inclusion makes it like a party taking place in the middle of the film. It's as if you're in your neighborhood, and all these people you know just start turning up. Wouldn't it be great, she thinks, if all the people you loved were in the same place? But it's not possible—places hold people, topography grabs them, and some people respond better to certain places, certain cultures than others. Just as she wouldn't be satisfied to move back to Brookline, her sister would never feel at home in Paris. Maybe some people can do this, maybe they are stronger. Their families are first.

Alternative families are created in these films, alternative families through alternative culture. A mix of race, culture, gender, and definitions of father, mother, son, sister. She thinks back to Josephine Baker again, sweet and powerful *Joséphine*; the woman had four husbands with different racial, cultural, religious connections and identities. But what was more incredible was the beautiful family she had adopted. She adopted twelve children from different countries and backgrounds - French, Moroccan, Korean, Japanese, Israeli, Algerian, Ivorian, Venezuelan…these children all became French, they all became part of Josephine's family. This family that stood for love, contradictions embraced. Two of the brothers continue her legacy in New York with their restaurant Chez Josephine, interestingly without the French accent, giving her back to America as well.

In *Smoke*, the widowed white writer facing some sort of identity crisis brought on by the death of his wife, is saved from oncoming traffic by Rashid, a black teenager and a runaway, looking for his father who abandoned him long ago. Although they eventually find his father, he stays with Paul, the writer, to make an alternative family that extends to Auggie and the others who frequent his cigar shop in Brooklyn. The idea of the alternative family extends to the neighborhood where cultures and people interact, talk about stereotypes openly, and make surprising connections. It is an idealized crucible of the notion of the American melting pot. In *Blue in the Face*, mock interviews with Brooklyn citizens reveal these ideas they have about each other until they all come together in a street dancing extravaganza: the Brooklyn Cha Cha, led by the famous drag queen: RuPaul Charles. Everyone comes outside for this dance, they come together in simple celebration, in that basic human instinct to dance. It is as if this whole neighborhood has created a collective identity, realizing they can reclaim the active part of their identities.

The dance is hope. It continues beyond the film, captivates the viewer, gives us a hint that culture might not be stagnated here. It makes her want to have a Paris dance, to bring all the characters she knows so well, all those who are a part of her life, not only a part of this city, to some street corner she loves and have them start spontaneously dancing to improvised music. To dance is to express oneself, liberated. To create, to be, to move together, to freely interact. It is beauty, multiculturalism, the extended family of humanity. She feels like she's dancing when she's painting as well, moving in new ways, creating new visuals, that people can look at and dance to if they wish. At least there would be a dance inside their heads, she hopes. She wishes she could bring her family to this experience next week. At least their images would be there; in a way, they would, too.

Jazz does this, too, not that she plays. Undine had been a phenomenal piano player in grade school, and singer, an early Janis Joplin. She thinks of her now as jazz runs through this film. Undine's curls bouncing up and down gave the impression that she was born for this art, creating her own compositions freely while the family ate dessert after Sunday lunch. She decides it may be time for some jazz at Sunset one of these nights, like they had gone to during Undine's one trip to Paris. The outdoor festival would also be going on this weekend at *Bois de Vincennes*. Groups from all over the world, even some from New England and New York. The jazz in the film, and maybe elsewhere as well, reflects the idea of family - improvisation celebrated, making something beautiful. It also has roots in Black American culture, like Josephine Baker who improvised her life through a difficult history and made a herself a unique identity.

And then there is the drum. The drum is like a heartbeat that runs through the film and expands beyond the edge of the screen. Its inconsistent beats, all those of jazz music, reflect a life filled with surprises and improvisations. Life is a syncopated experience, it doesn't flow in even eighth notes and constant four-four time. Sometimes the beat happens before or after we expect.

She closes her eyes and listens to the film's music. What she really loves about jazz is the dissonance. The strange sounds created from notes that typically shouldn't be played together. Its freshness awakens her. Like chiaroscuro is for color. When people ask about a particular jazz song, it is not what it *is* but what it *does*. However, even the title for each piece of music gives it new careful meaning from the authorial standpoint, and she stays now to find out what the titles of the songs were at the end of the credits, a detail she has not noticed before, or at least not remembered.

As the credits and music end, she slowly gets up to walk home. The other patrons - mainly students and retired people - have already exited.

It's now about six and aperitif is just beginning on the terraces of Saint Germain. She walks in a different way than she came, as usual, and travels down the cobblestoned cachéd *Rue de l'Ancienne Comédie,* traveling by *La Procope,* one of the oldest restaurants in Paris filled with the ghosts of many great artists from *La Belle Époque* and the 1920's 'Lost Generation.' The street's exit, an archway, seems like something created for an amusement park, like Euro Disney, but, like the restaurant, it is genuinely from the seventeenth century.

She turns left, passing by more cafés with people talking, laughing, enjoying champagne or a *jus de fruit.* Suddenly an overwhelming desire to share a discussion of these films with a partner takes over. To share an aperitif with a friend who will also be sleeping by her side during the long night. It changes the energy of discussion. Its subtleties of dancing words, sips, glances are like magic. These films have stirred her up, reminded her of Esmé's absence here in Paris. Paris who has become her life partner.

She identifies these feelings as toxins trying to surface. She wants to talk with Pascal about this, or both he and

Edmond, but she knows she can't until he makes the first move of retrieving friendship. So, she does the next best thing; she goes to purge these feelings at *Le Prince Regent*, a small spa with sauna and hammam on *rue Monsieur le Prince*. Near the giant *Mosquée de Paris*, but with more intimacy. At this one they also have a cedar sauna before entering the baths.

She skips the massage and goes straight to the sauna. The only other person who shares this room that smells of warm, wet cedar is a Chinese woman, fat around the middle, who is slapping herself in a systematic direction that eventually covers her entire body. There is no acknowledgment of her entrance into this previously private space. She wonders briefly about this woman — is she an immigrant, too, or just a visitor? But the thought quickly leaves her mind through the sweat that beads off her body, starting at the little crevices behind her knees, elbows, armpits, and then continues from her entire body. Only their energies mix in the open heat of the air. Her steam in shades of orange mixes with the whiteness from the hot rocks in the corner.

She started to go to the sauna when they were living on the military base, before she was making any money and could go to Maria for the massages. The sauna was free and gave an ironic sense of freedom in the tiny windowless room. She needed to escape and couldn't always leave the compound. Or if she did, although Italy fascinated her, she still was not sure how to handle the machismo on the streets at that point. She found it was the only place she could avoid talking about politics, children, or spa treatments, ironically.

The women on base were shadows of themselves. She

loves to *debate* politics or read about it, but here there was merely a regurgitation of the inferred message from 'Military TV', the American network provided by the government so that they could profit from this while in Italy. Not that Italian television was much better, since all of it was either run by Berlusconi or the state, and Berlusconi ran the state. Somehow the media there missed all the scandals about his ladies and his liaisons with Muammar Gaddafi.

On the subject of children, these women were insufferable for her. It wasn't that she didn't love children herself. She already had her baby and she enjoyed teaching art part time at the base school both primary students and teenagers. Kids unpredictability made her sane in a base that felt very far from real life.

But she did not want to hear about how many hours of sleep each newborn in the community could sleep before waking up. She did not want to hear the exact amount of formula and baby food that both went into each child and came out, either end. It was amazing to her that these women wanted to talk about it. There's no way they wanted to, she thinks, but they must have had no one at home to bounce the information off of immediately. Beyond that, they always asked her when her second would be or how many she wanted or, worse, simply how many *he* wanted. It was hard to satisfy a military man, they said, hard to have the legacy he wanted and make yourself presentable for him. Their ambitions were different than her own. They were quite lonely and she pitied them. Most of them would not be *allowed* to look for a part time job like she had. Actually she pitied herself sometimes as well, but she hated to do that. She would try to embrace the problem and tackle it head on. If she felt lonely, in the intellectual sense, for there were always people around, she would go to the art studio and paint her feelings. She would also call her parents or her sister just to bounce ideas around, but not too often since Thomas reminded her that it was expensive.

No one could get to her in the sauna, though. She loved the feeling of sultry heat and the purging of toxic thoughts. Toxic thoughts, like the way her mind danced around the ways to get off this stupid military base where people's dreams were to die for their country, to be included in the hair salon gossip, to find the latest great products from 'home' at the base supermarket, or, in the case of the young people she knew, to earn mediocre grades and join the military.

She had pondered many times how to get off of this base, as if breaking out of a prison. She could only think of divorce or death, of her husband. What was happening to her? The base was poisoning her mind, or bringing out the evil side of herself, that animalistic side we control until the balance shifts. She wondered if any of the wives who were constantly talking about how worried they were about their husbands deployed somewhere were actually secretly hoping this as well.

The idea to leave had surfaced during one of these sauna sessions and she wasn't able to go back for weeks, afraid that the space had a kind of poisonous energy. She tried to push those thoughts aside, but they kept coming back into her conscious mind like a paint spill, once the thought was there it was difficult to take away any trace of it. That was when she had decided to go to Florence for a few weeks with her art, to make sure she wasn't really going crazy.

She knew Thomas would be off duty for a while and she presented it to him as a business request, for the possibility of selling her artwork. It was just before the spring holiday break at school as well, so not only would she have some of the time already off from work but they also would have some cheap childcare available for base children during the week.

Thomas was actually a great father, she realizes, and more indulgent of her than the others. Many of the other military husbands would never have 'allowed' this. But the others were slowly converting him. We all readjust to what our communities tell us is right. She could see them mocking her and her work. Well actually maybe it was her own personality that would never have stood for something that extreme in the first place. Thomas was fine to support her until he started his political career. He enjoyed time with Esmé, even if it was solo, and for that she felt forever indebted to him. Esmé may not have many memories of her father but she could relax knowing that he was loving and did actually spend time with her. When she was born, he was the first to cry and call each of their parents. And he never was disappointed she wasn't a boy. Boys seemed to be the desired little doubling of oneself for the other officers. When they would go to the park, he spent hours pushing swings, playing on the slide, and who knows what else while she sat sketching the landscape. He never asked to see the sketches, though.

He had taken Esmé to science museums and patiently sat with children's books to jumpstart her education. This was usually while she was making them dinner or shopping for some people he had invited over. On other days, he had generously used his salary to take them to restaurants or on small trips.

How could she wish such awful things on such an innocent man? She should be proud he had his ambitions. She should be grateful for his love.

The most frightening thought surfaces now. It takes hold of her and makes it hard to breathe in this now oppressive heat. The Chinese woman has left and she is all alone with no one to call for help or calm down her reflexes. It is as if she is choking on the cedar itself, as if a sap has oozed out from the walls and taken hold of her lungs. She opens the door for air, inhaling deeply. The breaths come faster and she feels the need to jump into a cold, shocking shower, which she does for a few minutes before drying off and returning to the sultry heat to face this thought, this nugget of truth in a solitary room where she cannot escape it. She closes the door tightly and bravely pours more water on the stones. Lying on her back, she allows the frozen moment to come back, slowly unthawing and arriving in the form of a question.

What would life be like if he had lived? His presence imposing judgment on her everyday. His exterior brilliance allowing everyone to think *she* was crazy not to appreciate him more. His career moving forward at lightning speed. Would she still be on that stifling base? That was not living. That was life, waiting. Or, worse, would they have moved on to his next agenda in military academia and its politics? Would her artwork and the personal time she held onto have disappeared completely?

And the worst question of all: would she have resented her child?

But she would be a family. Isn't that what she had

always wanted? A house all to themselves, lazy weekend mornings and lunches on the terrace. Trips to the lake together. Celebrations of Esmé's success at school. A husband's shoulder to rest or cry on. Someone to be proud of her, by her side.

Where is her family now? A plane ride away. Or in her paintings. And this is her replacement. Hyperreal colors swirled into impressions of people she loves. People who share some part of her name.

Catherine Vitalia Poulain James. The first two names, of course, given and chosen by her parents. Catherine for Saint Catherine and her feminine strength. And Catie, the nickname that only her father used for her; her nephews, too: 'Auntie Catie!' Her mother had often, in the other direction, called her by her first two names and added an extra Italian rhyming -*a* suffix to her first name. Vitalia was also her maternal grandmother's middle name, whom she had never met but who was supposed to share her artistic eye. She had been a seamstress, but really more of an underrated fashion designer. Poulain brings her to her father's side again, and their French background, the one she had felt that instant cultural connection with. The name she shares with the famous chocolate company as well, apparently started by a 'cousin,' who could be related in any number of ways but perhaps explained her love for this indulgence.

These three names were easy to love, easy to connect with her family who have echos of them in their own. Esmé also keeps Poulain as her middle name, and her first name had been Catherine's choice. Thomas didn't care much about the significance of these things. But he had cared that she take his name, and she felt it was a great idea at the time. She wanted to feel their love more deeply, make their marriage matter more, and thought that taking his name would make it all feel more romantic. She had even felt defensive when they left for a Paris honeymoon, her first trip to the city, not long after their marriage and she had his name on her passport but her maiden name on the airplane ticket. Despite the fact that Poulain was still on the passport as well, a female immigration officer was visibly annoyed by the difference and asked her to show her marriage certificate, which she had packed in her bag just in case. As she riffled through her carry-on items to produce it, the officer, a grumpy feminist, said harshly, 'You know what I did when I got married? I *kept my name.'* She glared down at her impatiently while Catherine felt the anger toward the unfairness of mankind that was directed at her at this moment. Or perhaps it had been to warn her somehow. She wasn't sure, but at the time, it made her angry that someone else would question her choice. She felt embarrassed, as if she were being judged for giving up her life and identity to someone else. Wasn't it enough that she had kept her maiden name as well? Her mother in law who had erased her own Greek heritage from her name by subtracting Delichatsios from her own designation had said, 'I don't know why you don't just take our name, dear. Now your name is so monstrous, so messy.' But her parents had both loved the idea, and anyway she prefers it. It lets her take on different identities; it gives her a history. At the moment at the airport, her innocent romantic view of their life together had been questioned and she wondered why no one she was close to had helped her to question it before. She

190

knew, however, this would be fruitless. Her independence had always been evident to others, keeping them from trying to control her decisions. The marriage and this name had been her choice, not his, not anyone else's.

However, as soon as he died, she felt like freeing herself of that name. She wanted to get rid of it, clear her name from his influence. But even well after the emotional funeral and its aftermath of ceremonies, she continued to feel the touch of his mother's grieving hands, fat but cold, looking for the warmth of her little boy. She saw his reflection, too, in her own little girl, who need not know of her doubts. She could not bring herself to change to erase the name from hers. James became the scarlet letters she wore on her documents, reflecting her history and connecting her further in name to her daughter. To remind her also of her freedom.

It was with that full name, the one on her passport and plane tickets, her prescriptions and medical records, that she had accepted her fate one day in the middle of her trip to New England. One day during all the visits with relatives and friends, the trips to the doctors, the chemotherapy, the attempts to seek what one should seek for comfort in the place of her roots. In boarding the plane for Paris, so many of them thought she was running away from reality. She had gone crazy or was hardened and angry by disease. They did not realize that Catherine had learned to live with the growth that is not foreign, but something that her own cells had created. She cannot deny this fact. It is a new way to live. A new framework of experience that she is forced to take on.

And so she has moved back to the place where she has always uncannily experienced comfort with displacement

191

and acceptance with foreignness. In Paris, life is eternal. She moves between portholes, tricking Time and spreading her energy through the city where visitors from the future will feel the infra-red and ultra-violet rays of her presence.

And just as much as she wishes she could erase this last name, she realizes she is free of it: it is just a name. In fact, many Parisians know her only be her maiden name, partly for the functionality and fluidity of its Frenchness. And proximity is just relative, she is free of space, too. Free of fleshly connections. Is her mother not still with her? The people still alive in New England as well, although she cannot touch them here. In Brookline, would she constantly be fighting to spend time with Esmé or tell herself not to bother her and let her daughter be independent? Would she be constantly disappointed by what her sister might say, or not say?

In Paris, she has her family. She carries them with her into the studio everyday. She has made new family, too. Family is mutable, is changeable, is always growing, not just dying. Where does one even start to create a family tree that really covers all the roots and all the loving connections we make in life?

She takes these thoughts that have emerged from her skin in small droplets of sweat, have dripped down the back of her calves and the curve of her spine, she takes them into the shower to wash them away.

She dries herself off, dresses, and emerges into the bright evening. This time when she passes the couples sharing a bottle of champagne and the groups of friends laughing at stories, she does not feel sad or alone. She feels she can share these emotions with them. Her burdens are not gone, but she is proud of her name as she glides down the street and continues to live with kinesthetic perception.

XII

Les Pierres

The day comes to her with her head still on the pillow. Today will start with a long walk before she will begin her painting in the afternoon, but she's not sure where it will take her.

Before leaving, she goes early to buy a *tradition* at the *boulangerie* - the baguette made exclusively from wheat flour - and comes back to her apartment to take her time over breakfast at home. The *boulanger* chose just the right loaf for her with his expert fingers, the perfect consistencies of hard crust and soft interior. '*Voila Madame Poulain! Avec ceci?*' he says as he places the naked bread directly into her hands. It is the custom to ask what else the customer would like, not to capitalize on the sale, although this is another result, but to lack the attitude that the customer should feel rushed in her payment or decisions. She has the right to ask for consultation or suggestion, to waver between pastries in the window; it is all allowed for a pleasant experience rather than just the purpose of buying bread.

At her small table near a courtyard window, she breaks open half of the baguette with her hands. She skips the butter and spreads chunky *mirabelle* plum jam on one side, drizzles honey on the other. She gets up to fetch the milk that is warming on the stove and pours it slowly into a red ceramic bowl with chicory. She sits and eats slowly, refilling the bowl after finishing the bread with *confiture* and reads *Le Monde*, which she bought on the way home. She reads all the articles that interest her, cleans up her breakfast, and puts on sunglasses and a sweater for the morning cold.

Catherine begins walking across the wooden beams of *Pont des Arts*, She looks out at the still quiet Seine on either side of her. A few early tourists stroll by and snap photos and a man in a three-piece striped suit sits on a bench reading *Le Figaro*. He has his long legs elegantly crossed and has placed his fedora hat to his right. On his left, a cane leans against a worn leather shoulder bag. The bridge approaches its apex here. Matching empty benches continue toward the stony bank and *Quai François Mittérand*. The old wood still has life in it, springing her forward toward the Louvre.

To the right of the museum, open space breaks into a geometric puzzle of triangles, rhombuses, and trapezoids.

She weaves back behind, onto ancient streets. With no path in mind, she catches various angles to feel the light or shade a different way, to disorient her inner compass. She glances at closed storefronts, passes dog-walkers and early commuters.

Eventually she finds *rue St. Denis* behind *Les Halles* and decides to take the long road north. Later in the day, this street will turn into a flea market where bohemians and poor sell bricolage, mostly junk, although she has found a pair of vintage crocodile loafers and pearl tear-drop earrings in the past. She pauses at several restaurants to look at their menus, something to try in the future or a meal to imagine at that moment. Passing one called *L'Évidence* where she and Esmé had enjoyed a lunch on the terrace before she left for college, she remembers the gazpacho, her monkfish, *lotte*, served with sesame sauce and Esmé's lamb, the exquisite patisserie they had shared, a vanilla tart with a sculpture of chocolate and raspberries piled high. She recalls the crisp white wine from Chinon that reminded her of a *vino verde* from Portugal, one that she had tasted in Macau on another trip to sell her work at the Hong Kong galleries. Beautifully understated, just like the perfectly tailored black blazer that had been her parting gift for Esmé. An item to mark her sophistication and adulthood. One that she was disappointed not to have seen during the past few months in Brookline.

Her steps move forward in the soft rhythm of iambic pentameter. As if barefoot in these well-worn flats that are molded to her feet. But she does not take their comfort and longevity for granted; they have been polished and resoled several times already.

Continuing up St. Denis, the arch enters her vision,

Porte St. Denis of the old city wall. She realizes this is the reason she chose this path even though she was only aware of it for a fleeting second fifteen minutes ago. The arch was made by Charles V with the fortifications of Paris. Who has entered through this porthole? In those days, an archway was erected for every king who entered the city, though they were usually made of *papier maché*. She would love to see one like that before her here, not so that she would be a queen entering the city but so she would be able to touch the molded paper and peel away a small portion to place on her window or to use as a placemat that evening. The weathered cream-colored paper could help her boiled carrots and peas, her plate of tomatoes with fresh basil and cold-pressed olive oil from Umbria and aged balsamic vinegar from Modena to jump a register of color. Its softness,too, would give her a fitting place to rest her forearms and place her bread. She could use it later to wipe her mouth clean or dab a droplet of wine slowly trickling down the open bottle. What would the king do if he were able to experience this sensual solitude?

Walking on the stones that laid the foundation of Napoleon's development of the city, she feels comforted by their hardness. It is not a manmade hardness but one that only geological formations could provide, steadying her within the mecca of culture. Only when she is wearing high-heeled shoes does she prefer the pavement to the uneven rock from long ago.

She eventually arrives at the arch. It has been years since she came here or to its twin close by at the end of *rue St. Martin*. There is not usually a reason to continue all the way up this street, and she conveniently forgets spots of beauty in the city so that she may re-discover them by mistake. Its symmetry and smoothness impress her and would have likewise impressed the King. A regal entryway. Passing underneath, she enters a new zone, a new energy of being. She passes underneath again rather than circling around - more energy is granted from the city - alive and generous.

She feels compelled to walk further afield, deciding to visit one of her favorite places of solitude - *Père Lachaise* cemetery where she can visit some of her favorite people from the past. It is four kilometers away, but this calculation does not enter her mind. She moves down *rue Château d'Eau* past little markets, bakeries, restaurants preparing for lunch. Men with bellies that extend out like pregnant women stand outside their shops, arms akimbo, looking at something in the street and waiting for customers. A tiny young woman reorganizing her displays of cards and posters on the sidewalk with rapid finger movements and frequent bends downward or reaches up on her tiptoes. Then an old baker whose rosy cheeks and round bottom have risen slowly like the dough she prepares daily. The woman is half-humming, half-singing the tune of *La Bohème* from Charles Aznavour as she brings out fresh batches of bread and files them into the proper baskets.

On the way, still thinking of the famous stones of the city and anticipating her encounter with its famous souls, Catherine's mind drifts to her first trip to the Catacombs, another cemetery of sorts. It had been with Thomas, during their only stay in Paris together on their honeymoon. The entryway in Montparnasse was difficult to find, like a manhole with a tiny office to take the entry fee and hand out a small brochure. The tiny opening revealed a spiral staircase down into the depths of the city, under a large circle where cars were driving and people were going about their daily lives. She had not wanted to go, finding it morbid. He insisted and she complied. He got what he expected, but she was surprised at her own fascination. Down that rabbit hole, death and merriment intersected in secret during the war. The Catacombs were built in 1788 and have become secret hiding places, including their use by the French Resistance during World War II.

Thousands of skeletons - all body parts - crumpled together, stacked up and lining the walls. A young woman before her had said 'disgusting,' it was the reaction she had expected to have; another young family before them was visibly excited, the children pointed and made faces at the skulls. She somehow felt a calmness in the cool dark passageways, not unlike the one she had now come back to Paris with. She lingered over the Latin inscriptions, calling on her high school studies to decipher their meanings. They had been warnings for the Germans during the war. In defiance of death, French soldiers had drank wine until they were drunk, taking in the strangeness so that death and life blurred into one, losing their fear of guarding their principles through any (violent) means necessary.

Flashes of her other favorite Paris stones run through her mind swiftly — Église de la Madeleine; the impressive Pantheon, especially Voltaire's tomb and his lecturing statue with a hint of laughter; the *Arc de Triomphe*, where the flame at the tomb of the unknown soldier is always lit and where you can climb to the top to look in all directions of *l'Étoile*— toward *Défense*, the Louvre, *Trocadero*.

But in addition to these well known monuments with signage and visitors, each street has stony building façades and pavement that hold the secretes of the people of this city who have lived here and will in the future. The contrast of ephemeral everydaylife and permanence in these solid structures creates an intertext of immortal vitality. Their juxtapositions and interactions create a timeless understanding of the ages.

Nowhere is this more apparent than at Paris' grandiose cemeteries. Parisians have a special relationship with death. Perhaps it is because they really know how to live. The world is neither boring nor filtered through rose colored glasses. They take it all in, just like they take in life and death at the same time.

The one in Montparnasse was another favorite. Here she had visited Sartre and Beauvoir. Buried together in eternal peace, though the famous feminist was manipulated by her womanizing lover in life. How can they define this love? Is it something about women and men? About ambition, fate, and nurturing? How are these traits connected through the sexes, why are they complicated? Why are they made into a game?

She eventually arrives at the entrance on *Boulevard Ménilmontant*. There are a few tourists roaming about with maps of the cemetery, a few groundskeepers. She ignores the map at the entranceway, not because she remembers where the graves are but because she prefers to stumble upon them freshly. There is no one she needs to see here. Immediately, she leaves the main road to the smaller paths that put her right in between the graves. Tombstones with poems, family crypts, sculptures — there are all types of stones to mark resting spot of Paris' rich and famous. Most of the names she does not recognize. She passes one grave with a pianist called George Enescu. His photograph lies on top of a huge stone slab with a carved piano and music. She finds one of a photographer with large modern-style camera sculpture inside a small crypt. Others list many family members with fresh flowers from the current generation.

In her path, a man with long straggly hair, sunglasses, and ripped jeans glides by stones, one hand holding a clipboard, the other a cigarette. His hair flies behind him as he seems to leap down the hill toward her, like an angel of Death. She is fascinated but turns to avoid him and rejoin a larger, populated path.

Here she hears tourists discuss their desire to see Jim Morrison's grave. She wants to tell them she has been there before. She wants to tell them they are on the wrong side. She wants to recount the story of coming across it the first time on his birthday, when the other members of the Doors had played music at his tomb, an anual tradition. One of the best concerts of her life. But she wants even more that they can discover their own stories and take their own route, so she stays silent and continues.

After rambling over another quiet hill, she reaches another main route where a Japanese couple holding a map breaks her silence. 'We look Oscar. You know?' Oscar Wilde. Yes, this is who she has come to see today. 'Sure, I can help you. Can you show me the map?' She looks and tries to orient herself, unsure of where she has arrived, and looks around for street markings and numbers that identify the sections. As she looks up, she sees the long-haired man approaching again in the distance. He points down a pathway, still too far to have heard them. And before they can get close enough to him to say a word, he turns off in the other direction to help the group of Americans still looking for Jim. He seems to work there or do research there, to somehow inhabit this space with information ready to transmit to others.

Without looking back at the map to verify the direction on the map, she asks the Japanese couple to follow her. They move briskly toward the spot where the man had been standing and turn left down another main route, slightly downhill, where they eventually see the large rectangular stone with the art deco style angel, a naked man who seems to be swimming forward, eyes closed, face of a pharaoh. They thank her with several small bows, take a few photos, and continue on their way.

She is making her way slowly around the tomb, looking at each individual kiss of bright lipstick that has been planted on the grave. Later, in fear of defacement, the caretakers will place glass around the stone to protect it from these kisses, but Catherine sees it now in its pure, approachable state. She feels this is what Oscar would have wanted.

She recalls Oscar's quote that Françoise Sagan includes in *Bonjour Tristesse*, which she finished re-reading last night: '*Le péché est la seule note de couleur vive qui subsiste dans le monde moderne.*' She always thinks of this quote of his in French since that is how she first encountered it, but he had written it: 'Sin is the only note of vivid colour that persists in the modern world.' He had worn his 'colour' in his dandy attire - top hats, smooth canes, flashy shoes. His sin was his indulgence in late nights and in love. He was not afraid to reinvent love as a non-linear, non-normative phenomenon. It popped out of the pages of his writing in unexpected spaces and could be discovered between the lines.

Wilde's literature is some of her father's favorite; the entire oeuvre lines his writing room's bookshelves and she discovered them there as a teenager, starting with *The Picture of Dorian Gray* at the age of fifteen. Perhaps even more interesting than his own writing, though, was the *Irish Peacock and Scarlet Marquess*, compiled by Oscar's grandson about his trial for homosexual relations, although the 'crime' for which he was being tried was actually 'acts of gross indecency with other male persons.' The trial is Oscar at his best in the face of danger - funny, subversive, and beautiful in language and expression. When she read this book, she felt she were in the courtroom with him, watching him answer questions in a purple suit. She wanted to jump to his rescue! In his ensuing imprisonment, he had eventually died at the age of forty-six. A year younger than she. Too young, too many stories left untold, too many people left without the graces of his love. But his bravery publicly broke the mold without apologies. And for that, others followed him to Paris - Gertrude Stein, James Baldwin, Christopher Isherwood.

It's not just about being gay or dressing differently; Wilde told the world you could come to Paris and be yourself without shame. Without that Puritanical shame that makes people afraid to expose their bodies, makes them scared to veer from old-fashioned definitions of sex and pleasure and desire. Desire — that can take so many shapes and colors, that can be realized in so many ways.

In Paris, you can be exactly who you want to be. When Americans go there, they mistakenly feel that Parisians are constantly judging their inferior fashion or food. But if they are ridiculed, it is for a lack of pride in themselves. *À chacun son tour.* If you hold yourself with purpose, proud of your clothes, your hairstyle, your choice in a small delicacy to eat or drink, then you are succeeding in being French, or more correctly, in being yourself. If you instead try to follow the trend, drink because others like something, not for the joy of trying something new, or hide what you see as weakness although it is just the love of something, pure Becoming - *Devenir*, then you will be ridiculed.

Like Oscar, Catherine belongs in Paris. In this city everyone is *un petit peu* sensitive, sensual, proud, emotional, particular, dramatic, nostalgic, confident, fashionable, philosophical. In a word: *formidable*, in the French sense. People interact more - constant Bonjours to be polite or say that you are pretty, explanations and friendly advice, regards and smiles, observations, approvals, disapprovals, debates - and find truth in the spaces between. But they also leave you to your private affairs - with money, family, politics, time, space, desires. Judgment is both strong and absent; cultural ethics lies at the heart of this. It cannot be simply explained.

You can be any shape or age, any profession or nationality, and still be sexy, sophisticated, intriguing. You can still be heard. It is how you carry yourself and how you hold yourself up. Because if you do not love yourself, no one else will. She has learned these things in this city.

She begins to feel a tear well up, for Oscar Wilde and his beautiful truth that died in that prison.

She reaches the stone with her unpainted lips, leaving

an invisible trace of her love for his thoughts. The action is more important than leaving her mark. And she continues on her way toward the opening on this end of the cemetery.

Near the exit, there is a garden of mourning for whomever you choose rather than only the esteemed who are allowed to be buried in the cemetery. The flowers laid there are plentiful and personal. The placement by family members allows them to feel, and to spread memory or share in sadness. One bouquet catches her eye. It is large and heart-shaped, pink roses with a sash like Thomas wore during his first military graduation ceremony. It has a photograph of a happy-looking round bald man and on the sash it reads: '*On t'aime toujours. -Ta femme et tes enfants.*'

She thinks of Thomas. She did not always enjoy his company or how he made her feel but she had love for him all the same — she hopes he knows she and Esmé both love him...somewhere, wherever he is. She bends down to inhale the odor of the flowers and as she looks around and sees no one, she takes one flower out and holds it in her hands a few moments.

She tosses it back on the lawn and finds the exit, exhausted. She gets on the metro to head back to her studio. Staring out the window at graffiti-lined walls and advertisements, she also catches the reflection of herself. It is not as young as she remembers. The lines near her eyes are made of laughter and tears. But the ones that sometimes appear on her forehead — those are the ones that could be erased. If she could only, if she could fully...but it may be too late.

The White Night

XIII

Grand Café Crème

She feels the *abyme* of the apartment's emptiness, weightlessness. Its void. Or is it possibilities and memories, mixed into one present space? Whether good or bad, it is too much for her to take right now. The endless abyss makes her a bit lost. And so she leaves it. She cannot take the turmoil of spinning colors of light, creating a whiteness that only light can do. It is too bright.

She heads out to *La Palette*.

There, she finds the art dealers, celebrities, tourists, and waiters she knows well. Alone - she often invites conversation from neighborhood acquaintances or strangers. Today, she stays solitary - her sunglasses on, fresh-cut fringe covering half her face. She only exchanges brief pleasantries with the waiter. Incognito, she stares out at the imagined horizon. She then focuses to notice the walkers, street cleaners, and other patrons. But she does not acknowledge their existence, seeming to engage in a silent conversation with the building façades, graffitied or vined, and the ornate rooftops. Through an archway that has become a galerie's glass window, a charcoal sketch of a reclining nude faces her with simple confidence, unapologetic. Other patrons may think Catherine is posing, her chin in the air, or pensive, her slight movement of hands suggesting thought. But in fact, at this time, her mind is empty, happily *vide*.

The arrival or her *grand café creme* is seamless, as if it comes without command to her as the saucer slides onto the small circular table. She holds the edges of the cup with both hands, staring downward, dissolving the froth with her breath ever so slowly. The faintest hint of swirled espresso reaches through the top of this crest. All she can see is the whiteness in a perfect circle contained in the perfect ceramic circle of the white cup, and further whiteness at the exterior and interior of the white saucer, which she has moved directly to the center of the circular wooden table.

She leaves the coffee for a moment and tries to read the headlines of *Le Monde* that she has picked up off the counter. But the words twirl in spirals like a science fiction film or like a movie where we are to imagine we're all on drugs while we watch it, *The Big Lebowski* or *The Unbearable Lightness of Being*. She puts it down, putting her sunglasses back on to block out the reflections that seem to come from all directions, the sun overhead bounces off the newspaper and the table top as if brought together in conspiracy to burn a hole through her forehead. The rays are strong and their contrast to the cold air surprises her. She keeps her trench coat on but removes the scarf to feel their power.

The foam breaks with the insertion of her tiny, perfect spoon, parting softly. It cuts the burning sensation from all the natural forces around her that seem to be reflected in the heat of the drink captured underneath this soft layer. It does seem to dissipate marginally as she allows some heat from the espresso to escape. She sips with the steadiness of both hands, afraid she will drop it if only bearing the handle. She allows this sip of coffee to enter her slowly, hoping she can refocus this white noise that has overtaken her on this overstimulating morning.

She refocuses on what is tangible and present. She enjoys what is in front of her as much as most anything in the world: a café table in Paris with coffee and the newspaper on a morning with no time cap. She stares down into the frothy whiteness just level with the top of the mug and pauses her fingers on the handle. Her only movement is her heel slowly pulsing up and down in tune with the clank of the waiters inside. The second foot, crossed over the other, moves like a shadow. Her eyes open wider letting more of the steaming milk enter deeper into her head. She stares, neck craned with her head tilting downward just slightly. One would think by the angle of her intense gaze that she is watching a bug floating in her coffee, but her face is smooth, utterly relaxed.

After a blink, she is suddenly transported to the Alps on a brilliant day of freshly laid powder and glowing sunshine. She smells the pine trees, hears distant laughter, and sees an open piste with a sharp edge. Hanging on to this moment, until she allows herself to lean forward into the mountain, courageously pointing her skis down to gather speed. Attacking steep terrain, long graceful drops, followed by snappy zigzags, then calmly floating over the leveled out areas where her concentration can dissipate to soak in the view of whiteness all around her. It is many memories trapped together of skiing days, long indefatigable days of meditation, that allowed her to function when the marriage got bad, and allowed her to carry on after he died. The escape to the rough edges of national border that instead now bring together so many Swiss, Italians, French, Austrians, and Germans with shared slopes and après-ski fireplaces, wine, and stories. There are no boundaries on these summits or in these chalets.

They swirl and twist like the snow before her. She sees no skis nor people, just the landscape's sublime expanse. She tumbles through it, weightless and disoriented. It engulfs her, chilling her face, and while she expects a frigid burial under snow, trapping her face in an immediate headache that would race down her spine, she instead experiences cold kisses of snow that melt instantly on her skin and evaporate in sublimation to the indigo sky.

The waiter reappears with the bill forty-five seconds later and she snaps back upright. What has happened for the last minute or so? Why can't she remember? She is perplexed, causing the waiter to repeat the amount she owes him before he goes on his break. She reaches into her purse for some francs and tries to remember what was happening. All she can envisage is whiteness, elusive, like Ahab's whale and that chapter about the white painting.

Suddenly, she realizes she has been having many white outs recently like this. Not black outs; it's not that she doesn't remember what she was doing but that there was nothing narrative going on in her brain at these moments to form memories. The white space felt almost meditative; calming and blissfully ignorant. She enters it willfully. At these moments she is unaware of her brain tumor and unaware of the passing moments of time.

But the white moment changes as she drinks the coffee again and as the caffeine already in her blood starts to take effect. It alerts her senses, clarifying the enjoyable turmoil in her head, making sense of thoughts to take her to memories that please her. First they are a swirl of colorful images of people's faces and snow outfits, of warm meals, wine, and hot chocolate, and of the trees and the different colors of the sky as the sun or clouds' positions change, but this palette mixes like light rays into whiteness again. Time stops moving as her mind is transported into another realm triggered by the same color of the white marble walls of the buildings that surround her. From behind her sunglasses, her gaze at the wall spirals inward.

The mountain landscape takes her back to another experience on the Alps that led her to her life in Paris. While in Florence, she had heard of a group of mountain artists who hiked with equipment on their backs to new summits of the Alps. They came from different countries to create art in shared, naturally fantastic landscapes. She received their newsletter and joined first a small local hike in Tuscany near Lucca, where she mounted a small pathway with charcoal, colored pencils, and a large notebook. Some came with paints, others carried impressive cameras – each capturing a sentiment of the shared sublime space from an individual artistic perspective. The results were varied in subject – a historic Renaissance church, empty skeletal grape vines, distant mountains, and even parked Ferrari – and the sentiments likewise – nostalgia, cultural reflection, energetic expressiveness, sadness – each capturing the human experience of the sublime.

She kept in contact with the group through their newsletter and her letter once a year and when she felt remarkably stuck in a life of the alarm clock, feeding her child, grading student drawings, and paying rent, while having a downward heading affair with her art teacher, she decided to go on a more ambitious excursion they were planning at *La Tournette* in the Alps, near Thônes. She decided to bring Esmé with her, who at four years of age was an impressive walker.

They embarked by car, traveling through the Mount Blanc tunnel after stopping for a night in Alba. Its glistening white glacier in the summer sun was remarkable. The climb had taken a considerable number of lives. It easily captivates hikers who don't understand the risk. The tunnel likewise held risk. A risk that was fully realized this March in a massive fire for which it is being rebuilt.

On the way, the had stopped in Annecy for a day, where the color of the valley's lake seemed to change every hour as they sat in the medieval town looking out at boats, mountains, and French families on holiday passing by. Later, they swam in the lake and looked up at the mountains surrounding them - *Les Dents de Lanfin, the Semnoz, the Parmelot* - wondering which peak they would be going to with the artists.

And on the day of the event, they began by stopping at a *boulangerie* in Thônes for a picnic lunch. The baguette sandwiches were filled with ham and the town's special Reblochon cheese that needed no condiment to fill one's mouth full of flavor. She had placed the sandwiches in her pack with the water, two peaches, and a chocolate bar with hazelnuts. In the outer pocket, she had brought her small sketchbook with just a few pencils, wanting to focus more on the experience than her artwork, although mediating it somewhat in this way would give her joy in appreciating the moment.

They followed the written directions up the steep mountain and the car's solo excursion suddenly socialized as it parked behind at least a hundred other cars that weaved in ascent up the road toward an open field. People were strapping on backpacks with cameras or sketchbooks, lunches, and water, like their own. In the open field, a piano and its player were waiting for he helicopter to arrive, to take them up the mountain to a small clearing by a refuge where three hundred artists and their friends would be picnicking and taking impressions of their surroundings. At the lower field, there was also the start of a *chemin* that led, rather steeply, toward the refuge, which they climbed in the company of the others who had recently arrived. Two hours later − a bit slower with Esmé's small legs but more enjoyable with her noticing things Catherine would not have seen: a hummingbird, a fossil of an ancient mollusk, and another toddler who happened to be from Paris and whose mother began conversation with Catherine.

As they mounted, she heard about the Parisian art scene – its economic struggles but culturally romantic freshness that never died – and as they picnicked together on a rocky ledge above the refuge, she heard of the lifestyle as a single mother made possible by the public daycare, easy transportation, and helpful, adoring elderly neighbors.

The helicopter arrived suddenly and in such proximity as it maneuvered as a boomerang that they thought, for a split-second of motherly instinct, of futily running for cover from a perceived mortal threat. But as the artificially created wind descended on them, blowing open the pages of the empty sketchbooks, they relaxed into the trance of the next hour's exalted mountaintop concert. Her mind took in the music with the surroundings and her recent information as she held Esmé between her legs to keep her warm. There was snow on mountaintops in the distance.

She cannot now recall the words exchanged on the descent – a burying fluff of noise exchanged somehow to allow her to occupy the space her new acquaintance was leaving, to occupy her studio as well in the Marais. Seeking a small sum of money for the property, needing to go to a new place. Catherine had money as a military widow, and she had saved money from her work as well. It was an easy decision. The woman had given her a new life, a future. She, in turn, had wanted to try something else, move to Tahiti for a while, see where it would take her. A gap had opened between parallel universes, and both of them were slipping between.

Now strangers, she hopes the woman's life had continued without a twinned poisoning in her brain. Why had the tumor chosen her? Or had she created it... something within herself without explanation from the outside...the brain, the most personal piece of her body, had turned on itself, created its own killer. Does she secretly want to die?

Her questions had morphed from desperate attempts at understanding why she was chosen into curiosity. She now rarely thinks of it, but when she does it is with this kind of fascination at its strange existence within her. Something she is incapable of sensing.

She stares down at the empty white cup and saucer. Here are her answers. Again, the permanence of the white cup, the ephemeral quality of the hot beverage now moving through her body. Awakening her faculties further. The creamy milk allowing for a slow release of caffeine that will keep her slightly in the hyperreal for hours. The waiter does not disturb her as she continues to move her eyes upward, lightly over the horizon. Hidden behind dark lenses, she can stare or move her pupils as she wishes. Everyone is looking at each other in this city. Observing. Mimicking. Admiring. Trying out new faces of their own identities.

They judge, too. She judges. And why should she not? Are we not all being judged all the time?

Catherine scans the current cliental. A woman with an exquisite red pantsuit appears to her right. It is not a fashion statement she would ever make nor does she think it is in fashion now, but the woman clearly adores it. She rests her elbow gingerly on the table, opens her body toward the street, awaiting a passerby's glance.

To her left a man with shocking white hair, a cigar, jeans, and black t-shirt reads the newspaper. He occasionally fixes his hair in the mirror created by his aviator sunglasses on the table.

A man on a motorcycle passes by, pausing for others to admire his Honda Gold Wing and revving the engine in case anyone missed him. He stares off in the road as if unaware of the café and her cliental.

Next on the road, a truck arrives with '*La Ferme d'Alexandre*' written on its white side. The subtitle is '*Produits laitiers - Fromages affinés.*' The truck driver smiles brilliantly as he dismounts and nearly skips into the café. He explains which cheeses he brings from the countryside today, and the proprietor happily buys several for the week's cheese board selection. As he opens a particular favorite, the café owner breathes deeply with his eyes closed, then nods in affirmation of the selection. As the truck moves off, the pungent smell drifts wistfully toward her, leaving a trace of his presence. He has no need for a card, the smell is his signature that lingers in his wake.

Parisian pride is all around.

Just in front of her, however, a woman has clearly abandoned her appearance. She is slightly overweight, but that's not a problem. She wears last year's trendy colors, but that also does not bother Catherine. It is the way she holds herself, awkwardly. Her shoulders are slooped, her eyes move anxiously toward the others around her. She orders a *café creme* like the others even though she wants a tea. She looks at *Vogue* though she wants to read an Agatha Christie mystery. This is not admiration, it is futile attempts at assimilation. What she really needs is to look inside herself and find what is already beautiful there. Catherine considers how she could help her and realizes kindness is the only way. The woman has noticed her gaze, so Catherine smiles warmly and briefly, offering her approval, trying to move that energy into the woman's brain, to spiral there and implant itself. She imagines that this tumor has given her special powers of internal mesmeric capacity. In fact, it has. Although she is unaware of many of these transformations, Catherine's choice to *live* has impacted many individuals around her.

She needs this help, too, these superpowers from beyond that are immortal, that live on from inspirational souls in museums and libraries. That power from within has told her today to seek this gift, available to her just around the corner.

.....

In the Mazarine library, there are many empty eyes staring coldly out at her from statues of dead writers. The eyes' dullness always seemed a sad unfillable emptiness when Catherine had tried to work with sculpture. Here, Caracalla's black onyx bust oversees her thought process at desk number ninety-six, which she was given with precision in choice by the attendant. He wants to make a perfect matrix of those who inhabit his library. Her selection in this spot at a table shared with a young writer and an Italian professor is not at random.

This is the library she goes to when she is looking for titles. On her square leather desktop, one of eight on the long wooden table, she has three books out and an open orange Semikolon journal to trap her titles when they arrive. She likes to read with constant multiplicity, like the way she paints several projects at once. She is always reading at least three books, so she may match the one she picks up with her mood. At minimum, there is one novel and one non-fiction narrative or detective story in English, and one French philosophy book, but there may also be the addition of a French novel, a biography, or an indulgent suspenseful mystery. She usually kept a few magazines at bay as well, *Art News, Beaux Arts, Vogue, The New Yorker,* and *Philosophie* are her staples. But these would never travel to the Mazarine library. Instead, she might pick up an academic journal off the shelf, but the books are her own. She does not come to this space to look at its books; they simply surround her with their ancient odors and ghosts of the past.

In the L-shaped room, under the gaze of the attendants, she takes a walk, carefully looping around ladders that reach twenty meters up into the bookshelves, to peruse the journal titles on display. She picks up a copy of *Les Temps Moderne,* the journal founded by Jean Paul Sartre and Simon de Beauvoir. Without looking at the essays included in this edition, she knows there is always something there for inspiration.

She walks back to the desk and slowly, as quietly as she can, pulls out the chair and begins to float through the pages a bit awkwardly, since it is contained in a large red plastic covering to ensure its safety. This is the method that seems to work for her to find titles. She comes here within the week before a show's opening and selects a title for each work she has created. She has never used 'untitled' or 'Paris #45' as some artists do. They want the work to speak for itself and for the audience not to be 'tainted' by their subjective interpretation of what they have created. A type of artistic formalism.

Catherine is instead struck by a concept that Derrida talks about in the beginning of his essay on judgment, 'Before the Law.' She had enjoyed reading his ideas about framing and titles both in this essay and in *Parergon* but had not come across a poignant concept about the title until reading the French version of the essay that has a much longer introduction. Her favorite young waiter named Martin, who has since left *La Palette* to continue his studies, gave it to her one time as he left the café in the morning. He said it confused him but he loved it, 'Read it. Tell me what you think.'

In quoting and discussing Duchamp, Derrida talks of the title as an invisible color. It is not like an indigo that exists as a certain wavelength but only certain insects can see. Instead it is a nameless, faceless color that may in fact look different to everyone who sees it. In this sense, the viewer still has autonomy, but is given another color to play with as they enter the space of the gallery or wherever it is on display, then the proximity to the painting, moving from the title on the wall, to the frame, to the image itself. We all wonder if different people see colors the same way we do, and this is the same concept on a more obscure level. How does the naming of *Guernica*, for example, make Picasso's masterpiece different for each of us? Perhaps more interesting, how does our viewing of a painting change when we hear that an original title has been translated differently: 'Mona Lisa' is actually '*La Jaconde*' when we go to the Louvre.

Duchamp's readymades were of course changed by their titles, or the act of giving them a title.

She tried to return the book to Martin, but he said, '*Non, cadeau,*' and turned gracefully on his heel. She still sees his ghost weaving through the tables on foggy mornings.

In an article in the journal, she comes across that term she adores, '*L'Ousia*', meaning being or essence, and jots it down in her journal. She then finds discussions of bird migrancy as a metaphor, and notes this concept. The phrase also makes her think of a twig like frame that could be used for her paintings. Sometimes she draws the frames here as well.

A frame is important to her, and like with the many 'untitled' posts that pervade the galleries these days, she is struck by the complete lack of framing. A frame gives a space to play with what is outside of the artwork and what is inside. To make sense of the themes in relation to our own world. Before reading about the philosophical implications of this in *Parergon*, she had felt the effect first hand when she visited the Gardner Museum in Boston after the famous Rembrandt robberies in 1990. She had gone with her father, an avid museum goer and admirer of anything strange that had taken place; it filled him with excitement to see a living mystery. It was the winter after her mother's death, and they also both welcomed something to do out of the house that would give them a different subject to talk about.

Having seen the works before the robbery, she could imagine them there in the open frames, and the emptiness of them still there on the wall where Madame Gardner had ordained they be kept in her will, was frighteningly hollow. The frames still seemed to speak of what was there, they held the stolen images within them. They held Rembrandt, Gardner, and all the visitors who had previously come to see them. This was fascinating. But what was sad was imagining the paintings either rolled up in a tube or on display in a hidden room without their frames. Rough edged as if not worthy of reflection. Made into mere commodities or materials to be owned, even if admired. The language of these paintings had been cut short and she waited the day with impatience that they should be found out. In sudden epiphany, she had a second career idea as a detective to specialize in art thievery, much like the wonderful character in *The Thomas Crowne Affair*. Like Steve McQueen and Pierce Brosnan. It was likely more the sense of wanting to escape her sorrow - as it passed, so did this strange passion. She knew her father would have disapproved silently and distantly.

For some reason, although she knows its silly, she feels like because of these museum visits together when she was a child, and still today, her father would only be satisfied with her artwork if it were hanging in a museum like this one. As she now looks around the library, she sees the books that have lasted for centuries. Her father's stories were in magazines, not as popular as *The New Yorker* but still archived officially by definition of the medium. And the books he published are in libraries all over the world. She knows that he wishes he could be one of those authors whose names were immortalized, on best seller lists and taught in English classes, or at least recommended by a popular book review. But he hasn't talked about these aspirations for years while he still continues to write in his study when he doesn't have a manuscript to read. She wonders if he is satisfied with himself. She feels the need to satisfy this artistic immortalization for him, but time is running out.

At least she is nearly satisfied with her work for this opening. She cannot believe it is already coming next week. The month seems so long and so short at the same time. It has been long enough for her to finish the paintings, except for one - the painting of her daughter. This pause to fit words with them could be fruitful. She likes to write the titles in English when she is showing in France or Italy (which is almost all of the time). It gives just enough distance between the reader of a title in a different language, one which they usually can still speak, to create meaning in the act of translating it into their own. They may then guess if there are extra allusions in the original language or if there is a second meaning in English they are unaware of. The twists and turns of the words in this way allow at least a few extra seconds to focus on the titles before jumping to the frame, before entering the image. Then there may be further conversations between people, possibly of different cultures to make her work come alive and bring active meaning to the display.

She has been able to finally complete most of the painting of her daughter on a rainy evening, lasting well into the night. The light plays over her face in an invisible undulation created by the underpainting she destroyed and rebuilt. The quality of the painting is nearly photographic, like paintings of Gerard Richter, giving it a hyperreal element that draws in the viewer. She writes many phrases that have to do with light and systematically crosses them out until settling on a simple idea: Awakening. It might be her own awakening she is referencing, or the way each morning she witnesses her daughter waking up again, she feels the joy of her birth rush through her.

She has two self-portraits in addition to the blue one she has done most recently. One of them is in reference to this birth of her daughter, but also a deeper meaning about the universe. Well, maybe those are the same thing for her. It is of her belly, evoking the womb or nourishment, but focusing on the belly button, a popular subject of Indian art, especially in sculpture of female deity. They call it the *omphalos*, meaning belly button in Greek, but also evoking the center of the world and the circle of life, like a Zen Enso. So this is what she calls this painting with the Greek letters bracketed.

The next is of her calf, as if the power of her metaphysical movement in the world were contained there. She's not sure what to call this one yet and hopes it will come to her over the next few days. She makes a note of this gap in her journal.

The blue painting became an image of her about a month ago, her face at its thinnest, sickest, but ironically still full of life, perhaps more than ever before. It is the proud face of her fight for survival. It surprisingly evokes Spanish dancing culture and the form is something like Picasso's blue period, so she takes survival into Spanish: '¡*Sobrevivencia!*'

For her sister's portrait, she has done something special. She already knew what the title would be before she began the under-painting. 'Antigone.' Her favorite Greek tragedy with the principled heroine willing to fight for her family through passive resistance. Her family, her core. She painted Undine as she was in high school, innocent but powerful. There was something captivating about her spirit that made it easy for her to make friends and made her a sort of carefree, understated strength at the center of her family. The youngest, perhaps most in tune with her intuition. The painting is a cross between a photograph when they were on vacation in Vermont and from the image in a memory of a particular night. There was nothing especially significant about the photograph, simply that she looks powerful, young, and healthy. On the night of her memory, Undine became Catherine's big sister. Catherine was eighteen and Undine sixteen; it was Catherine's winter ball, her senior year in high school. Her date was someone she had dreamed about for years, and when he asked her to the dance she was thrilled, though she hardly knew him. His friends were in a different crowd; the girls welcomed her because he had chosen her. Usually with the artsy crowd or the swimmers and related nerdy-jocks, this cool crowd had once seemed untouchable. She had a genuinely good time at the dance and was excited for the party after at a friend's house, whose parents were conveniently out of town. Catherine drank a beer or glass of wine here or there, but had never been drunk. Here, she felt pressured to go out of her comfort zone, both by the other girls drinking vodka with cranberry and by her date who made sure she had a drink in her hands. As the night quickly became blurry, she ended up in a room with him. She still didn't know him, she felt cornered, she saw him swaggering toward her, taking off his shirt, she remembers backing away, seeing him beckoning her, feeling him pulling her, holding her down, trying to take her against her will, then kicking, throwing open the door, and running downstairs to another empty room. There, she had found a phone. She had called Undine on their private line they shared. Undine said, 'I've got it under control. Meet me outside in five!' Her sister had told their parents it was a friend from school; she had completely forgotten about a group project. She took advantage of their trust. They were disappointed, annoyed but let her go; she said she would stay over there so it was safer.

It was after midnight then. She drove to find Catherine as promised. She took her away and they showed up at Undine's boyfriend's house. Peter was a stoner but a nice guy with hippie parents. They let Undine stay over whenever she wanted and would even make up excuses to their more protective and traditional parents. Actually they weren't sure how their parents would react to this event or the idea of sleepovers, because they felt the subject was taboo. While they talked at length in their house about many topics, some topics - death, sex, drugs - were not discussed. Maybe everyone was tiptoeing around everyone else for no reason, but in any case, they did not want to tempt it and especially not all at once with a situation like this.

When they got there, Peter was waiting in the kitchen with his mother. They were playing cards and did not know the girls were coming over. Although Catherine was drunk, she was embarrassed, she remembers this much. But they simply took care of her without question. They put her in the guest room, brought her pajamas, even made her breakfast in the morning. By the time she got home, she was feeling fine and the acceptance by this family and Undine's easygoing rescue almost seemed worth the terrible events of the night before. Undine never teased her about it or brought it up again, except to ask how she was feeling later that week. They had their fair shares of jealousies and fights, annoyances and fatigues with one another, but they also had their warm memories and shared experiences. This night stood out as a remarkable show of character that she hoped she could always count on if she needed it. They often kept their distance now, and they had in high school. She wonders if Undine knows she could count on her in the same way.

Even though her family has changed her, Undine's nephews are like her own sons, or at least she feels that they could count on her in that way and she loves them that way, even if they do not spend that much time together. The painting of them together makes her think of her own mother.

She has only told Pascal this Buddhist revelation, but she is certain that her mother's soul is contained in her sister's younger son. The energy must have been placed there after her death. Catherine had prayed to the Buddha and meditated and left oranges at the temple near the Marais and again in Boston under Pascal's suggestion. When Charlie was born just a few weeks later, his skin had the tinge of blue, having not received quite enough oxygen when he was born. Because of this, they pampered him, and she visited him at the hospital where he stayed for three weeks. Catherine went to visit one day and there was a nurse on duty who was singing a religious hymn to him in Italian. She said he was soothed right away. But the one he really preferred was *Ninna Nanna*, an Italian folk song. Catherine had gone white at that moment before again allowing the blood to rush to her cheeks as she bent over the crib to sing the song. It was her mother's favorite lullaby. Of course any baby would respond well to this soothing music, but she was struck again when on his fifth birthday, he was allowed to lead them through his choice of streets in the North End only to end up at a little known trattoria. He said, with a huge, innocent smile, that he wanted to eat spaghetti and meatballs there. It was the same place their mother had taken them many times, most notably for her own fifty-eighth birthday, seven months before the stroke. Catherine had exchanged a smile with her sister. They didn't say a word about it. Her sister didn't believe in these silly energies and they would just get in a fight, and even more so with her husband there. And their father made it clear that in his unceasing mourning, he was uncapable of discussing his wife with anyone, beyond, 'Wasn't she beautiful?' in looking at her photograph on his desk. No one knew what he really believed in anymore, a former Catholic swayed away by the philosophical readings he had dove into during his student years. But he wasn't quite atheist either. This was another unspoken area for him.

She looks out at the horizon of books on shelves for an answer, both for this title and for the questions about her family she still holds in her heart. For this energy of her mother within, she calls the painting, 'Sons,' so the viewer would think of the lineage.

The image of her father that she has captured is at his writing desk, where he is most happy, immersed in an idea that has come to him. Working out the details of the twists and turns of language with careful ink delivered from his mind to his hand to his moleskin journal, precisely capturing the tone even further through the style of his hand. Many books, many ideas of many dead writers may go into just one phrase. As he squeezes them all through his mind, it is like an elephant going through a needle and coming out as gold thread. She sees his brow furl as it works its way through, and the release is magical. The painting catches a moment of release. When he works like this, she always thinks of Paris's Pantheon that contains the bodies of so many writers whom he loves, whom he reaches toward for knowledge. It is also where the famous recreation of Foucault's Pendulum is housed. She calls the painting, 'Pendulum.'

And then the painting of her mother. A memory of her cooking eggplant parmisan, a moment when it smells perfect. This memory of smell is contained in the painting as we see her mother inhale deeply from a raised spoon. At the side of the stove, their dog's eager eyes look up between her mom and the food. As the memory continues, her mother goes into the other room to set the table and when she returns, their dog has eaten half of the dish. That night, they order pizza instead, but it is even better with the lingering smell of her mother's dish as they casually grab slices of mushroom or pepperoni. This painting is called, 'Memory.'

Finally, there is a painting of Edmond and Pascal sitting together on a blanket as they watched a jazz concert at *Parc Floral*, next to *Bois de Vincennes*. She had taken the photograph — their shirts off in the June heat, leaning back on their elbows, Pascal's eyes and mind on the concert, Edmond's focused on the camera. This title is also simple; it will be called 'Love' but in Tunisian Arabic.

She just needs to ask Pascal what this would be. She wishes she could ask Edmond, too. She wonders if he will come to the opening, if she will see him again before she dies.

She quietly packs up her things, goes to collect her ID from the librarian, and leaves the library with all but one of her titles and two sketches of frames for the still unframed latest ones of her sister and daughter. The show would also include a few older ones of landscapes that haven't sold yet but were kept by the gallery who usually promoted her. She asked them to place these in between the portraits because they held shadows of people, too, whom she wanted to include more subtly. The landscapes were her memories of Italy: a lego-like multi-colored building façade in Cinque Terra, a hidden brick tower in Siena, one of Firenze's outer bridges, and, finally, the Napoli seaside where they had picnicked as a family so many times. Those were happy times, Esmé a baby, Thomas just starting his career and happy to escape it. She would run into the water while he took photographs. They would eat *braseola* and *gorgonzola* with ripe tomatoes. Esmé discovered sand, a natural fascination for any child. They shielded themselves from the sun with a brilliant yellow umbrella and their floppy hats. They would read, look, walk, sometimes swim, together.

This calmness and beach life she loved, even in her escapes to Paris, she captured in a series at an opening she had of beach scenes from Napoli and from Crane's beach, where her parents used to take her and her sister as children. Her father still went there for walks early in the morning every now and then. Her relationship with the sea has grown over the years. In Italy, she found that women enjoyed lying topless. Thomas seemed titillated by it even though he condemned the behavior as strange and shameful. He told her she should only do it when he was around, and at those times, she didn't feel like doing it, as if it was for him to watch. She had not come to the beach for him. Instead, she tried it on her own, first when hardly anyone was around. It was liberating! She found that nobody seemed to really care, that everyone was into their own thing or at least they hid it well. And when she went into the water…this was the best part. She was happy when a rich Italian widow had bought the painting showing this moment.

The painting at Crane's on Gregoire's desk was the only painting that remained from the show because the gallery owner had bought it from her themselves. In this particular piece, Gregoire said she captured here a *bonheur* like none he had seen before. If it didn't make her famous, he said, it would at least make them happy when they looked at it.

He had kept one other painting from a show on Paris itself. She had made this paintings more for the American market, but even Parisians found something fresh in her depiction of their city. She had not painted any tourist locations; rather she captured her favorite little streets and shops as if she were inside of them and as if we could feel her emotions as she captured them. Gregoire kept one with a personal connection. It was a tiny, detailed close-up of two round tables from the terrace of La Palette, one with a man that could have been himself. Sitting alone, enjoying a silent, pensive morning, but also feeling the absence at the chairs next to him that may be the wife who has divorced him, or the lover who has died from an overdose when they were young and involved in the May '68 uprisings.   Or perhaps the absences were his grown children whom he rarely saw, one in London and the other in Marseilles.   Even with these gaps, though, the painting made him feel good, like a reminder of love he once had.   He keeps it on his desk in the back of the gallery because she gave it to him.

She wants to call Edmond, to ask if he has received her letter.   She could use the pretext of asking Pascal about the Arabic title.   But she can't.   She wants to call Esmé, too.   She hasn't been able to talk with her since she came back.   But it's five o'clock in the morning there.   Their lives have moved to different planes of existence.

XIV

L'Arc en Ciel

As Catherine skates through Bois de Vincennes, she is
not aware of any brain tumor that may or may not be
continuing to jiggle around incessantly. Its friction or the
fast movement of her body through space creates feelings
toward Enlightenment, of the Buddhist kind. It comes to
her as light in magnolia paint pumping through her flesh
and into her sweat, making tiny pools that glide swiftly off
her skin at the elbow, off the lining of her shorts, from the
tips of her hair; hyperreal sensation of movement; her
black rollerblades gliding like stealth weapons that cut
through dissonant noise in her way. She attacks the
surface with deep angled one-leg squats and the full
extension of her leg as she pushes off with her calf,

232

leaning into the turns as fluorescent sweat glides off the tip of her elbow to land on the soft grass at the right.

Her mind jumps into the Château before her while her body stays strapped into her skates that stay on the path, as if magnetized. Louis VII's hunting lodge in the twelfth century. Big enough for a small kingdom. She imagines herself in a different life in the middle ages, Lady of some protected castle on a hilltop in Italy like Castello dei Conti Guidi. People cooking for her, dressing her, taking care of her children. Living in a tower, subjects working the field. Guarded, protected, and simply waiting out a lifetime to die. So stifling, suffocating. She prefers this outside looking in.

How will it change further into the future? She glides, losing sight of the path's twists and turns, yet continuing to seamlessly maneuver the skates around them and even around the pebbles moved to the pavement by bicycles. Her mind spins into the future rather than twisting a spiral of the past's imprint on her present daily experience.

She imagines Esmé at the hospital. Her patient husband greets Catherine and offers to bring her a coffee while they wait for news from the doctor. Esmé is not sick; she is having a child. After the child arrives, they go to see mother and daughter, calmly sleeping in Esmé's arms.

She imagines the way they all huddle together in an inter-generational embrace as if they four are one being for an instant. She can't wait to see how the granddaughter grows up.

But it brings tears, real ones, that blur the path before her. So much that she must stop on a round peg placed to keep cars off of the path. As she sits, the salt water begins to run down her cheeks, clear and unbrilliant like her sweat had been in reality. It is normal human crying. Nothing seems special about it. This sadness of mortality is real without a silver lining. She will never see a grandchild being born because there is no future for her. It has been written in the shaky looped handwriting of her wise, old French doctor, and likewise in the haphazard print of the young prodigy in America. Prescription: rest, healthy foods, the drugs, chemotherapy. Outlook: months. Not years. It would take years to see Esmé graduate, find a profession, start a family...the thought of this escaping her feels like a robbery. A violation. By whom?

The tears glaze over her eyes and through this warped vision she sees a mother running next to her son on a bike. She replaces the blurred faces with those of herself and Esmé, transported back to excursions they used to take here or to the park outside Versailles. At Versailles's park, open to the public, she had taught Esmé how to bike. She would bike faster and beckon her to follow, weaving between other visitors, the gardens, and the ponds. They sometimes rode for two hours before stopping for apples or ice cream.

She doesn't remember how she learned to bike; it just happened in the driveway or on the streets nearby, gradually taking off the training wheels. She still has the same old bicycle she had used then; it stays in her father's garage waiting for a grandchild to use it someday. Her bicycle here she rarely uses. Instead, she started skating just a few years ago, like many Parisians, and found it easy in its similar sensation to skiing.

Her father had taught her how to ski. They had gone to New Hampshire for a weekend to stay in his publishing friend's ski house. Catherine was four years old. She had gone on ski trips before and stayed in the house with her mother or at the daycare on the mountain. Her sister was still too young to put on skis, so she went alone with her dad. They started on a side hill, unoccupied, unattended by workers. Just a small open hill that perhaps had been cleared for an old tow-rope. They climbed up in the hard boots, falling deeply into the snow every time she took a step. But after she put on her skis at the top, she could stay afloat. She felt light as air. She followed directions to angle her skis in slightly and her father held her as she kept her skis between his. It seemed too easy. They did it again. Then they moved toward a different spot. He told her to wait; she looked at her ski tips and suddenly she was lifted off the ground! She had looked down as they were moving high up into the air, but just as she was about to panic, her father's face told her this elevation was to be expected. He did not bother to explain what they were doing, instead telling her to look at their personal view of the treetops as they passed by. He carried her off the chairlift and they skied down the mountain just like they had done on the small hill. She loved it. They went again and again until it was time for lunch and they rejoined her mother and Undine in the lodge. She would go many times with her father, getting faster and faster. They would share many chairlift rides together, looking at the mountains and sometimes talking or sometimes remaining silent. He does not say much; he leaves it for his writing, it seems. But on the chairlift, she heard stories about his parents who had both died when she was young. She was asked questions about her high school boyfriend. Together they would ponder ethical situations. Things they didn't talk about in the house.

235

When he said good-bye this time, he also didn't say much, and during the months in the house, talk was rather simple, ordinary, refracted. She felt like he should talk more, talk about her treatments or ask her how she was feeling. She realizes now it hadn't been necessary, that this is the way he is.

Clouds have come in quickly as she skates by the lake, now far away from the castle. She can feel the rain coming, a terrible combination with skates. She sits down at a bench and changes into her white canvas sneakers in her backpack, replacing them with her skates and sliding the heavy load onto her shoulders before walking into the tree-lined trails.

The woods are empty before her. She walks toward the immensity. Toward the dark clouds in the sky. It is as if this universe before her, absent of other humans, is a reflection of her soul. Her bag is heavy on her shoulders, so she ties the waist strap as well. The adjustment makes it easier to push onward, forward, into the abyss. Then all of a sudden, *tout à coup*, the rain breaks over her head. It is cold and windy; it could be autumn the way it comes down and blows around. The trees sway and the leaves dance under the rain as the roots begin to shift underground to reach for water in their thirst. She personifies them as if they move like those in *The Wizard of Oz*. She welcomes branches to snap across her face to reprimand her, but they do not come, only water and wind, pulling her hair straight, exposing a naked face to the elements. She looks up toward the Heavens and closes her eyes tightly like two little prunes in the middle of her face. The dark crimson insides of her eyelids transports her deep into a hidden crevice of her brain that become her reality.

She slams the front door and runs into the cold November rain that numbs her, stopping the tears from running down her face in a sort of freeze, frightening but welcome. She wanted this punishment. He was dead and she needed to feel terrible physically. This was the way to do it. She had gone out too early and stayed out a little too long on the run that day, to tempt the fate of catching pneumonia or worse, until she remembered her daughter at home with her own father. Esmé would be waking up soon, she would be wanting her mother to eat breakfast with her.

It was the morning after she had heard of his death.

She's mixing up time. It feels like it's happening right now, but all the pieces of the memory are coming to her at the same time. How many years ago? Sixteen.

And now as she walks in the woods of the forest, a twenty minute train from her apartment, but another world, where wild boar sometimes appear and people pray in the Buddhist temple, she wants to feel uncomfortable again. It is as if she cannot believe the thing inside that is killing her sometime, at an unexpected time. She wants a reminder of it so she knows it is real. She should be worrying, asking the gods *why her* and contemplating life and death. Instead she frolics in parks and sits on terraces as if nothing were wrong. She walks into the rain to feel it on her skin and smell the way it changes the earth around her rather than feel her curse is following her to the city limits. She questions this sureness of her feelings that must be a falsity, must be a disguise.

That November, she didn't know how to feel; she was completely lost. There was numbness and too many questions. She had been trying to leave the base for years, but then she just felt stuck and wanted to live with her father forever. She wanted to be his child again and live in her childhood bedroom and live without alarm clocks or bosses or even adult discussions. She just kept running and running, sometimes going twice in one day, often leaving Esmé with her father. Those woods became so unfamiliar to her as a grown up self. Weren't they supposed to seem less scary as you age? Like monsters under your bed, the mysteries should became clearer with age, but she felt more confused and unsure.

It's getting darker now. She had not looked at her watch when she started off from the metro exit near the chateau, feeling the freedom of what felt like endless summer days. But there would be a limit, and she seems to be reaching it. She has to stop at the fork in the trail and remind herself which direction to go. The ground becomes less clear in the enveloping shadows and she quickens her stride though she should actually slow it to take care of her ankles on the hidden rocks and roots under the leaves. It is a narrow pathway, a shortcut behind the military horses. But with the rain masking their smell, she has a hard time confirming if it is the correct direction. She has to focus just a few feet in front of her stride and loses track of what might be before her.

On one of those mournful, or pre-mournful for she has never reached acceptance, runs in New England, she actually did lose herself completely in the dark. It was early December then and the darkness came early and fast. It came without warning, taking all prisoners in its cloak. The coyotes came out earlier, too, and as she lost track of the path both before her and directly under her feet she had heard their howls. True that they would only attack small animals, or children, but because she felt so small inside, she was afraid they might go after her.

In the late Paris dusk, the rain now stops, the water welling up in her eyes from fear and realization block her path even more. She tries to wipe them away and stumbles on a stray root, completely blinding herself for an instant. She has the sensation that the heavy skates on her back had knocked her out, but in fact she just has a small scrape on her knee. Regaining composure, she sprints ahead to shake away the coming tears and try to make her mind go blank. She feels the wild boar all around her, waiting to chase and knock her down.

But again she blinks her eyes and returns to that coyote-filled night before finding the bigger path. She had stopped then in her tracks, trying to turn on her inner-compass and spinning like the needle, hoping she will stop in the right direction, but she just span closer and closer to the forest ground until fully collapsing on the layers of dead vegetation decomposing in the cycle of life. Completely disoriented as if the devil has taken hold of her eardrum.

She hears the coyotes coming for her...in a pack...that is how they attack their prey...closer......she has nowhere to go...she can hear their footsteps nimble on the damp earth, blessed with night vision like the vampires in Transylvania. She wonders why they do not howl, instead silently haunting her with their approach. Her face is wet and she is sobbing, nearly hysterical in hyperventilating breath.

But there had been the sound of plodding shoed feet as well, awkward in rhythm and placement on the ground, and then suddenly a bark unlike what she imagined a coyote would be capable of producing. It sounded like the bark of a beast who was communicating with man, relating some human emotion that brought its energy closer to what was known as the intellect. It was eager, concerned.

She felt its breath just inches from her face when her cognizant self had literally turned to mush. A wet, thick tongue licked her face, her exhausted muscles. Then came the voice of man himself: 'Eunomia, what is it?'

He arrived as well, emerging from the brush, and asked who was there, was she hurt. He held a cane; he was blind. This darkness made no difference for him, there was no more danger than during the day. His dog, a large Bernese Mountain Dog, would protect him from the coyotes anyway.

She could not answer him right away, but he and the dog both helped her up and half carried her toward the path from which she had strayed. They walked in silence for a while before he spoke again. 'What is troubling you, child?' He could not see her aged face, but it's true that she could have been his child. He was older than her father, upper seventies at least. A feeling of shame overwhelmed her. She replied that she had lost her way. How could she explain these feelings that she herself did not comprehend? She had been running from them for days, and only now at this scary moment was she suddenly trying to make sense of it. How could she be a mother to her fatherless daughter with these volatile emotions? She was a danger to herself, to her family. She was a freak of a woman, unable to mourn, unable to mother, unable to return the calls of all her caring friends.

'I understand child. We all lose our way if we really want to live.' They walked on as she gripped his arm in fearful desperation and in her complete inability to see the path before her, but her breathing became easier. She began to relax with the ease of his stride, the wagging tail of his dog at her side.

'My child, I want you to search within yourself. I can feel your pain in your fingertips. I often turn to those men who used to frequent these woods for my answers. I think of them when I walk in their woods. Do you read much, my dear?' She told him that her father is a writer; she was brought up reading many of the classics and imagines he is talking about Thoreau and Emerson, or maybe Hawthorne. They had all occupied these woods, or those connected to them. Their manuscripts lay in these libraries. Their descendants inhabit these towns. She asked him if he meant the way Thoreau had gone to live at Walden Pond for two years. Thinking of them had distracted her from pain.

'Yes, child. I do enjoy reflection on *Walden*, but I also think of how the strangeness Thoreau felt in his canoe and on the trails in *The Maine Woods* gives us even more truth. The challenge of it is brave. Remember what Emerson, his dear friend, has said: *What lies behind us and what lies before us are tiny matters compared to what lies within us.*' And with that, they continued in silence until they reached her father's door and before she could question his knowledge either of where she lived or of anything else, the man simply stated, 'Your father, the writer.'

As they reached the porch light, she noticed his wrinkles from many years of expressing his emotions, now lightly smiling. His dog remained by his side, ready to be of service to his kind companion. She had invited him in but he kindly refused, saying her daughter was home for her. She wondered how he knew this, too, until she heard Bette Midler singing *The Rose* as she opened the door. As she turned to thank him, he vanished back into the woods.

Esmé is watching *Beaches* in the little closed in porch off to the side of the entry way. She is not three years old, as she was when Thomas died. The image of Esmé in this memory tells her it is recent; it must have been a cold spring rain instead. She knows the seasons can intermingle in New England. What had appeared as the coming of winter was simply a cold delay of its thaw.

She is crying uncontrollably and gets up to wrap her arms around her mother. This mother whom she needs so much, she now understands as a real person rather than the being needed to care of her. '*Je te comprends, Maman. Vas-y. Je te joindrai.*' She would come to be with her in Paris when she could, but her mother has to live as an individual. Her mother needs to be set free, so she speaks to her in the language of her mother's freedom. Esmé does not need her at this moment and has allowed the tables to turn.

It was toward the beginning of her trip home. They slept together on the couch that night wrapped in each other's arms, and in the morning, Esmé left her mother to sleep there, later bringing her a breakfast of fresh bread, fruit, coffee, and yogurt at ten o'clock. They had enjoyed it together once her father had come back from meeting an editor; they all watched old cartoons on television in their pajamas. Catherine had forgotten this night; she had fixated on the end — on Esmé's absence at that last dinner as if it had been payback for her absence as a mother. It was one dinner of many; it should not bear more weight than the others.

She senses a foreign being crossing her path and takes her eyes slightly forward from their comfort zone. If it is a wild boar, it is not interested in harming her. Is it anything at all? But after a few more steps she is out in the open and realizes she is near the horses, and one is galloping freely along the fence. She looks up and sees blue sky in the distance. In fact, it is not as late as she thought. The dark clouds had masked a sunset, but they were merely passing by.

Even though her clothes are soaking wet, her canvas sneakers have small puddles inside, she feels better as she makes her way slowly toward the Metro.

As she looks up at the château again, walking around its exterior, she thinks of one of her favorite quotes from Thoreau that her father is always quoting: 'Things do not change; we change.'

.....

She exits at St. Paul for a nice walk back to her flat, but as she exits the station, there seems to be a buzz in the Marais. Drawn inward, she moves down *rue Pavée*. The movement of the crowd takes her in a zig zag until she sees the multi-colored balloon archway over *rue Saint Croix de la Bretonnerie*. *L'Arc en Ciel* — a rainbow, but not from the rain that has passed. It is too early for the annual Gay Pride Parade, still almost a week away. But something in this district is happening, as if they are practicing for the upcoming event. She sees a sign for the *pacte civil de solidarité*, the civil union rights that the gay community is fighting for.

Before her, she sees the crowds. Her aimlessness turns into the direction that the crowd takes. Turning a corner down a blocked route, more rainbow flags, balloons, and outfits adorn the spectacle. People are dancing, watching, and drinking. Many are dressed normally, but all the focus goes to those wearing neon colors or group costumes. Many are also drenched from the rain like herself, but it hadn't hurt the spirit of the event.

The happiness is like a virus. She is suddenly smiling along with everyone around her, including the cops and the homeless drifters. It is a source of power to don seven inch platform stilettos, she notes, as one man with a purple velvet pair stops to allow photographs. More than power, this space has given freedom, not to be gay, but to be whoever one wants to be. It tells her that human nature must be good if this is what happens when all inhibitions are let go.

Many people walk arm in arm and shout out to friends; she is suddenly overwhelmed with loneliness, much more so than she has experienced on her way back from the cinema last night. She drifts off like being pulled in the undertow, winding up on a side street where drunk sailors on the left dance to the Village People and butch lesbians occupy the curb at right. Laughter, songs, cheers.

Her overwhelming joy is suddenly replaced by unbelonging, not that these people are unwelcoming, but she has realized she is reaching the end of her life having never found that soul mate. Thomas was young love that could have easily been lost in the wind, if not for his calculated anticipation of his military career. And their love had faded rather than grown like a true soul mate's should.

She mazes in and out of the streets, seeing balloons, costumes, ads for happy hours all behind the safety of her dark sunglasses.

Once she reaches the open square by Pompidou she has hit safety – no one is trying to interact or ask her to join the party, so she doesn't feel like such a lone floater anymore. She notices her tired feet and bodily exhaustion and heads toward the bridge that would take her home.

But before she can leave the square , she is stopped by a young man whom she assumes wants a light. He starts, however, with 'You may find this really forward, I mean I don't usually do this, but I just find you so pretty.' He pauses unable to read her blank expression behind the sunglasses. 'I just think you're so adorable.' He is sweet and genuine in nature, unlike some of the over-confident men on the Parisian streets, and clearly not more than twenty-two years old — her sunglasses and casual festive outfit create the illusion of youth. She smiles, accepts the compliment and says she is married, walking on.

Her mind wanders to thinking maybe it wouldn't be too late to start again. She can still connect when she lets herself be open. A new chance at romance, maybe easier since Esmé is at school. But the sound of a church bell is the chime of reality, and she knows this romance can only be a daydream now.

She continues drifting toward the bridge, but decides she is not ready to go home yet, and weaves back toward the middle of the Marais once again, now finding comfort rather than isolation in the people around her.

.....

* * *

His gaze cuts through the crowd. His smile is open and raw, like it used to be; it is directed at her. Edmond. He has received the letter. She dances through the crowd to reach him as he envelopes her with his arms and smacks her with three kisses on her cheeks. There are no tears here, just celebration. Joy for their friendship that can endure.

'You are soaking wet! Where have you been?'

'Skating —'

'Ah, your guilty pleasure! I won't nag you about finishing your paintings, since, knowing you, you've already finished your work for the opening. Sis, meet my friends here...' She loves it when he calls her this.

She is introduced to three friends and the other two she already knows. They all exchange *bises*. Pascal is at work. He is coming by later. They tell the small anecdotes of their days, they talk of soccer and opera and politics, and sometimes they laugh so hard that they cry.

They order fresh beers and drink to their health - like a chorus from Sophocles, they chant in unison, '*Santé*!'

XV

Nuit Blanche

It is June twenty-first. *Fête de la Musique* and the longest day of the year. People are celebrating all over the streets of Paris. Her event has already officially started, but she is getting ready in her apartment nearby.

She enjoys the extra attention the city seems to ask her to pay to herself, especially tonight. The noise of the streets is her audience and she is theirs. She takes her time with her creams, perfume, makeup, and hair. Everything is simple, but each action is drawn out longer than necessary.

Evenings of *vernissage* - gallery openings with champagne that spill out into the streets - have been her favorite type of *soirée* for a long time. They are happening all the time in Catherine's neighborhood. It is a way for her to party and drift among friends with little commitment and with a secondary possibility of being inspired by the art. It is always, at least, something to talk about with new acquaintances. To go to *vernissage* at any gallery, she would always go in confident shoes and jet-black eyeliner. These gave her mingling ability. Rather than the drifting, isolated artist who was typically more comfortable watching others indulge and laugh, she took on a performance of her own. Were the others performing most of the time then? When were they real? Or are most ever real?

   She enjoyed these performances. Suddenly, she was the understated artist with the long perky ponytail, champagne in one hand and sometimes a cigarette in the other. She let people come to her, playing the elusive figure in the corner or drifting over to a piece of art she hoped to discuss. She had not been able to live much of this lifestyle while living on the base, whether showing her own work or checking out others', but she did bring Thomas to one event in Naples and another back in New York. He thought everyone seemed so fake, especially in the way they talked about the art, but also in their incessant flattery of each other. He was right, to some extent. Performances were happening all the time, but they were not empty nor worthless. She loved to hear, 'Oh, darling, I just loved your show in Chelsea!' or 'What a *divine* hat! Real peacock feathers...exquisite! Tell me they didn't have to hurt the little darling for them...' or '*Do* come 'round with the children. They just have the cutest little manners and outfits. It's like something out of an old film, and we'll never have those darlings of our own.' Why not flatter each other? There were truths in these statements, overstatements, perhaps, but that's what art is.

In her paintings, she takes reality and blows up some aspect of it. Why not do that with ourselves? Otherwise life becomes too ordinary. Thomas went to these events, wrinkled his nose at the crowd, and really had a fit when someone told him to 'lighten up.' Grant it, she hated to be told to 'turn that frown upside down' or 'smile' herself, but it was true that he was grumpy and reserved for no reason. She had no problem leaving him at home, but he was always jealous if she did these things on her own. He would tell her to go and then ask incessantly what he should eat for dinner or what to do with Esmé, as if he wasn't the perfectly capable father he always was when she was around.

When she realized that she, likewise, would not want to attend political social events after having her first try at General Maverick's cocktail party, she knew they had a problem. If they could have gone to separate social events and have a balanced home life as a couple and parents, that would have been fine. But it *was* a problem if he held it over her that she was able to float in these fascinating artist circles and that she shunned his own crowd (although she didn't shun them, she just didn't connect with them). It was the animosity, started as a small ripple that night in Brooklyn that had turned into an ever-wakening fault line. When she realized this, it was then that she had decided to go to learn how to work with stones, to build walls and lay them neatly in the ground. Free climbing the Medieval stone walls, drinking too much wine, *rien à faire*, and the deep spirit of the dreadlocked stone mason. Wanting to debate about philosophy and traditions, feeling so strongly he sometimes stood with deep hand articulations to make a point. She would silently laugh. Reconnecting with herself told her the truth about Thomas: she could not be happy if she stayed with him.

She had started to compare how she felt here and there. Of course she missed her daughter, and she felt guilty for feeling better away from her, so she searched to make sure this was not what she was running from. In comparison to the meals around that large table that inspired all her senses and often engaged her cerebral interest, meal time or time on a café terrace was dull with Thomas. She always wanted to stay just a bit more, to feel something or talk about something, or just to relax.

She remembers a beautiful sunny day in Napoli, outside of the base, when they sat down on a terrace. She had her sunglasses on and was people watching, slowly rocking the stroller at her side so Esmé would continue to daydream in the warm sun. She had a magazine and a book in front of her, and sometimes switched back to these pages, sometimes commented on something she saw. It was a Saturday afternoon and Thomas had the entire weekend off, an increasingly rare opportunity to take time together off base. She had started to suspect the disruptions were really his decision.

After about twenty minutes of lingering with empty coffee cups, he said, 'Well, don't you think we should go?' She asked where, and his reply was just to get going, do something, be somewhere. 'But this moment is lovely,' she said, and he stayed, unwillingly, a while longer. He pretended to relax, but she could feel the tension in the way he turned the pages of his newspaper loudly and commented briskly on Russian spies and something about Reagan. She had turned to him and said of course he could go back to base if he wanted, or walk around. He wanted to know how they would get home, especially with the baby. She said she would figure it out, leave Esmé with her, who was so relaxed. They could get a taxi or go on a long walk. He got up quickly, feeling unneeded. Maybe it was easier, she thought, for him to feel needed by the military. This is how she had lost him. How could she ever compete with this enormous feeling of interdependence he had with them? She realized it as he left the café terrace that afternoon. And as the thought had formed in her head, she felt both guilt for not being able to provide the same feeling and calm at being left in his wake. It was peaceful. It was the first time she realized how much better she might feel if he were gone.

But why is she thinking of *him* on this night? Why does he still seem to seep into her conscience, trapping her from full enjoyment? She thought she would have been over it by now. But she replays these moments, the disappointments and *mal entendus* that separated them long before his death. She blames him for attempting to ruin her night, then she blames herself for blaming him. Lost in a circle of blame and guilt that she usually succeeds in hiding, even from her conscious self.

Although she has already washed her face in the shower, she throws cold water on it again before patting it dry and applying the dark black eyeliner and mascara. It cleanses her mind, brings her back to the present. She brushes a light rouge on her cheeks and gloss on her lips, looking *vivante*, as if she has just returned from exercise. The last touch to her simple black outfit and slicked-back short hair to reveal her sharp profile is the shoes. Tall summer heals. Long stilettos with thin green crocodile straps that reveal her dark violet toenails and a tiny tattoo on her pinky toe - the Chinese characters for 'double happiness' to remind her of her mother's mantra, and hence, of *Mama*.

She heads toward the door, then turns back for one more addition. She takes off her shoes to stand on the bed and reaches high on the bookshelf. There lies a small jewelry box that is rarely opened. An opal necklace from Thomas; he had given to her on her birthday, the first year they were together. The silver chain is slightly tarnished, but she doesn't mind. She fiddles with the clasp, then checks her reflection quickly in the mirror, satisfied. She looks a moment longer to internalize this feeling of anticipation for her big event. It was what her mother had told her to do before her wedding day, to take a minute to look at herself in the mirror and feel that it was real. She buckles the fine straps of her shoes again and heads toward the door.

She doesn't go far at first, simply crossing the corridor to Cecilia's apartment. She is accompanying her there, although Cecilia is perfectly capable of going by herself. It's nice to arrive together. The door opens before she is able to knock.

'I heard you coming. Are you ready? Are you excited?'

'Yes...' and at that moment, Catherine begins to think of her family members across the Atlantic. How could this be her most important show without them? What has she done, coming back here?

The moment of self doubt is obvious on her face and Cecilia ponders how to handle it. She begins to insert the large golden skeleton key into the door, then pulls it back and turns toward Catherine with her finger pointing toward the heavens, 'Ah...I forgot my hat!' She shuffles back inside the apartment calling out, 'I won't be long!' And true to word, she arrives back at the threshold a few seconds later. 'Ok, all set now, I thought the red would be a nice accent for this special occasion.'

Catherine stares at her, stricken by the object placed artfully in the center of Cecilia's wavy set atop her head. She is quite sure it is a shoe, a single red patent leather pump. Is Cecilia going blind? Is she really moving toward dementia like she had alluded to...

Catherine reaches her hand out to her. Her eyes eminate a look of concern. They link hands, quietly.

But just a few seconds later, Cecilia bursts out laughing, giggling in a high pitch. She grabs Catherine's hand to reassure her, 'You thought I really lost my marbles didn't you?' She winks, 'No dear, but you looked white as death. I had to stir you up a bit. Like my hat?' She twirls and curtsies, removing the shoe as she pliés her legs.

Catherine attempts a smile or some words but her lips just part silently. She wonders if Pascal and Cecilia could have conspired of if this moment is just another instance of karma and the strangeness of the universe.

Cecilia breaks into her thoughts: 'I know you have had a lot on your mind lately, but this is your night! Try to live in the moment, *bella*. I know your mama that I met once long ago would be so proud of you tonight.' She gives her a wet kiss on the check, smooths the hair back from Catherine's face, and beams at her while looking into her eyes before retreating to her closet to retrieve a silk-lined peach Cloche hat.

While she is gone, Catherine gets herself together. '*Grazie*, Cecilia. Thank you for much more than tonight. You look beautiful and timeless.'

'And you are radiating! *Andiamo ragazza!*'

As they turn out from the courtyard, Catherine feels something inside her rising, as if this moment before her is the one she has been waiting for - not anxious but anticipatory. She notes the movement of her body's approach to the gallery. She feels each foot step with determination; her arms glide with satisfaction. She holds her shoulders back and chin high.

They come quickly within hearing distance of the party already started at the gallery and she sees Cecilia's eyes get wide. She has noticed something through her acute senses. Rather than ask what it is she enjoys this anticipation even more and holds Cecilia's arm tight. She adjusts her scarf's easy drape on her neck and tries to make her gait look effortless as her legs swing like pendulums and the tiny heels of her shoes brush the ground quickly, hovering from one foot to the next. Her calves flex under tight jeans with every step. They are forty-five minutes late, to let the crowd warm up. She feels the buzz and hears the testing of instruments in front of the gallery. The approach is closer and she has been spotted by Pascal whose warm face rises above the others. He doesn't say anything. He just nods and the rest start to turn her way. Before they have a chance to greet her, she takes in the scene — a celebration of her work, not herself, but the actions of beauty she wants to share.

Cecilia leaves her arm, saying she has spotted one of

her suitors. Gregoire is toward the back talking with a potential buyer, engaged deeply in conversation after handing over a business card. The canapé are floating around the room. Laughter, looks of deep thought, small groups, solos networking.

Only in Paris at one place on an evening in June can one find black fishnets with a crisp blue dress, shades-of-orange pants on *all* the Italian men, women dressed in black from hat to shoe, ripped jeans with a Dylan T-shirt, and two serious berets, one atop a man with pipe hanging from his mouth and the other atop a Swedish six-foot model with stiletto heels and something like Otto Dix going on with her outfit. The photographs of the event could be a show all in their own. Tonight the fashion scenery was even more interesting with the band, who had each brought out some form of chain and glitter and grunge all mixed together atop Doc Martens.

The energy shifts as soon as she arrives, breaks the plane by stepping off the opposite curb. Those who know her flash a welcoming smile, congratulating her. Those who don't are told in whispers that *she* is the artist and their questioning glances shift to admiration. After seconds taken to find a resting spot for glasses and place cigarettes in mouths, careful applause actually commences like an accelerating Paris summer rain. Quick echoing beats refreshen the air and remind her of living.

But as the applause breaks after her humble wave and shy *merci beaucoup*, and people move about again and the band begins to play a warm up song, a cover of The Doors' 'People are Strange,' Pascal and Edmond approach her, gripping each of her elbows. She's confused, but in performance mode and goes with it.

They enter the gallery together, the portraits of her family surrounding her, and two doubles appear like hallucination in the middle. She blinks and blinks again but is careful not to touch the thick black eyeliner giving her the illusion of mystique.

And then she sees them. She can hardly believe it, looking so adult and sophisticated in her black jacket, the gift Catherine was sure had been thrown in the back of the closet or given away, her daughter who had said she would come to Paris 'when she had the time,' Esmé — and then, smoking a pipe while engaged in some sort of storytelling with a stranger, her father, the one who could never tell her how he felt about this cancer, about her artwork or her choice in friends and lovers, but who could show her his love on this night.

They embrace. Her father, by way of greeting, starts singing a couple of lines from an old Scottish folk song about 'Catie' that he has always sung to her. They are whisked into the back room by Edmond who leaves them for a moment, but warns 'not to take too long so you don't miss the party!'

There are no tears this time, only brilliant sparkling eyes that would continue late into the night, into the small hours of the morning. They all start laughing instead. She gasps a few times with hand over her mouth, incredulous. Is it a dream? But their touch reminds her it is real. All her daughter says is, 'Papi wanted to come, too, so I changed my ticket to come with him.' And all her father says amidst the laughter is, 'I am so proud of you. I always have been.' And she knew it was true, all those years when she worried that he felt she had wasted her life first following her husband, then going for a career that was wistful. 'Maman, don't worry about us, we'll be around for a while, go back out to the party to see everyone. They are all waiting for you!'

Catherine takes her daughter's advice and returns after introducing them both to Gregoire. She runs into Rebecca, the American artist friend who was supposed to go to the play with her. Rebecca has ringlets of strawberry blond hair springing outward like a dandelion, her *équipe* is Bohemian and loquacious. Catherine is introduced to several friends, musicians, writers, and teachers in their thirties and they decide on a good day for lunch next week.

She continues to shift through the crowd to find Gregoire. He reaches effortlessly for a glass of champagne off of the server's tray that passes him at just the right moment and hands it to her and tells her she is a 'knockout' with his thick hand on the small of her back, 'Well done.' He gives her arm a little squeeze and moves off toward a circle of women in their sixties with Gucci bags and pencil skirts.

'You look younger every time I see you. What is your secret to eternal youth and beauty?' She hears in a male voice. His lips just next to her ear and his hand gently tucking her hair behind it. She turns to face Henri. He has a way with flattery that is both obvious and also makes her melt. It is his silver hair, his soft deep voice. It is the way he gives his full attention to her when he is speaking. These light flatteries turn into deep conversations in a heartbeat. He maintains this mock look of curiosity about her magical powers until she kisses his cheeks warmly and thanks him for coming. He has already seen many of the paintings, but he wants to know more about them. She says it would be better if he comes again when it's not so crowded. '*C'est fait.* It's a date!' he says, then adds, 'Do I sound American? I've been watching a lot of *Friends*.' She gives her silent approval of his play with culture.

They decide to go outside to get some air and hear the music. The band plays a Radiohead cover and then two originals while Edmond and Pascal come over to be introduced to the attractive stranger by her side. Edmond explains, 'We are like Catherine's brothers,' and kisses her cheek.

Much like this group in the audience, the band is filled with unanticipated harmonies. They sing in French, English, and Moroccan Arabic. A clarinet, classical guitar, bass, percussion - tambourine and a kettle drum. They take turns singing or created richly toned textures together.

She feels lost for conversation with anyone. She just wants to soak up the night, feel close to them all. Edmond grabs her hand to start moving to the beat together. Suddenly, everyone around her on the street starts to move. Some take partners or dance in groups. Some just move their arms and their heads, others their entire bodies. People join them from other gallery openings nearby. They shake their hips and raise their hands up high. They make eye contact with strangers occupying the same space through their movements. Catherine spins, looking up at the summer night sky just starting to darken, losing herself in the music and the champagne and the celebration.

. . . . .

* * *

They dance into the night, twirling together down the street to a sing-a-long already in progress. Swaying to '*Oh, Champs Élysée!*' then '*La ballade des gens heureux*' with people circled around Gérard Lenorman, who had made the song famous. He croons as if lost in a trance, but coming back to Earth to connect with his audience, while his friends pass out sheet music. Esmé comes up next to her and they reach arms around each others' shoulders. Her father comes over on the other side, already singing with Cecilia. Much of the party from the gallery has come over here. Pascal and Henri are toasting each other with champagne they have carried over, while Gregoire stands nearby with his glass held pensively at his side as he looks up toward the rooftops, exhaling smoke. Edmond dances with some of Rebecca's friends. She catches them all, then loses them to the stars and the music and the champagne. She is alone and also with everyone at this moment.

Closing her eyes, the music enters and swirls through her blood to reach her heart.

.....

With Edmond leading the way, they sing themselves over to Pharmakon, an old fashioned cocktail bar on *rue Mazarine*, just behind the library. It becomes the after party. The door opens—a vibrant, loud party – closes – the street, more calm but still occupied and living. It opens and closes again. Beckoning them in. Once a frame, now a mouth, not to swallow them up, but allow them to become a type of nourishment for the external world.

Catherine always notices the beautiful vintage wallpaper as she enters, and this time is no exception. Peacocks and pineapples made to look like embroidery. Faded shades of green and yellow and a still brilliant aquamarine accent. It lines the only space that is not made of old dark cherrywood, the rippled beams at waist level, which continues as spools that line the stairs rounding up to make the banister on the left. A mirror on the stairway gives the perception of a grand entrance, a *tromp l'oeil*. Upstairs, there are a few tables offering a more intimate gathering. Downstairs, there are several tables in little nooks, sometimes with wooden separations between them and surprisingly placed arches. The bar is of this dark wood as well, where the bartenders create their drinks with an artistic flair.

Everyone is here, but she sits at a table by herself, momentarily. She rests her legs and looks at the menu in front of her. The cocktail list here is exquisite. Each season a new list comes out from the bartender who creates concoctions such as the Penicillin and the Pimscothèque. As usual, she looks at the offerings out of curiosity but orders a Negroni instead, for which she had acquired a taste in Italy. Gin, vermouth rosso, and bitters - simple but just the right mix of flavors. Or sometimes the gin was replaced with champagne, a *sbagliato*, meaning mistake and named after the mistake a bartender in Milan luckily made one night. The waiter tells her it is a '*très bon choix*', with a serious tone, and swiftly maneuvers through guests toward the bar where the concoctions are carefully mixed, shaken, stirred, and poured. The dark orange drink here comes in a scotch glass with a single ice cube that fills much of the cylindric prism's space, displacing the strong, bitter drink toward the edge of the glass. As she sips, her upper lip softly glazes the wet cube, which is especially pleasant in the crowded room after dancing on the streets. It is a moment to herself in this night that is overwhelmingly active with so many people she loves and with reflections of them and herself on the walls. All these people coming together to support her, to see her work, which means they might also be able to see inside of her head, to understand her. Is this not what we all really search for? For people to understand and share our innermost thoughts, rather not pieces of identity but the way we see the world? This is why visiting a museum devoted to a single artist is so incredible or why reading a writer's entire oeuvre is satisfying.

As they drink and talk, the Pharmakon consumes them as we may consume a fruit, peeling the layers, leaving the pit.

As she sips the Negroni, she leans back against the banister to the stairs, slowly allowing the swirl of summer colors before her to swirl in her head, giving the sudden sensation of white before her. She loses track of the outline of forms before her, and cannot hear the conversations around her as a Frenchly-accented white noise takes over her ears. The feeling is like that present-absence at the sing-along moments ago, only now it is more intense. This energy shift seems to release a trapped memory or thought. She imagines it is like a tiny capsule that has been floating through her blood, pumped through her heart a thousand times a day, all the while containing this memory. She had many of these and they burst at these moments of whiteness.

White powder,
white paint,
white light,

white glass,

white stone,

white bubbles…

The whiteness is like the night they had been driving to Lugano from Italy. Snow was all around - on the road, swirling from the sky, stuck on the trees from blowing horizontally. In a frightening trip up the mountain pass, she was at once both awed by the landscape and scared for the life of the child in the back seat. The trip was slow in the blinding storm and they arrived late, fatigued. But the prize was skiing in the beautiful powder the day after. The thickness of it lost the athletic speed she was used to and instead after moments of looking off into the vastness that the Alps had to offer, she pointed ski tips down and dropped willfully through the powder aided by the verticality. Her body and mind both seemed to revert to childhood. Completely carefree - living through this corporal experience that lifted to infinity higher and higher the faster she descended.

Kathleen Clare Waller

Snow is creative, destructive, it is out of our control. Even man-made snow quickly becomes uncontrollable, part of the mountain after it leaves the jet on the side of the trail. That is what makes it so beautiful − we can never expect to control nature. As this thought crosses her mind in a rough form, she also tumbles into a blown mass of whiteness. Her skis fall off, a chill implants on her neck then all around her, but almost feels warm from its insulation, and she takes a few seconds before deciding to emerge. Upon her exit, like a groundhog, she laughs, looking up at the sun and smiles at the teenage boy who hands her one of the skis that had cartwheeled several meters up the mountain, defying gravity.

Her frame of vision decomposes in and out with the beat of the house music coming from a DJ in Pharmakon. As she blinks it is like the shutter of a manual camera slowly revealing a new vantage point outside of herself. In one moment the frame is a twilight blue and the stone walls of the old façade are before her. Her life feels like discontinued fragments of hypersensitivity to the physical world followed by blankness. *Is this what dying is like?*

She sees Esmé still dancing carefree at the club's threshold with her friends from high school. The next beat refocuses and she sees a jet black frame around swirling whiteness that frightens and excites her at the same time.

Click.

More people enter the frame − strangers bearing martini glasses, moving to the music, laughing. As the aperture changes back to the soirée in Saint Germain des Près, Edmond comes over to ask her if she wants another drink but she is fine. She steps outside for a moment.

Click.

She is back in the space of her mind she recognizes as Thomas' avalanche. The melody becomes white noise and the cold scene is a plea for help, something is lost in there. It calls to her. Cold snow blowing in the wind blocks her view. His last moments, he calls to her, but she is unresponsive, not knowing how to reach him.

Her eyes tear in the cold wind and as she again cuts back to the Parisian streets, Esmé is trying to tell her something. She can't hear. She still hears the cries from the avalanche though she hadn't been there.

And she enters it again, now willingly looking for an answer, or to answer its call. She wills the whiteness aside and faces not Thomas but herself.

'Save me.'

But why are you suffocating?

'I'm frightened.'

Then her daughter before her.

They look into each others' eyes. 'I'm so lucky,' she says and embraces her. But she is dying, she is leaving Esmé, alone. It's not fair to her; *I haven't given her enough.*

Catherine grips her daughter's arm as she loses sense of the world around her. The snow of the avalanche dumps into images flying through space around her.

264

Mama's angel food
cake, smelling sweet out of the oven on
Sunday morning

creamy milk

her father's hair, lit by the
window in his study
the pages of his manuscripts stacked on the
desk

the white
whale - its elusive form in the pages of
Melville's book

Pascal's towels, his soft t-shirts when she
goes for her massage

a dove, the pigeon's brother, circling the
inner courtyard

seagulls at Crane's Beach, at Cinque Terre
Esmé's test papers brought home with pride
                              her white baby
pajamas, clean cloth diapers, her protected
baby skin

                              brie de meaux,
warmed in the sun and spread on baguette

            risotto on the stove, or at a trattoria,
gorgonzola creating a sticky web between the
grains

Davide, Venus de Milo, Psyché reanimée
par le baiser de l'amour — marble statues
that rest in the museums she has visited but
drift freely through her mind

            the magnolia painted walls of her

apartment that dance in the sun, sleep in the
dark

Dijon, the city absent of trees, a trip with
her daughter

the fence at the house where she grew up
                    clean cotton sheets on her
childhood bed

empty canvases

winter

Suddenly, everything is black. The shutter has frozen shut and she's not sure where she's stuck. She feels warmth envelope her and finally realizes it is an embrace from Esmé who is facing her – looking more and more like herself, but also with her father's eyes, as she grows older. Facing her now is the door to this 'Pharmacy' that instead of elixirs of chemicals to fix a malady, makes drinks to quench thirst and join people in celebrations of each other's ideas. But she realizes that many also go to forget. To feel less shameful, to escape their problems or their sins.

A poison, a remedy. Plato's Pharmakon.

She realizes she has blamed herself for his accidental death all these years. She is as much guilty of his as she is of the ice man's murder found eight years later not so far from the site of the avalanche. The Italians had named the mummified 5000 year old arrow victim Ötzi, because of the place in the Alps on the Austrio-Italian border he was found called Ötztai. And she is as guilty of their failed marriage as he is. They needed to be themselves first, understand the other, respect, allow time. No, he did not deserve to die so young, but he was doing the thing he loved, lost in a white out, frozen in presence.

Total darkness again, complete absence of color. Until little particles of whiteness float in to fill up the four-dimensional screen in her mind like snowflakes filling up the pavement -

('Maman?')

* * *

- until the whole pavement is covered and she is surrounded by light, not white anymore, no color can describe the intensity of the all-encompassing light she is bathed in.

('Maman —')

And the light splits again, as suddenly as it was pieced together from whiteness, it splits into a million colors, the components of white light. It splits into tiny memories of red vine tomatoes, blue painted doorways, pink ballet flats, her mother's green summer dress, deep brown melting chocolate, Thomas' yellow Camero in college, orange paint on her pallette, steaming green asparagus, the turquoise Mediterranean, Esmé's hazel eyes —

('Catherine!')

and then the color of the skin of all the people who had touched her — butter, olive, chocolate, cream, coffee, rose — like flavors of gelato swirling into an intense spiral —

Someone is shaking her shoulders. 'Maman!... Oh, you're back,' she looks relieved and softens her grip, ' You scared me a little but maybe you just had too much to drink or something. I just want to let you know I'll stay at Sophie's tonight. She's got an apartment in the fifth, so it's pretty close. I don't want you to have to wait up if I'm late,' here she smiles again, silently asking for some space of her own. She glances at Sophie at the table in the corner next to a boy she doesn't know and Simon, the tall poet from Esmé's lycée, now studying at the Sorbonne.

Catherine grants her daughter her approval, even though it is not needed, 'That's fine, tomorrow we're meeting Grandpa at *Le Relais de L'Entrecôte* for lunch at noon. Edmond and Pascal are coming, too. Do you want to just meet there?' She gives her a hug and a real kiss on the cheek, not the subtle hint felt during the exchange of *bises*, but a kiss that says, 'I love you.'

. . . . .

The party is winding down. Her father, Cecilia, the gallery owners — they've all gone home long ago. Edmond and Pascal chat with the bartender and try sips of exotic and esoteric liquors. Every now and then one of them glances her way and catches her eye.

Catherine sits at a table with many now empty chairs and her near-empty glass of a second Negroni. Across from her one chair is occupied by Henri and the dregs of his whiskey cocktail sits in front of him. He had been outside talking with Gregoire until he saw Esmé shaking her. Worried, he had come over after to see if she was alright and then made it a good excuse to invite her to sit down with him.

Their conversation has drifted toward the film they have each recently seen, *American Beauty*, and then Kevin Spacey's even better performance in *The Usual Suspects*. As they come to a pause, Catherine looks up to see Edmond watching her; he smiles approvingly this time and nods ever so slightly, silently pushing her forward. He turns back to Pascal, the bartender, and his drink just as he gets that feeling you get in your throat before you cry and takes form and moves upward to be released. He excuses himself to the toilet before the tears come. There, he has a deep cry — for his father, for Catherine, for Pascal, for himself. As the bubble from inside bursts free, he knows what he wants to do tomorrow but he will keep it a secret until the family lunch tomorrow.

Meanwhile, in the pause, Henri looks into Catherine's eyes and admires her, he moves a piece of hair from her face and lightly continues down her face and her neck then her arm until he is loosely gripping her hand. While still looking into her eyes, all he says is, '*On y va?*' They exit without any good-byes and walk toward *rue de Verneuil* where he lives. They hold hands like lovers or children; they talk about what they see on the streets, diversions from their thoughts; they hold silly smiles. Henri pauses as they reach *rue Jacob*, and as he moves forward, their elongated arms become part of a dance, begging her to twirl into him. He pulls her softly toward him with his free arm, so their bodies are pressed together. He looks at her again before kissing her and it turns off any inhibitions. She has not kissed a man like this since her time in Florence just after Thomas died and before Esmé was old enough to explain anything to.

He softly releases her, smiles as a reflection of her own, and they continue silently and with a quicker pace toward their destination.

They kiss again at the door as he reaches behind her to type the code. Again in the rickety elevator. Still without a word.

His cologne is subtle but sharp, not unlike the one her grandfather used to wear, and it mixes with a hint of his sweat from the summer heat and the long night. She is blindly led through his threshold, to his bedroom where the feather comforter welcomes her landing and his subsequent one on top of her, a welcome pressure that is both comforting and new at the same time. He has already taken off his jacket and pulls off a gray t-shirt. His chest is lean and strong with olive skin. He delicately unwinds her silk scarf and pulls her shirt over her head with a gentle press of his lips on her warm skin following each movement.

With his pressure they grope and glide in anticipation for several minutes before fully giving in to desire.

She doesn't know if she is making love or in love. Love is just *there*, between them, being created at this moment. She thinks of something Edmond had told her just after his father's death when Pascal had comforted him: 'Find the one you love and love the one you're with.'

The rainbow of colors return again as her body feels pleasure and the labyrinths of their souls come together like puzzle pieces.

The colors follow the path of their different wavelengths, gliding and intersecting, moving up and down like the ocean waves. They envelope each other.

Until the waves crash — and the crest sublimates into flashes of white, like a sun that is too bright to look at. The sun on a mountain summit, reflecting off the snow in the open sky so it is impossible to avoid it if you open your eyes. Colorless sun rays ricochet everywhere. She closes her eyes, but when she has the courage to open herself to it, it is *le petit mort*. The French way of explaining the orgasm. The little death. The title of the Alvin Ailey dance she had seen in Boston with Linda and Janice. Explosive, mysterious, and sensual. The dancers' bodies transforming the entire Wang Center.

Kathleen Clare Waller

Love at this elated moment takes over everything in her body and she is so high and filled with so much pleasure that instead of releasing an orgasmic yell or phrase like the women who enter the flat next to hers, she sings a single note of *juissance* as if she were rehearsing for Ada in Die Feen. They are pressed so tight with only their sweat between them; it is as if their cells have fused together. Flesh to flesh. And as the note comes to a close, she releases and lets her arms fall away, angled above her head, creating the form of yet another Ode to Joy.

Energy released through a euphoric physical connection. *L'amour.* It is the same love she feels for Esmé, for her family, the same feeling she had experienced at the Pharmakon. Love for herself. Taking over her body. It takes over all her cells, even those cancer cells that chance or fate, God or her own guilt, or maybe an encounter with disease or chemicals in the air or her food had created in her brain. The same space in her body where she can appreciate this feeling.

He holds himself over her, pushing the hair again from her face and tracing the undulations on her moist tummy that once carried Esmé for nine months. '*J'arrive toute de suite,*' he whispers and gets up.

In his brief absence, she sighs heavily in release, as if in a film. She feels the moisture on her body evaporating and giving her goosebumps. She rolls onto her stomach and rests her face on her arms.

He returns with a large yellow towel, covers her, presses it against her skin tenderly, then does the same to himself. It cools her off and the wind that sneaks through the window now open to the courtyard and rooftops of Paris in the early morning hours when most, but not all, are

273

asleep. With the window wide open, they dip under the crisp linen covers and fall asleep for a few final hours of darkness.

XVI

Le Rêve

Dawn's light guides them into consciousness. He says, '*Je t'aime*,' through the short hair that covers her ear. His warm breath gives her chills as he pulls her around softly for a last embrace before rolling out into faded jeans and a gray t-shirt and into the morning.

Catherine stays, half asleep. Questions about forgiveness, facing fears, and the difference between *juissance* and *bonheur* float in her mind. Images of people and places she loves equally jump around between sleep and wake.

He has snuck out to buy oranges, now returns, slices,

275

squeezes into tall glasses. And she wakes completely to the smell of bread toasting as Henri showers through the closed door. She stretches her legs in bed until he emerges from the misty bathroom in a white towel, smiling at her. 'How did you sleep?' Without waiting for response, he reopens the shutters he had closed on his way out and throws a large t-shirt at her before following, jumping like a monkey with a concave back that hollows out room for her body before he softly pulls her on top of him. '*Bonjour Mademoiselle Poulain* —' he kisses her, then jumps up again. As she pulls on the shirt and rolls out of bed, she sees him through the cracked bedroom door bringing a tray with the full breakfast to the little table in the kitchen.

They eat together like old lovers or newlyweds. Comfortable but flirtatious.

He has to go to work. 'Stay as long as you like. Here's a spare key. I'll see you very soon.' He kisses her again. They part without good-bye.

She pours a second bowl of *café au lait*. She watches the news but listens to the birds in the courtyard. She throws on last night's clothes before walking to her apartment.

…..

There is a message waiting on her answering machine. Before entering the shower, she presses play and listens from the bathroom. It's Gregoire. He sounds hungover, but excited. 'You'll never believe this, *chérie*! All the paintings have been sold. We'll celebrate later in the week. I'll bring a bottle of the leftover champagne over to *La Palette. Félicitations!*'

Catherine slowly takes off her shoes and sits by the

window.

She has heard of this happening to other artists in Paris but never to her. She had not seen anybody buying anything but had not really been paying attention. Rinsing the soap from her hair, from her face, she looks upward with her eyes closed like a sunflower in the rain, caught up in surprise and pride.

She changes her clothes and has half an hour to walk in *Jardin du Luxembourg* before lunch, trying to make sense of everything that happened last night, but abandons it as she passes by the Medici Fountain and feels the gentle movements of walking on the pebble path. She reaches her fingers out to the leaves of the trees and bushes surrounding her, letting the chlorophyl rub off on her fingers. Meditation takes over. The mind moves outside of the body; the body moves inside of the mind.

It is a hot day and perspiration lightly catches the back of her beige shirt dress. The moisture connects her back to the world around her. The statue of the lion rises before her and she stops to stare into his eyes for a moment before moving on toward the gates to the street.

. . ...

Her father and Esmé have already arrived at *Le Relais de L'Entrecôte* and secured a table on the terrace for five before the lunch rush. The waitresses in traditional black cotton dresses with white frilly aprons move with speed and purpose. Crisp, professional movements to match the neat buns atop their heads. One of them leads her to the table she points toward and pulls out her chair. The waitress asks her father if has decided on a wine. He chooses a bottle of red *Côtes du Rhône* and Catherine orders a large bottle of Badoit and a carafe of water for the table. There is already *rosé* on the table, ordered for aperitif, which the waitress pours into Catherine's glass.

They all stand up again to exchange hugs, moving about the table. As they sit down, they look at each other and laugh. Catherine breaks into language, 'This is like a movie; it's completely surreal right now.' She raises her glass and changes her tone to serious, reflective, 'This is to both of you and to our family. This is for your generosity and your support.' She puts her sunglasses back on to hide her emotion. They don't need to talk about why they came or why her sister hadn't. They talk instead about Esmé's work with the professor, the flight they had taken over (with good camembert for dessert and a celebrity passenger — Zinédine Zidane), the hotel her father is staying at on *rue de Cherche Midi* in a room with red velvet furniture and a canopy bed.

This was the first restaurant she had gone to in Paris; it was on a list of five recommendations left by the woman whose life she had taken over. *Cosi, Chartier, L'Auberge a Deux Ponts,* and *Chez Omar* had been the other ones. It was not in the tourist guides, but known as the best *steak-frites* by Parisians. In the future, it would expand to locations in Geneva and New York, losing some of its authenticity, but this original in the sixth *arrondissement* kept something special and secret, inimitable. She had gone alone the first day Esmé had stayed at the daycare. The only thing to order was the temperature of her meat, which she ordered rare - *saignant* - and which the waitress had written with a crayon on the white paper table cloth. The simple salad with a few walnuts had arrived just after her half bottle of wine, which she had ordered because she wanted the Saint Joseph rather than the house wine by the glass. Her empty salad plate was taken away and she looked out at the other patrons dressed in suits, Chanel dresses, and simple shirt and jeans combinations. Then her plate of sliced pink beef and thin crispy french fries had arrived. The beef was covered in a special peppery brown sauce and she took a big scoop of spicy dijon mustard for her fries. She had taken her time eating several bites, drinking a few sips of wine, looking out at the people around her. As she finished the last of six slices of meat she heard an older gentleman approaching, calling out a repeated headline as if he was from an old film. He wore a beret, held a newspaper at eye level of the cliental and another stack in a bag on his shoulder. He calls out, '*L'Italie et Vatican sont separés!*' repeatedly with the headline and photograph of the pope and Italian president facing the restaurant patrons. She was interrupted from her trance by the waitress arriving with her second plate of meat and fries, included in the meal. The server also poured the rest of the Saint Joseph into her glass. She finished the food and sat longer with the wine, being transported to another time or place, like a porthole to a parallel world. She had opened up the gap and it was too late to go back. Her life was now destined to be in this inbetween space, where she could be independent, creative, indulgent. Where she could be a good mother and still have time for herself. The waitress had arrived with the famous dessert card during this interlude. She asked what was best and went with it: a rich chocolate cake with vanilla ice cream. It was simple, exquisite. She followed with espresso. Aloof and abuzz at the same time, she had paid the bill and strolled over to Luxembourg, found a chair near the fountain, and took a cat nap. Never really asleep, the wonders of the new world she had opened herself up to came to her in daydreams, like something in a Dali painting.

Edmond and Pascal arrive and they all stand up again, disrupting her moment of memory while her father had been asking Esmé about her Parisian friends. Kissing, toasts, ordering the temperatures of their meat; it is convenient not to break the flow of energy and conversation by having to look over a long menu of choices. In the wake of the waitress's departure, Edmond reveals his secret: 'Last night, I realized what I want to do. I need to spread my father's ashes at St. Malo. I need to go there, to face my pain and let my father free. Pascal will drive me there after lunch. Catherine, will you come? I need you, too.'

She looks over at Esmé and her father. 'Go, Catie, I'm here for a week and I want to take Esmé to some museums.'

'Yeah, Maman, I've also got plans later tonight anyway, and I'm not going back until fall semester starts!'

The decision is easy, of course she would come. They would leave at three o'clock, stay overnight at his parents' old home, which he has to sell or to keep, he isn't sure. It is decided and so they can talk about other things — a recap of last night mostly but also recent trips and funny stories. They are like uncles to Esmé, and they tease her about boyfriends and her more mature look. A lot of laughter. Quiet pauses, toasts, pleasure in their food.

When the dessert card comes, they decide to share a *tarte citron*, profiteroles, and the chocolate cake with ice cream. As they wait for their dessert and coffees, her father brings up Undine in an offhand approach. 'You should call her after lunch.'

'But it will be eight or nine. You know Undine will go nuts if I keep the kids awake.' She doesn't really care about the time but thinks it is up to her sister to call her. Her father insists, 'Please, Catie, call her. You know she is not comfortable dialing international numbers.' Catherine thinks to herself that all you need to do is add three numbers to the front, decides it is more the cost of the call holding her back, but agrees to do it all the same.

The desserts are quickly devoured. Coffee cleanses the palette, wakes them up after the wine. She pays the bill on her way to the toilet and comes back to find her father and Edmond politely fighting over paying it as well. She tells them they can stop since it is taken care of. The couple goes home to pack for the overnight trip and the rest go to Catherine's apartment to relax while she calls Undine and packs her own things.

.....

Her nephew answers: 'Aunt Catie!'

'What are you still doing up?'

'Mom did something so crazy last night! You are gonna love it, Auntie Catie!'

'What are you talking about, Jimmy?' She glances at her father who is smoking a pipe by the window.

'She let us stay up and we did something funny! Haha! I'm not s'posed to be up now, but I ran out of bed when the phone rang and now Mom has seen me, but I don't think she's mad.'

She hears Jimmy give Undine the phone and tell him softly to go back to bed to read before lights out. He seems to comply as he is heard yelling, 'Good night, Auntie Catie!'

'What's going on Undine? Suddenly your kids are night owls?'

'Oh, Larry is on a business trip again, so no big deal!' She cannot remember the last time she had heard her sister in disagreement with Larry, having become one and the same person as 'the family' years ago.

'So, what's up? Dad said you wanted me to call you.'

'How was your show last night? I'm so sorry I couldn't come, but you know…the kids, Larry, saving for college…'

'Yeah, don't worry about it. I didn't think anyone was going to be there from home, so it was great to see Dad and Esmé. You didn't need to stay up to apologize.' Catherine was starting to feel like this phone call was only intended to relieve her sister's guilty conscience. Although, she is already a little surprised and maybe comforted by this new awareness of her personal impact on others' well-being.

'No, that's not why. Oh, I mean I'm still sorry though! How was it really?'

'Well, honestly it was a huge success. Not just to see everyone and the party after, but all my paintings were bought in that one night. Dad bought one to give Esmé, an old pretty portrait I had done of her, and my neighbor bought one of Mom. But then all the remaining were bought from an anonymous buyer. It was incredible! But surreal, almost like a dream….'

There is a pause on the other end. Then, 'Oh really? That's just great, Catherine. I'm happy for you.'

282

She sees her dad turn toward her and ask softly, 'Did she tell you yet?'

'Tell me what? Undine, what are you supposed to tell me?'

'Oh, I just wanted to make sure your show went well.'

'That's sweet....' She is ready to hang up.

She hears her father pipe in more strongly this time, 'Undine! Just tell her already! No need for humility.'

'What, U.?' This was her nickname for her sister from childhood.

'Well...ok, if he insists.' She giggles a little, something Catherine hasn't heard from her sister in a long time, 'So, what I did was, you see Larry was gone and I don't know what he would have thought, but I don't care!'

'What did you do?...' Catherine starts to feel a little concerned.

Another pause.

'I bought all your paintings!'

A few silent breaths.

'Oh, U. — I'm so...I don't know what to say, Have you been drinking? Is everything alright?'

'Yes! Couldn't feel better! After I called and bought the paintings, well I haven't had this much energy in years.'

'But, why? I mean what will you do with them?'

'I want to put them up all over the house! I know I haven't seen them all yet but I love your work. I always have. And...I...the kids...I mean, I'm just going to, I mean I *do* miss you so much. I have never felt so hollow as I have in the days since you left for Paris. But I feel like I'm going to, like I do, have you with me, with us.'

She should feel annoyed that her sister wouldn't think other collectors would want to buy her work. She should feel humiliated by the realization that the anonymous buyer is not necessarily a fan of her work. She should seek further explanation. But these feelings pass through her faster than she realizes they are even there.

'U. —'

'Yeah?'

'I love you. I'll see you soon.'

…..

They get into the car and Catherine turns to Pascal: 'I think I'm beginning to understand that koan.'

'Oh I knew you would. You already do, you're just not sure how to put it into words.'

They each settle into their seats with Edmond in the back, quietly looking out the window. Catherine is the DJ and finds CherieFM, which is playing Indochine, to start them off on their excursion. She thinks about how she had felt in Henri's bed last night, replaying the evening in her mind but not able to recreate all the details. She wonders if he is thinking of her now.

She pulls a blanket up to her shoulders. Rests her head on the window. The peaceful humming of the wind.

…..

Four hours later they arrive. They park near the city walls and see the tide is still too high to walk to the island where Edmond wants to spread the ashes. Besides, it is dinner time. So they leave the ashes and their bags in the car and go to a *crêperie* called *La Malouine*, which had been Edmond's father's favorite and where they would often meet for lunch. As they look over the menu, he tells his friends that he would always order the *boudin noir* (blood sausage with stewed apples) or the *St. Jacques* (scallops with cream and leeks) and his father always got a *complète* (egg, ham, and emmental cheese) with potatoes; they would share a bottle of cider and his father would finish the meal with Calvados while Edmond opted for a caramel crepe and café.

When the waiter arrives, they skip the cider and opt for Perrier. Edmond orders the *complète avec pommes de terre,* Pascal orders one with mushrooms and roquefort cheese, and Catherine chooses the ratatouille filling and a small salad on the side. She craves vegetables more and more these days. Edmond shares stories of his childhood while they eat: getting up early with his dad to find mussels, walking the perimeter of the wall with his mother before going to the beach on Wednesdays when he did not have school, going to church on Sundays with them both where he would pull the hair of the girl seated in front of him and run off to play on the rocks with the boys once the service was done.

The waiter comes back to clear the plates and ask about dessert. Edmond gets a sweet crepe with caramel and a scoop of vanilla ice cream, Pascal orders one with frangipane and chocolate, both made in house, and Catherine orders another buckwheat crepe with goat cheese.

They prefer to go outside for a café or drink, still waiting for the tide to go down. Edmond makes the suggestion; maybe his nerves need to calm down as well. Catherine remembers a terrace near the passage to the beach where they will cross over to the island. A few old men drink calvados and British tourists drink kir and pints of beer. They order their coffees from the friendly waiter.

When he comes back, Catherine says she remembers him from last year. It breaks the ice. He's actually the owner; the father of the little girl who often chases the seagulls in front of the terrace. He's French with Moroccan parents who immigrated to Normandy. His bar is successful but he wants to move around - go to Japan or Colorado and ski or bring his bar to Cassa Blanca to join his brother. Business is good but the weather is always gray. Edmond offers that he loves this weather; the grayness. That he loves the wall; its history, stability, artistic expression. He surprises himself with this love for his homeland. The owner is impressed, refreshed by this attitude and starts singing to the jazzy music as he excuses himself to take the order of a large group that has just arrived.

Edmond bums a cigarette off of one of the old men. Catherine has no desire to join him, but enjoys the sweet scent while she listens to Pascal telling a story of a voyage to Morocco.

In a way, it is always warm here - the community is close - in this little bar, community comes to the proprietor - his friends arrive in sequence, sometimes expected, sometimes not. She sees some of them this evening and remembers the morning she had spent there, sketching, waiting for Edmond to finish helping his dad fix something in the house. A young man had put on a little piece of theatre for them all in that square. In his white painting outfit, he took a beer break at ten thirty. He spoke loudly about his work, still not done. He became the center of attention, a mock-tragedy under the rain that kept him from his work.

Waiting for business, for news, or a joke. Watching life pass by these windows, in the square, into the bar or the terrace.

They pay, stop by the car to collect the urn, and turn toward the small archway leading down to the *Plage de Bons Secours*. The island is already visible through it, and they soon see the concrete pathway over the sandbar has just opened up.

They walk down the stone steps. They take off their shoes and leave them there. The sand is still wet from the quickly changing tide.

On the sandbar, the Atlantic stretches out on either side. Shells and seaweed are collected at the edges of the path.

They reach the stairs and path spiraling up. They move silently up, careful of the placement of their bare feet.

They reach the stone panel with a warning for the dreaming writer who may become trapped on this little island, finding beauty only to reach death. The ghost of Chateaubriand buried nearby whispers to them. A reminder of mortality for the immortal.

Edmond stops here. He uncovers the urn and throws the ashes out over the cliff. Most of them blow back into their faces as if he doesn't want to leave them, so instead they run back to the beach, no longer timorous, and jump in the *piscine plein air*, a tidal pool, which will then be carried out to sea at the next high tide that night, but for a while he can rest by their side as they lie in the sand.

As the three of them lie side by side, the tide safely retreating, Catherine begins to unconsciously sift small amounts of sand through her fingertips. The fine grains fall in smooth trails as if from an hourglass, but the amount and the speed of emptying her palms is not constant. This movement and the wind passing over her face lull her to sleep. She is both present and not. The salty air deposits its minerals into her ears, her nostrils as she lies motionless.

. . . . .

The fatherly timbre of Dr. Caillot's voice comes to her in the wind: 'The X-ray shows no sign of a tumor. It has completely disappeared.'

I must be dreaming…

But she feels weightless, as if someone has extracted this three pound weight from inside her head that had been infinitely multiplied in its position at the top pin of her body. Just like a sunflower, she feels the pressure to hold up the delicate, immense flower with her body as its stalk.

Her daughter opens the door to her apartment and enters with a newborn in her arms. 'Maman, I've brought Lynn over for today while I go to work, OK?' The baby is beautiful, of course, with eyes like her father's, and has the calm face of one in complete balance with the world. No sign of interference from the outside has made its way into this sleeping beauty, or if so, she has counteracted it with her innocence and her mother's nurturing touch. Her eyelashes are crystalized with reminders of the length of her sleep.

Tiny granules of sand rise up and graze over her face. She lies motionless while Edmond and Pascal get up to put their feet in the water.

Suddenly, she is atop Chamonix, looking out at the magnificent Alps. There is no other way to describe them, this jagged line that tore through the countryside ages ago and has since stolen the lives and hearts of so many humans who think they can conquer this stagnant force. The pass she imagines where Frankenstein followed his monster, his mind's projection of his inner guilt, his Freudian double, is marked by her gaze. She glances out at the whiteness, the covered evergreens, the strange pointed formations. She examines the path below her, at once steep and soft. Anticipation gives her adrenaline and vibrance, putting her into a hyperreal moment of sensitivity. Snow on her red helmet melts and drops down quickly to her nose. The surprise of its coldness in the mountain summit sun shocks her, bringing a smile in response to its freshness.

Glancing left to wipe the snow away, she sees a puff of what appears to be smoke on the mountainside that is shining under the brilliance of the sun. It is as if the ice is smoldering in the heat.

An avalanche.

Her heart races. What is this feeling that suddenly consumes her? It is not fear. She is safe on her mountaintop, miles away from danger. She is the right combination of a warm core and chilly wind on her face. She has the right equipment to slide lightly and nimbly down the piste. She has a daughter, and granddaughter, waiting for her somewhere, in a lodge or at home, she's not sure.

The feeling grows deeper into the pit of her stomach until she feels she will be sick in this picturesque landscape, ruining its purity with her disgusting reaction to this force of nature. But why if she is doing the activity that brings the greatest sense of inner calm through her ability to lose herself in the world and at once be at one with the world in the greatest way possible?

Thomas. *She says it out loud.* Thomas? *What does she have left to say to him? The sight of the avalanche has sparked this response.*

His unit had been engaged in an emergency response to some American climbers that were lost in the Italian Alps. He had parachuted down, she imagines the delight he must have felt at that moment over the clear mountains, not knowing where he would land but that it would be on pure snow.

But the landing had been taken out of his control by the violent winds on that day. They propelled him toward the sharp decline he never would have chosen as a landing.

She imagines how at first the snow's consumption of him and his equipment upon his impact must have felt as refreshing as the piece of ice falling on her nose on that mountaintop. How the whiteness and lightness of it would be like a dream. But once he was covered completely, panic must have set in. An expert in this business, he was suddenly powerless against the forces of nature. His training, his guns, could do nothing against this snow that had decided to devour him at that moment.

She had used his story to help sell special new safety equipment to the military, a balloon that you could open up if caught in an avalanche, giving you air, space, time to survive.

But this was for the ones who came after him. For Thomas, there was no balloon, there was no company of support to keep him happy in his final moments, to share his life's feelings and experiences. Why was she not there for him? What would he have to say to her? No doubt it would have been more meaningful than any of the arguments they had been having about schooling, eating at the dinner table instead of the television, the value of art (and her art), and living as expatriates. Why wasn't she there?

But of course she was not there. She was keeping their daughter safe. And like a voice from the avalanche on the mountainside she was now fixated on, she heard Thomas. She heard him say, 'I forgive you. I know you forgive me. Forgive yourself.'

She feels water on her face and opens her eyes. Edmond is splashing her with water. He and Pascal have buried her legs in the sand while she is asleep. She laughs,

'What are you doing?' They all laugh. Then he pulls her out of the sand and the three of them hold hands to run into the tidal pool to wash away the sand.

The sun is setting behind the island. They run up to the wall to watch the colors dispersed through several clouds, making this daily occurrence still unique. In the colors, she sees love in her memories, of her present, and of her future. How many sunsets will she watch with Henri? Will she ever see one with a grandchild?

They sleep that night at his parents' house. All three of them collapse on the bed. She sleeps deeply and calmly with the knowledge that Edmond and Pascal are at her sides, with the knowledge that she shares love with her family.

. . . . .

She is awake, ironically with a dulled sense of the world around her. She climbs out of bed without waking them up and moves into the living room.

Forgiveness. And love. Those were the answers. Those are the concepts she had always taught Esmé. But why had she always stopped short for herself? Why would these concepts not apply to her own well-being? As if it were a self-inflicted punishment, she ignored the advice she gave to everyone around her, family, students, friends, and even strangers on the street. Somehow she held herself partially responsible for this lonely death in the Alps. Somehow the breakup caused by his death felt like a divorce where she had left him in the lurch, or worse, like a murder. Hadn't she sometimes wished he were gone before the accident? She had wondered what life would be like without him. If they had never met, if they would divorce, or if something would happen...

But she did not kill him. She also did not make all their problems. The living must live.

She is dying but she is alive. She is alive. Is she dying? They tell her she is dying. Her dream tells her she is living. She has to be sure.

She calls Monsieur Caillot. No answer; no wonder, it is only six in the morning. She goes back to sleep.

She wakes up. Alone. She hears the church bells eleven times. It is eleven o'clock. No light comes from the window. Eleven o'clock. In the evening. She has slept more soundly than ever in the last few months, or maybe ever. She goes back to sleep, easily.

.....

Translucent red, mandarine orange, a purple the color of fresh plums, and green the color of plump olives. All those colors swirling upward from the depths of the ocean into the open sky.

The sunrise over the Atlantic. Atop Mount Desert Island, the first place to see it in America. People she has never seen before at her side. And Henri holding her shoulder in the cold morning.

Henri wakes her up. She was talking in her sleep, an early morning dream. He had left the apartment early to get fresh bread for breakfast. The smell of the toasting bread and fresh espresso in the kitchen gives her an added feeling of safety and comfort. As she enters in a white silk slip and Henri's extra robe, she sees the fig and apricot jam, the butter, the warm milk, the yogurts and blackberries all on the table for them to enjoy together.

.....

She wakes up again. This time in her own flat. She sees Esmé asleep on the other side of the bed. It is eight o'clock in the morning. A normal time to wake up. She makes toast and goes around the corner to La Palette for an *allongé* and buys the newspaper on the way, taking her time to read it as if it really matters.

Morning light travels through asymmetric openings in the rose trees. Business discussions, the day's tourist route, and breakfast selections surround her. But she is remarkably quiet, simply nodding as her *allongé* arrives. As she hears the clock chime again, the once knell of passing time has turned into a resonating celebration of this moment that now feels so infinite in front of the repeated scene before her. As days shift, the ebb and flow of people also change dramatically, but some things stay the same. Her spirit is settled. The illusion of so much time—long summer days—dance before her and make her feel immortal.

XVII
La Nécrologie

It happens under a tree one day in her daughter's arms. Catherine dies.

During a walk in the New England pine forest, they stop for some water and orange slices, but she is so tired. She rests her head on Esmé's shoulder, then softly moves her head to her lap, smiling up toward the face she had created, toward the evergreen needles and the sky overhead.

It is like the times during her childhood in the large colonial house in Brookline when she would start upstairs in the middle of the night without turning on the light - she knew the way - and the times during her adulthood in the Parisian apartment building when she forgot to press the light button on the way up. If someone had left it on, it might snuff out as she reached the second flight of stairs. She would continue after pausing a second to calm herself and find pleasure in this blind mountain climb.

Esmé spreads her ashes in the Atlantic, like they had done together with her father's. She spreads more on a journey through France and Italy - at various ports of the Mediterranean and carried by the wind from mountaintops in the Alps. Esmé travels with her husband, and they take turns carrying their young daughter on their back as they hike toward the peaks she revisits from her childhood, documented in the sketchbooks of her mother. At the end of the trip, they reach Paris where they will live for a year in Catherine's apartment and where on certain weekends they will visit Edmond and Pascal who have retired in St. Malo.

Catherine was forgiven because she forgave herself. She was loved because she loved herself. How long did she live until this very moment? She's not sure because she lost track of time. Had she loved Henri for months, years, or just that single night in June? Time, like love, multiplied before her every moment she paused to reflect or found joy after passing through immigration that first day in June of the last year of the twentieth century. Space multiplied, too. She was lost in endless dimensions between the Paris streets, between her home countries, and over the Atlantic. Jumping through portholes and histories, she lost track of mortality and forgot of its existence. She had conjured the strength of a heroine, an Antigone of her time without the tragedy.

She has lived a Long Life.

The White Night

Printed in Great Britain
by Amazon